hidden talent rediscovered

Bello is a digital-only imprint of Pan Macmillan,
established to breathe new life into previously published,
classic books.

At Bello we believe in the timeless power of the imagination,
of a good story, narrative and entertainment, and we want to
use digital technology to ensure that many more readers
can enjoy these books into the future.

We publish in ebook and print-on-demand formats
to br   nderful books to new audiences.

B E L L O

Ann Cleeves

Ann Cleeves is the author behind ITV's VERA and BBC One's SHETLAND. She has written over twenty-five novels, and is the creator of detectives Vera Stanhope and Jimmy Perez – characters loved both on screen and in print. Her books have now sold over one million copies worldwide.

Ann worked as a probation officer, bird observatory cook and auxiliary coastguard before she started writing. She is a member of 'Murder Squad', working with other British northern writers to promote crime fiction. In 2006 Ann was awarded the Duncan Lawrie Dagger (CWA Gold Dagger) for Best Crime Novel, for *Raven Black*, the first book in her Shetland series. In 2012 she was inducted into the CWA Crime Thriller Awards Hall of Fame. Ann lives in North Tyneside.

Ann Cleeves

ANOTHER
MAN'S POISON

BELL◎

First published in 1992 by Macmillan

This edition published 2014 by Bello
an imprint of Pan Macmillan, a division of Macmillan Publishers Limited
Pan Macmillan, 20 New Wharf Road, London N1 9RR
Basingstoke and Oxford
Associated companies throughout the world

www.panmacmillan.co.uk/bello

ISBN 978-1-4472-5022-7 EPUB
ISBN 978-1-4472-8900-5 POD

Chapter One

Ursula Ottway drove the Land Rover over the cattle grid, then got out to shut the gate carefully behind her. Back in the vehicle she paused for a moment before carrying on. It was late afternoon and the hills threw long shadows over Crow Water. Now she was almost home there was no hurry. She savoured the relief of her return to the valley.

She hardly left the farm now apart from these monthly shopping trips to Appleworth and each time the excursion became more of an ordeal. The drive along the dual carriageway to the Superstore was a nightmare. Everyone seemed to go so fast. Traffic passed her, horns blaring, lights flashing, the drivers apparently irritated beyond reason by the slowness of the Land Rover. Once, she had been so shaken by the journey that she had driven into the back of one of the sleek, new cars queuing at the entrance to the supermarket carpark. The woman had been as polished as her car, quite beautiful Ursula saw, long legged and golden haired, but when she opened her mouth she spoke incoherent filth.

'I'm sorry,' Ursula had stammered. 'It's my fault. I'll pay.'

But that, it seemed, would not do, The woman was determined to draw attention to them both.

'I only passed my test last week!' she screamed. 'Do you know what my husband will say?'

'I'm sorry,' Ursula said again. Once, she thought, I would have been able to deal with this. I might even have enjoyed it. What has happened to me?

Still the woman would not get into her car and drive away. A crowd had gathered and most of the shoppers stared at Ursula.

She struck a strange and compelling figure and realised suddenly how different she was from the rest of them. The girls wore designer track suits and smart white trainers, and the middle-aged women were smart enough to be at a Conservatives Ladies' Luncheon. No one, it seemed, was as old as she.

She was as tall and strong as a man, dressed in loose corduroy trousers, working boots and a thick woollen jersey. I should have changed before I came out, she thought desperately, but none of her clothes would have appeased these hostile women. At least she had taken off Fred's old tweed jacket before getting out of the Land Rover to face them. She knew it had holes in the elbows and smelled of sheep.

Eventually the woman had run out of steam and the audience had disappeared, leaving Ursula bewildered and frightened in the middle of the carpark. Each time she returned to the supermarket the memory of the confrontation returned, making her blush with shame and embarrassment.

Then she had to face the hot, airless shop. She could, she supposed, go to the small, family-run stores in Appleworth High Street, but she had a horror that there she would meet someone she knew, someone who would trap her in conversation. The supermarket at least was anonymous. She recognised none of the women who jostled past her, disdainful of her inability to make a choice between the competing brands of cat food.

She always bought the cat food first. She had nothing of value left now but the cats. The other residents of Crowford thought she was mad to stay in Back Rigg after her husband had died. How could she survive up there on the fells, all alone? Especially in the winter. Some family could move in there, make a proper go of it. But for the cats it was home and she could not consider moving them elsewhere.

The thought of the cats cheered her and prompted her to move. She started the Land Rover and began to drive along the track to the farmhouse.

She could see it ahead of her, surrounded by the spindly and wind-blown trees they had planted when they first lived there, to give the house some shelter. The track ran parallel to the road, which followed the edge of the lake. It climbed gently. At one time all this had been Back Rigg land but she no longer farmed it herself. When Fred had died she had handed it back to the estate. The lambs on the fell were fat and healthy and she felt momentarily jealous of the farmer to whom the land had been leased. She missed the ritual of dipping and clipping and sending to market. Still, she thought, as she pulled up in the farmyard, she still had Lottie and Belle.

She swung open the heavy door of the Land Rover and jumped down on to the yard. It was still muddy after the winter rain. She rolled up the canvas flap at the back of the vehicle and fastened it with a webbing strap, then began to lift out the plastic carrier bags. All the time she made the soft, cooing noise that let the cats know she was there. She expected them to come racing out of the barn at the side of the house, but the place was quiet and she thought they were getting old, like her, and they were probably curled up in the kitchen next to the Aga.

To get to the kitchen she walked through the garden at the side of the house. It was overgrown and unkempt, the only colour provided by daffodils, blown almost flat by the gale of the previous week, and some spindly twigs of forsythia. In one corner there was a hen house with a corrugated iron roof and a wire mesh run where six bantams scratched and pecked.

The kitchen door was unlocked. She had never felt any need to keep the place fastened. She had nothing she would miss if it were stolen. The kitchen was at the back of the house, built into the hill, almost dark. She left open the door to let in more light. The room was old, shabby, not what people expected to find these days.

There was linoleum the colour of pea soup worn through in places to the stone flags. There were the cupboards Fred had put up when they were first married. Once they had been painted white but they were discoloured now by the smoke from the Aga and grease and cobwebs. Ursula had stopped taking people into the kitchen – even her daughter Sally, on her rare visits, was kept firmly in the drawing room. The visitors' looks of shock and disapproval

3

made Ursula uneasy. Perhaps there *was* something shameful about the room, something she could not see. But it had always been good enough for her and Fred. Now it was good enough for her and the cats. She knew it was dirty but thought it had never been very clean. Farmers' wives were too busy to be over-obsessed with hygiene. It occurred to her that recently she had let things slip and she thought vaguely that she should have a good tidy out. It was the time of year for spring cleaning. The cupboard at the side of the range, for example, was full of damp and disintegrating *Farmers Weeklys*. The scout group in Appleworth collected waste paper. Perhaps she could take it to them on her next monthly trip to the supermarket. And if she washed the windows she might let in more light.

She went back into the yard to collect the remaining bags of groceries.

'Lottie!' she called. 'Belle!' She was more concerned about the cats than the state of her kitchen and there had been no sign of them by the Aga or on the scullery roof.

But still they did not come and she stamped back into the house and crouched awkwardly to stack tins in the cupboard under the sink, because that was where the mice always seemed to get, despite the cats, and only tins were safe in there.

She filled a kettle at the deep enamel sink, lifted the lid on the range and put the kettle on the hot plate to boil. While she was waiting for it she took a tin opener from the drawer in the table and began to open a large tin of cat food. She picked up the cats' earthenware bowls from the corner of the range and rinsed them under the tap, then spooned in the food. She had chosen their favourite flavour and knew nothing would keep them away now.

By the time Ursula made up her mind to go and look for the cats the light had nearly gone. At first she tried to persuade herself that her anxiety about the animals was foolish. They were hiding, playing some sort of game with her. What harm could they come to here? One might go missing but together they would be safe. So while she waited for the tea to brew she put away the rest of her shopping and went to feed the hens their layers' mash. Then

4

she poured out the tea and opened a packet of supermarket biscuits. She sat in the chair by the Aga and must have dozed off because when she awoke with a start her tea was cold and the room was almost dark. The cats' food was still untouched in the corner and she was thrown suddenly into panic. She went upstairs, switching on lights, peering under beds, calling them, then, knowing that she would settle to nothing until she knew they were safe, she decided she would have to go out to look for them.

On a hook by the door hung a large gaberdine coat, which she had always used for going out at night during lambing. There was still a torch in the pocket. She pulled on heavy wellington boots which were so wide at the top that they flapped around her legs, then she left the house and set off up the hill. It had been clear all day, and now, out of the house, there was enough light to see the whole of the valley spread below her. There was no real village. That had disappeared in 1963 when Crowford was flooded to provide a reservoir to supply the cities of the industrial north-east and Carlisle. The church and chapel were under the lake, visible only as ruins in times of drought when the water was low. At the bottom of the valley, below the dam, was the Cadver, the big house. She could see it better from here on the hill than from the road, where its privacy was protected by high stone walls and acres of woodland.

Bloody Grenville, she thought, as she climbed steeply through the field behind her house to the dry-stone wall where the cats hunted sometimes, prowling delicately over the top, attracted by the small birds that nested there. Grenville owned most of the land in the valley and she blamed him, irrationally, for all its ills.

At the wall she paused to catch her breath and looked down. It was very cold. She felt in her pocket and pulled out a length of string which she tied around her waist to act as a belt. She looked almost directly on to the roof of her house and saw that she had left the lights on and the kitchen door open.

'Lottie!' she called. 'Belle! Where are you, you infernal animals?'

In the school house, on the road between Back Rigg and the Cadver, the lights were on too, and were reflected on the lake. The school had been built on high ground and was saved when the valley was flooded, but with the destruction of the village there were no children to use it, and it was closed and sold. The class rooms had been turned into a pottery and showrooms and the owners lived in the adjoining house where the old school master had stayed.

Bloody Grenvilles, Ursula thought again. The valley's full of them.

She began to walk along the wall, shining her torch along the base of it, because by now it was too dark to see anything but the shape of the hills and the dull gleam of Crow Water. She was not sure, even, what she was looking for. From the direction of Appleworth she saw a vehicle's headlights, reflected first in the lake then turning towards her where the road crossed the dam. She had a brief glimpse of the towers at each end of the dam, then everything went dark again as the vehicle stopped by Keeper's Cottage on the edge of the Cadver Estate.

That would be the ambulance, she thought, bringing young Cassie Liddle from the special school in Appleworth where she stopped during the week to spend the weekend with her parents. It was late today. Marie would be waiting. From here on the hill she could see everything going on in the valley. She thought she knew them all, was aware of all their secrets.

She decided to give the search five more minutes then return to the house. Her feet and her hands were freezing. She was too old for this sort of nonsense. She should have checked all the farm buildings before coming out on to the hill. Belle and Lottie were probably back in the kitchen, waiting for her. She walked on, shining the torch ahead of her, and came to one of Vic Liddle's gibbets. The sight shocked her and she stood for a moment, holding on to the wall, trying to recover her composure. She had never seen one on the hill before; usually Liddle strung up the birds and animals he killed on a wire near the wood where they reared the pheasants. She muttered to herself disapprovingly. Why did gamekeepers have to make such a show of the vermin they destroyed, stringing the crows and jays and stoats on to a gibbet until they rotted?

She had always got on well enough with Vic Liddle and thought he would know better. Perhaps it was some sort of pagan superstition. This was a pole, stuck into the ground where two dry-stone walls met at right angles. All the corpses were fresh, most were crows. Then she saw the buzzard. It had been tied by its neck, so the wings and the great claws hung down. It was still beautiful. She shone her torch over it, stretching the wings, looking for signs that it had been shot. There was nothing.

She was so furious that for a moment she could not move, then she took a penknife from her pocket and cut the buzzard loose.

'Poison,' she muttered under her breath. 'That bastard's been using poison. I thought Vic had put a stop to that years ago.'

It was bad enough that the buzzard had been killed. Many gamekeepers hated them, suspected them of taking young grouse, and though it was illegal to kill them they were often shot. But poison was indiscriminate. The poisoned bait laid on the hill to be taken by the larger birds of prey was also taken by other birds, by farm animals, even by domestic pets.

Then her anger turned to fear and she knew that if Lottie and Belle had strayed on to the hill and eaten the poison, or one of the birds killed by poison, then they would be killed too. She turned the right angle of the dry-stone wall and walked on up the hill, past the keeper's gibbet. Tears streamed down her face, and she shouted and swore into the still night, promising them vengeance, imagining bloody Grenville strung up by his neck on a pole.

She found the cats curled up together in a nest of grass. They were cold and lifeless, surprisingly small. She lifted them gently into the large poacher's pocket inside her coat, her anger blown out, still crying. She walked back to the farm, carrying the buzzard over her shoulder, sliding over the frosty grass.

At the house she went into the kitchen without taking off her coat or her boots. She found one of the plastic carrier bags that had contained her supermarket purchases and put the buzzard inside. Even with the neck bent the claws stuck ridiculously out of the end. She tied the carrier bag at the top with a piece of string, fastening it around the horny legs, then put it carefully into the large chest freezer in the scullery. This was evidence. She was quite calm but determined that Marcus Grenville would pay.

She went outside again, this time locking the door behind her with the heavy brass key. Now there was a full moon and she could find her way on to the hill without difficulty. She retraced her steps, walking very slowly, giving all her attention to the search. Cars moved along the road towards Appleworth without her noticing. She moved along the dry-stone wall, inch by inch, moving the long tufts of juncus grass with her boot, shining the torch into the crevices between the stones. She was not wearing gloves and the hand holding the torch was very cold, but still she persisted, towards the keeper's gibbet, just a silhouette now in the moonlight. She found what she was looking for when she had almost reached it. Set in a nest of grass, similar to that where she had found the dead cats, were four white hen's eggs. On the open ground some yards away were pieces of broken shell. She lifted the eggs carefully and wrapped them in a large and dirty handkerchief, thinking as she did so that as she usually supplied Marie Liddle with eggs they might have come from her own hens. Ursula began to feel very cold and tired and she turned and made her way back to the house. There would be other poisoned eggs on the hill, but these were enough to serve her purpose. She was sure that when she got home and held them under a bright light she would see the tiny holes in the shell where they had been injected with poison.

She would arrange for them to be tested like the buzzard. That would give her all the proof she needed.

After the cold of the hill the kitchen seemed very hot. Condensation ran down the windows. Ursula stood by the Aga until her hands and feet tingled. She moved the kettle back on to the hot plate and padded into the drawing room in thick woollen socks to fetch a bottle of whisky. She missed Fred desperately. It seemed a daunting prospect that she would have to see the thing through by herself. She had taken all the decisions in their marriage but he had been there, behind her, giving her unquestioning support. She was not sure how she would face Marcus Grenville alone.

The sound of the telephone broke into her thoughts and she went unenthusiastically to answer it. She supposed it would be her daughter.

'You care more about those blasted cats than that lass of yours,' Marie Liddle had said when she had last been up to the farm. Now, guiltily, Ursula wondered if that were true. Would she be able to grieve so unequivocally for Sally? For more than a year Sally had been trying to persuade her to leave the farm. She sent glossy brochures advertising private retirement homes and estate agents' details of bungalows in exclusive sheltered housing schemes. There was never any suggestion that Ursula should move in with her daughter. Sally lived with her accountant husband and their son in a sterile flat in Docklands. Sally worked full time and the spare room was needed for the nanny. Ursula supposed that the telephone call would be an attempt to see her mother neatly tidied away.

'Hello,' she said, non-committally. She was in no mood for a long conversation about the pressures of Sally's work and the early signs of genius displayed by Joshua, her son.

'Aunt Ursula.' It was not Sally. The voice was female, calm. Ursula recognised it at once.

'Molly,' she said. 'My dear. What a pleasant surprise.'

Her relief made her lose attention and like an old fool she had to ask Molly to repeat what she said next.

'We would like to come to stay with you tomorrow night,' Molly said without a trace of impatience. 'George has a conference at the Cadver. It seemed too good an opportunity to miss.'

'Of course!' Ursula said. This was like magic, wish fulfilment. She should have thought of George and Molly at once. Molly was the child of Ursula's elder sister. Now, in later life, they seemed almost contemporaries, though there was perhaps fifteen years between them.

'Why don't you come tonight?' she asked. George and Molly would advise her.

'But it's late,' Molly said. 'And we're booked into a hotel in Teesdale. George has been doing some birdwatching.' She paused. 'Is something the matter? she asked. 'Has something upset you?'

'Yes,' Ursula said. 'It has rather.'

'We can come now if you like,' Molly said. 'It won't take more than a couple of hours,'

'No,' Ursula said. 'That would be ridiculous. I'll tell you all about it tomorrow.'

Molly accepted that without a fuss and rang off.

Back in the kitchen Ursula felt happier, but still could not settle. The cats were still in the pocket of her coat. She could not bear the thought of some scientist from the Ministry of Agriculture, Fisheries and Food cutting them up. She drank a large whisky, pulled on her wellingtons and went outside into the cold again.

The moonlight was very bright, the shadows of the house and the trees were black and sharply defined. She took a spade from an old pig sty which she used as a shed and began to dig a grave in the garden, underneath the daffodils. The earth was hard and stony, and it took her longer than she had expected. She laid the cats inside and was stamping the earth down on top of the grave when a car went past her, along the road by the reservoir.

Marcus Grenville, on his way home from London to spend a weekend in his constituency, saw Ursula Ottway, caught in the outside light of her cottage, a spade in one hand, bending over the black earth. To someone less preoccupied with his own concerns, less self satisfied, she would have been an object of some curiosity, and anxiety. She had always been eccentric. Perhaps this showed she was a danger to herself. Marcus Grenville, however, took some pleasure in the old lady's bizarre behaviour. He had wanted to get Ursula out of Back Rigg for years. He pulled into the side of the road and watched her. She stood, quite still, looking over the lake, her head bowed.

'What's the old witch up to now?' he said to himself, not really caring, only glad of this indication that she was mad as a coot, and needed locking up.

Ursula was thinking that she could not possibly wait for George and Molly before taking action.

Chapter Two

Marie Liddle hardly moved from the kitchen at Keeper's Cottage all day. Vic came in for his dinner at twelve and she had soup and bread ready for him. He ate in silence but she could tell he was worried.

'Have you had a good morning?' she asked carefully.

He shrugged. 'Bloody busy,' he said. Then, 'It's not Jeremy's fault. He's only doing what his old man tells him. But this should be a quiet time.'

They had hoped for some improvement when Jeremy Grenville had taken over the management of the estate from his father. They both liked Jeremy, had done since he was a lad. But if anything the situation was more awkward now. Marcus Grenville interfered and Vic was caught in the middle, given conflicting instructions by both men. He had never got on with Marcus Grenville but with him as boss at least there had been a certain security. You knew where you were. Now it seemed he could do nothing right.

'Mr Grenville phoned from London this morning,' he said bitterly, 'with a list of instructions as long as your arm. There'll be some important visitors up at the weekend, he said. He'll be hosting a Conservation Conference at the house. He doesn't want any mistakes. It's a bloody liberty. And I could tell Jeremy didn't like it.'

'They should know by now that you can manage on your own,' she said. 'They should let you get on with it.'

'Aye,' he said. 'Chance would be a fine thing.' And he went out, closing the back door behind him with a bang, calling to the dog that had been waiting for him in the yard, leaving Marie in the kitchen to worry.

In the beginning she had tried to make light of the new arrangements on the estate, jollying Vic along as if he were a child with a new teacher. Now she was starting to wonder if things were so serious that they would have to think of moving. There was Cassie to consider of course. She was settled at the special school. But Marie knew that she could always care for Cassie at home and in some ways she thought of Vic as the most vulnerable of the two. Perhaps she should broach the subject of moving with Vic. He would never think of it for himself.

'Who would want me?' he would say. 'At my age?'

He had been born in the valley and had never lived away from it. His father had worked at the Cadver as head gardener. Without her he would never have the imagination or the confidence to consider breaking away. She rehearsed in her mind what she would say to him:

'Anyone with any sense would want you. You've been running this estate almost single handed for years. The upland and the lowland. Even now there's only Danny Craven to help you and what use is he? You know you run the best shoot in the country.'

It was true, but would his skills transfer to somewhere strange? Here, she thought, he could walk the estate blindfold and not falter once. He knew every tree in the woods in the valley where he reared pheasants, every outcrop on the fells where the rich Italians and Germans came to shoot grouse. If he were uprooted to a quite different landscape she felt he would be lost and rather pathetic.

She stood at the sink to wash the lunch dishes and looked out at the garden where Vic worked every evening until it got dark. He had enjoyed gardening once, but now he dug and weeded with a compulsive restlessness. He knew he would not relax indoors unless he was physically exhausted. He brooded to much, she thought. That did nobody any good.

It was to stop herself brooding that she decided to have an afternoon's baking. The freezer was almost empty and she liked to cook something special on Friday ready for when Cassie came home. She lit the oven and set her weighing scales on the table, then began the therapeutic business of sifting and mixing.

Once she was married it never occurred to Marie that she might have a career of her own, though she knew she was brighter than Vic, quicker at picking up facts and ideas. She had taken him on when they had married and even though she was younger than he she had known that he was a responsibility.

'Whatever do you see in him?' her sisters had said when she had first started courting Vic. It was 1962 and their heads were full of pop music and boys. They went to village dances with teenagers in black leather and came home late on the back of motorbikes.

What had she seen in him? she wondered now as she rubbed fat into flour in a large, china bowl. Someone gentle, steady. Someone who needed looking after.

She had done quite well at school, moving from secondary modern to the grammar when she was thirteen and staying on for the sixth form. She had thought she would go away to Carlisle and train to be a teacher. She had always liked little children. Her father ran the garage in Crowford Village and encouraged her, proud to think that one of his daughters would go away to college. Even when she started going out with Vic her plans were the same. She could come home for weekends, she said. She would see Vic then.

The flooding of the valley changed everything. Her family had been forced to move and used the compensation from the Water Board to set up in a new petrol station on the A69.

Vic was frightened of losing her. He thought she would never come back. On the summer day when she left school he asked her to be his wife, explaining in a strange, old-fashioned way, what his prospects were. He was only under-keeper, he said, but in six months his boss would retire and they could live in the cottage on the estate. She had been touched by the emotion in his voice and his need for her. On her nineteenth birthday they were married in Crowford church, the last couple to have a wedding there before the waters came. Now, nearly thirty years later, she would have wished for nothing different.

She scattered flour on the table and began to roll out the pastry in firm, hard movements. She was a large woman, big bosomed and hippy with strangely fine ankles and small feet which she squeezed into patent leather shoes. Shoes, she always said to Vic, were her weakness.

At half past three when the oven was full she went into the garden to fetch in the washing. She saw Ursula Ottway drive along the road from the dam and turn up the track to Back Rigg. Marie waved at her but Ursula did not respond. Marie was not surprised. Since Fred had died the old woman had become more eccentric and isolated. Besides, she would have been out to Appleworth to do her shopping and that always upset her.

On the way back to the house she stopped, setting the heavy basket of washing on the grass, to shut the outhouse door. The wind had caught it and it was banging. The outhouse was stone built, part of the cottage. Vic should clear that place out, she thought. Most of the stuff inside had been there since before they were married and he never used it now. There were snares and traps, long since illegal, and on a shelf at one end dusty glass bottles which probably contained poison, the labels faded so they were illegible. He should keep it locked, she thought, briefly, and went back into the kitchen, wiping her shoes carefully before she went in. She piled the crockery on the draining board ready for washing then made a cup of tea and waited for the ambulance to bring Cassie home.

Cassie had been a surprise, a gift out of the blue. Marie had always wanted children but the years passed and no babies came. The doctors could give them no adequate reason. Then there had been Cassie. They had known from the beginning that she was brain damaged but by then Marie was so desperate for a child that she was grateful even for the chance to hold the baby in her arms.

'Are you sure you can manage her?' Vic had asked anxiously. Perhaps he was afraid she would have no time left for him.

'Of course I can manage her,' Marie had said. She was almost pleased to hear that Cassie would be dependent on her for ever.

It meant that she would never lose her. The decision to let the girl go away to the special school in Appleworth when she was twelve was the hardest she had ever taken. Vic had left the matter to her.

'You have the care and worry of her,' he had said. 'You'll know where she'll be happiest.'

The social worker had spoken about Marie needing a break.

'You deserve some time to yourself,' she had said. 'You've worked wonders with her. No one would have believed that she could progress so well. Now it's time to think of your own needs.'

It had been impossible for Marie to explain that she had delighted in caring for Cassie. Impossible, too, to say that compared with the effort of giving Vic the confidence to survive in the valley there had been a relief in meeting Cassie's uncomplicated demands.

All the same she decided to let the girl go. Cassie was becoming bored and frustrated at home and as she grew bigger and stronger Marie found her temper tantrums increasingly hard to control. And she realised that, although he tried not to show it, Vic was upset by the girl. When she was a baby he had been almost affectionate, holding her anxiously, buying her presents, taking her for walks up the valley in her pram. But now, as she approached adolescence, Marie could see that her uncoordinated movements and her slurred speech disturbed him. Sometimes Cassie would throw her arms around him, pulling him down so that his head rested against her cheek, damp from the saliva dribbling from her slack mouth. He would pull away without a word and go outside to stand in the garden, staring up at the hill. He would have liked a son, Marie thought suddenly, with a stab of guilt. A fit and healthy young man like Jeremy Grenville. Someone to take up on to the hill and teach everything he knows.

Vic Liddle spent the afternoon on the hill. He did not spend enough time there, especially at this time of the year. He thought it was too much work for one man – rearing the pheasants and keeping 2000 acres of heather moorland in a fit state to provide a decent day's shooting five or six times a season. The moor always had to take second place. Perhaps now he had someone to help him things would be different, but he did not trust Danny Craven further than he could throw him and he thought there would still never be enough hours of daylight to get it all done.

All the same he looked up to Crowford Crag with some satisfaction. The heather was just as he liked to see it. They had almost finished burning and the blackened strips showed up dramatically against the brown hill. Soon it would be replaced by the new shoots of heather that the grouse liked to eat. He burnt each year in strict rotation, following the plan left to him by the old keeper. He kept it on the wall in the cottage, though he knew it by heart and did not need the guidance of the crayon-coloured map. Marie complained about it good-naturedly and said it made the place look untidy but he would not let her take it down. Some keepers went in for November burning but he preferred to do it in the spring to leave some heather long to feed the birds in case there was snow. Now he wanted to check that there weren't any areas that needed reseeding.

He walked on towards the Crag, flushing the grouse which came lower down the hill in spring, looking all the time for signs of predators. There had been a lot of carrion crows this year and it was a bad time for foxes, just after lambing. Pest control was Craven's responsibility and if his gibbets were anything to go by he was conscientious enough, but Vic wanted to see for himself. They could do with some Samson traps to have a go at the stoats and weasels. He came to a shooting butt and stopped to get his breath. That would be the next job, he thought, repairing the butts. There seemed no end to it. As he set off again he saw Ursula Ottway's Land Rover drive up the track to Back Rigg, but thought nothing of it.

When he got down from the hill he was tempted to call in to the cottage and have a quiet cup of tea with Marie before the girl came home. Once the ambulance arrived there would be no peace for either of them until Monday morning. But he had sent Craven to build a new pheasant release pen in the wood at the east of the estate and he wanted to see if the job was finished. He took the van along the road past the cottage then set off across the fields by foot, thinking that they could do with a crop providing more cover here if they were going to release pheasants from the wood. Something like turnip would be best. If Jeremy Grenville had more authority on the estate he would arrange it, but he let the tenant farmers walk all over him.

The relationship between Vic and the tenant farmers had never been good. They came occasionally to work as beaters for the shoots but otherwise had little contact. Vic found it impossible to see the problems of the estate from their point of view. What did the drop in sheep prices have to do with him? He only thought the farmers should be more cooperative. His shoots made a profit for the Cadver and kept their rents down. They had no right to whinge. He walked on, brooding about this lack of gratitude, until he came to the small wood where he hoped this year to move the pheasants.

He bought in the pheasants as day-old chicks, when they were tiny, thumb-nail size, and kept them confined at first in very small pens, hardening them off as they got older, moving them into bigger rearing pens. You needed an affinity with pheasants to achieve his success rate. Each evening he would phone the met office in Carlisle and decide whether they could be let out at night. The release pen was the last step before they were returned to the wild.

He heard Danny Craven before he saw him. There was the sound of hammering and the low, tuneless whistling that a child makes when he's concentrating. It had been a cold spring and most of the trees were bare and the ground was thick with last winter's leaves.

Vic had known the wood since he was a child. It was one of the features of his landscape. There had been a fox covert, encouraged by the old squire, Olivia Grenville's grandfather, who had been more interested in hunting than shooting.

One summer holiday Vic had come to the wood each night at dusk to watch the cubs. It had been an obsession. While other boys watched television and played cowboys and Indians he came to the wood to see the foxes. Even now, when he should consider them as vermin, they held a fascination for him. If he had problems with a fox taking pheasants from the release pen he preferred to wait for it, in the special look-out he had built in a tall tree, and shoot it with a deer rifle, than put down poison which would kill them all.

At the edge of the wood Vic paused and looked back over Crow Water, preparing himself for the meeting with Craven. Vic found even the most routine exchange a strain. He had never had friends. There had only been one other boy of his own age in the village and they had never got on. When he had moved on to the secondary modern at Appleworth he had been even lonelier, out of his depth. He never knew what to say to the other boys, who all seemed quicker, more sophisticated. He had left at fifteen to work on the estate and had never shared the interests of other teenagers. He cared for Marie. And Cassie, of course. But there was no one else he felt the need to bother with. He went occasionally for a pint in the Crowford Hotel, and all the regulars knew him – he had been at school with most of them – but they never had any real contact beyond a nod and a chat about the weather. He got on surprisingly well with Jeremy Grenville, but he was hardly more than a boy and as shy and awkward as Vic himself. Otherwise he preferred to be alone, and though there was really too much work for one man he was happy that he had no assistant.

Then Marcus Grenville had decided that Vic needed an under-keeper. At first Vic dug in his heels and refused to have one. He was deeply suspicious of Grenville's motives in making the appointment and thought Craven would be there as some kind of spy. He had known Danny Craven since he was a child and had never taken to him. He had been the son of one of the estate workers, brash, cocky, always showing off. But Marcus Grenville had been determined and had called Vic into the Estate Office to discuss it.

'Look,' he had said in that soft, appeasing voice that Victor had heard him use on the television, talking to eager young reporters about the state of the Tory Party. 'I'd like you to give the man a chance. I know he was wild as a boy but that was years ago. He's been working for five years on an estate on Exmoor, running some of the shoots for them. His references are very reliable.'

'If he's that clever,' Vic had said, 'why's he interested in a job as under-keeper? You'd think he'd want to be in charge somewhere.'

Especially Craven, he had thought. Craven had always been an arrogant bastard.

Marcus Grenville had opened his arms expansively. 'Vic,' he had said. 'He wants to come home. I'm sure you can understand that.'

Not Danny Craven, Vic had thought. He couldn't wait to get out of the valley. His sister had been the same. She'd left for London as soon as she finished at Appleworth Tech. The whole family had wanderlust.

'I don't need an under-keeper,' Vic said firmly. 'I can manage on my own.'

'I'm not asking your opinion, Liddle,' Marcus Grenville had said, testily. 'The decision has already been taken. Danny Craven starts on the first of February.'

So Danny Craven had moved into the Lodge by the east gate and Vic could see no sign that his years away had made him more responsible. He was in his early thirties but he looked much the same as he had when he was a boy. His dark hair was still a little too long, his voice a little too loud. He acted as if he owned the place. Marie said it was all show, bravado. Danny Craven had always been a coward, she said. He was the same age as her younger sister. He'd always been one for teasing the girls, but if you stood up to him he'd run away.

Well, Vic thought. It was time to stand up to him. In the wood the hammering stopped.

'Hello!' Craven shouted. 'Who is it?' He must have heard Vic's footsteps or the dog snuffling through the leaves.

Vic walked on through the trees. The release pen was almost finished. Wire mesh was stretched between high stakes, folded under at the bottom. It enclosed a cleared area of the wood and was open to the sky. There were funnels to allow the birds in and out. They would need an electric fence to keep away the foxes, otherwise it was done.

'Oh,' Craven said. 'It's you.' He was squatting on a fallen log, smoking a cigarette. 'You're a bit late. It's nearly finished now.' He knocked the ash from the cigarette into his cupped hand.

'I can see that,' Vic said. He walked slowly round the perimeter of the fence, knowing that he was only putting off the time when he would have to talk to Craven.

'Well,' Craven shouted. 'What do you think?'

'Fine,' Vic said. 'It's fine.' It was true. When Craven set his mind to it he was a good worker. He seldom set his mind to it.

'Can I knock off now, then?' Craven said.

Vic had completed the circuit of the release pen and had returned to Danny Craven. He nodded. Now he was here he felt a fool. Craven had been perfectly capable of finishing the task without supervision. Marcus Grenville was always telling him that he should delegate more but Vic found it impossible to delegate to Danny Craven. He suspected him of dishonesty, of poaching, of being a better keeper than he was. He did not like the way he looked at Marie. There was something about him that did not ring true.

Danny Craven carefully put out his cigarette and buried it under a mound of leaf mould. He began to pack his tools into a grey canvas army surplus rucksack. Then he stood up, slung the bag over one shoulder and began to walk towards the open fields. Vic followed him without a word. Somewhere above the trees a buzzard was calling, and the noise seemed to taunt him. Buzzards were legally protected but they took more young birds than any other raptor. In the old days this would have been the time of year for getting rid of them. There were still keepers in the county who took no heed of the law.

When they came to the edge of the wood Danny Craven turned and waited for him, as if surprised to find him still there. The buzzard floated over the trees and hovered above them, its long round wings fingered at the edges to maintain its position against the wind from the lake. Danny looked up at the bird.

'There must be a pair breeding in that Forestry Commission land at the edge of the lake,' he said, challenging, mischievous.

'Aye,' Vic said, defensively. 'Well there's nothing I can do about it. Not now, Mr Grenville's orders.'

'It seems to me,' Craven said, 'that you take too much notice of Mr Grenville's orders. You're head keeper. He should leave you in charge.'

'Maybe he should,' Vic said. 'But that's my business. Not yours.'

Craven shrugged and they walked on in silence to the road. Vic felt awkward. He had managed the thing badly. He shouldn't let Craven irritate him. When they got to the van he offered Craven a lift up the road to the Lodge, as a way of re-establishing understanding, and was pleased when the younger man accepted. But when they got to the house the state of the Lodge garden, overgrown and untouched, with rubbish blown into the hedge and a box of empty beer bottles outside the back door provoked him again. He could not hold his tongue.

'You should do something to tidy up that mess,' he said, as Craven was lifting his tools from the back of the van. 'It's a disgrace.'

'I'm paid as keeper,' Craven said. 'Not as gardener.'

'All the same, I'm surprised Grenville's not had a word with you. What sort of impression does it give to visitors using the east drive?'

'I don't give a sod what the visitors think,' Craven said. 'And if Grenville says anything I'll tell him the same.'

He walked shamelessly up the overgrown path to the cottage door while Vic watched, astonished, from the front seat of the van.

Vic had still not returned to Keeper's Cottage when the ambulance came with Cassie and by then it was nearly dark. Marie had been looking out for it and went to help. She stood by the tail gate, tapping her shiny black shoes on the road to keep out the cold, as the ambulance driver let down the lift for Cassie and her wheelchair.

Cassie was still on the lift when she saw Marie. She began to clap, nodding her head backwards and forwards. The light from the uncurtained sitting-room window which shone on to her face showed she was beaming.

'Well, she's pleased to see you, that's for sure,' said the ambulance driver as he locked the back doors on the empty vehicle. 'Can you manage now?'

'Of course we can manage,' Marie said. 'Can't we, Cassie?'

And the girl began to clap again.

'There's a letter for you,' the man said. 'From the school.'

Marie nodded and took it. They'd be fundraising again, she thought. They never seemed to have enough money. She'd do what she could.

The ambulance drove off and she pushed the wheelchair up the ramp to the front door and through to the warm and brightly lit kitchen.

Chapter Three

Whenever Marcus Grenville came back from Westminster to spend a weekend in the constituency he liked to have all the family together for a meal in the Cadver on Friday night. He enjoyed sitting at the head of the table, listening to the chatter about the estate, holding forth about his week in the Commons, discreetly dropping names. More recently there had been some important names to drop. After years of being considered unfashionable, Marcus Grenville was coming back into favour. He had never been one of the forceful radicals in the party – not through principle but because he had misread the signs and failed to change his position in time. Now, however, it seemed that such radicalism was considered divisive. The party was looking to the solid, old-fashioned Tories, the Knights of the Shires, to hold it together. Marcus Grenville, it seemed, had been right all along.

When the tide began to turn Marcus Grenville emphasised his rural background assiduously. He suddenly developed an interest in the environment. With experience he had come to judge more accurately the direction the party was taking and was determined this time not to be left behind. He managed to get himself elected on to the Council for the Preservation of Rural England and was delighted to accept the position of Director of Westmorland Wildlife Trust. There was some comment in the local press that a landowner whose main reputation in the county was as someone who shot and ate birds with obvious relish should be so closely allied with the conservation charities, but Marcus Grenville said that there was no contradiction.

'It's all a question of habitat management,' he said easily when the question was put to him by a television reporter. 'If we manage the uplands for grouse we encourage all the other birds that we love to see on the hills. The same goes for pheasant and woodland.'

His advisers had told him not to be too specific in any of his replies in case he made a mistake. There were so many enthusiastic amateurs out there, they said, birdwatchers and greens and cranks of every kind, just waiting for him to mix up his curlews and his corn buntings. Much better to be vague and statesmanlike.

The television reporter accepted his answer without question. Nobody asked about predator control, about pole traps and snares and mutilated birds of prey. Marcus Grenville was a rising star, a potential Minister of the Environment, and nobody wanted to offend him.

Grenville drove the last familiar mile to the main gate of the Cadver quickly and without further thought about Ursula, preoccupied with his plans for the following day. He had invited a number of distinguished people to the house for what he had called an 'informal conference on the future of our countryside'. The people had been chosen for their power and influence. There was the head of the newly formed Nature Conservancy Council for Scotland, the Chairman of the Country Landowners' Association and a chief adviser to the Farming and Wildlife Advisory Group, besides the directors of a number of environmental charities. 'We are the policy makers,' he had written in his invitation, 'and I feel we should have the opportunity for an intense and informal exploration of our views before more policy decisions are taken.'

The more cynical of the recipients of this invitation reflected that Marcus Grenville was not yet a policy maker and that the conference was more about giving him the inside knowledge that would allow him to be one, rather than about any altruistic concern about nature conservation. Whatever his motives, he was determined that the conference should be a success.

He wondered briefly whether Olivia would put in an appearance the following day. The least she could do, he thought, would be to come in to lunch. She might enjoy that. It would remind her of the time when the Cadver was often full of famous people. She was always confident enough in the house.

He had thought, at first, that his wife's agoraphobia was a convenient excuse for not attending the constituency functions which she so hated.

'They're all such dreadful little people,' she would say after the annual dinner dance or garden party. 'I don't know what to talk to them about.'

The illness had developed rapidly after the flooding of the valley and it had occurred to him too that it was a sort of revenge because in the end he had been unable to prevent the reservoir from being built.

He had to concede that whatever the original cause of the panic attacks they must be real enough now. Olivia never left the Cadver grounds and her forays from the house into the garden were becoming more scarce. She could not still be feigning illness – it would be a disproportionate and irrational way of showing displeasure to make herself a prisoner for twenty years.

But she was an irrational and obsessive woman, he thought as the car pulled up outside the house. With regret he remembered other women he had known, women who laughed and danced and enjoyed his company.

Jeremy Grenville was nervous. Tonight would be Eve Theobald's first introduction to the family and he wanted her to understand them. He did not expect her to like them. That would be too much to expect, but he hoped she would get a clearer impression of the influences that had formed him. He knew that she thought him something of a coward. She called him, affectionately, a wimp.

'I don't understand,' she would say. 'If you don't like it you can always get out. You've got a degree. There are lots of jobs you could do.'

It was hard to explain that he believed he had a responsibility for the place, that although he had been sent away to prep school at eight, he thought he belonged there.

'I don't see why,' Eve would say. 'Your family's been exploiting that land for generations. So what? Why does that tie you to it too?'

Once he had made the mistake of using the word 'duty' in his conversation with Eve. His mother had been strong on the idea of duty. He had been brought up with it. Eve only laughed and said that he had been brainwashed by that crazy school of his. It was not duty, he thought now, but guilt which made him anxious to do his best for the Cadver. He had never lived up to his mother's expectations of him. She had made it clear from his childhood that her hopes for the estate rested with him, that he was connected to it emotionally, through inheritance, in a way his father could never understand. He had been three years old when the valley was flooded, and it was his earliest memory. He could remember his father taking him to watch the huge earth movers working on the dam and returning to the house to find his mother crying. It was the only time he had seen her weep.

Throughout school and university he had failed her. It was not that he did badly or did not try, but that he did not shine. She wanted a hero to protect the Cadver and there was nothing heroic about his shyness, his inadequacy on the sportsfield, his inability to inspire his fellows. Even now in the management of the estate he tried to please her and still her approval was half-hearted and grudging.

He stood by the window and looked down the drive to the Lodge where all the lights seemed to be on, and thought that it was not fair for Eve to jeer about his commitment to the place. She had her own ideals, her own idea of principle.

He had met her first when a party of Animal Rights Activists had come on to the estate to protest at the annual New Year's Hunt which always began from the Cadver. His father was away and he had been sent, imperiously, by his mother to deal with the protesters. He had made some unconvincing threats to call the police, then stood awkwardly watching, as if he, not they, were the impostor.

He had not noticed Eve at first. She was not one of the ringleaders. When the hunt moved off, the group had followed in a shouting, uncoordinated mob, but she had remained behind to talk to him. It had been freezing and he remembered that there had been ice on the edge of the reservoir. Against the frosted lawn she looked robust and healthy with dark wiry hair and cheeks red from the cold. She was wearing green cord trousers and a Barbour jacket, so she might have been one of the hunt followers, except for the anti-blood sports badge on her lapel.

'Aren't you going with them?' she had asked, nodding towards the red coats and the horses disappearing up the drive.

'No,' he had said, lamely. 'I don't hunt myself, actually.' He did not tell her that it frightened him.

'Why do you allow it to happen on your land, then?'

'I don't know,' he had said. 'Tradition, I suppose. My great-grandfather was very keen. And it's not my land. It's my father's.'

'Does that make a difference?' she had asked. 'You run the place, don't you?'

Oh yes, he had thought. It makes all the difference in the world. Then he had turned to her.

'What about you? Aren't you going to join your friends?'

'They're not my friends, *actually*,' she said, mimicking the expression of his voice. Then, smiling. 'Most of them are pains in the arse. I've made my protest. I don't see the point in chasing round the countryside getting cold.'

'Where do you live?' he had asked.

'Appleworth,' she had said. 'I'm a teacher. I work in the special school there.'

'You work with handicapped kids?'

She had nodded.

He had been going to say that she must know Cassie Liddle then, but she turned her back on him.

'I'd better get started,' she said. 'It's a long walk. I came in the mini-bus with the others.'

'Oh no,' he had said suddenly. 'Don't walk. I'll give you a lift.'

She had turned back and smiled. 'I don't know. It might be seen as a gift from the opposition. I'd be accused of being bought off by the enemy.'

'Oh well,' he had said uncertainly. He had never been very good with women. Perhaps she couldn't be bothered with him and wanted an excuse. 'I don't want to put you in an awkward position.'

Then she had laughed out loud. 'Don't be daft,' she said. 'I'm joking. I'd love a lift. The walk would kill me.'

In Appleworth he had bought her lunch in a pub crowded with drunken farmers. She drank pints of bitter and seemed perfectly sober. Afterwards he asked her when he might see her again.

'Are you sure you want to?' she said. 'What will your family say? I'm hardly the girlfriend they would choose for you.'

He could not tell if she were teasing again, but he took her seriously.

'I don't care,' he said. 'Really. I don't care.'

It was his mother who had insisted that he bring Eve to the Friday night dinner party. She had found out, somehow, that he was seeing a girl. His mother had a network of spies in the valley and though she never left the house she seemed to know, magically, what was going on.

'It won't do, you know,' she had insisted. 'You can't keep her a secret. Perhaps you are ashamed of her?'

When she spoke to him like that she could still make him feel like a six-year-old, and the stutter, which had made his childhood so miserable, returned to him.

'N . . . no,' Jeremy had said. 'Of course I'm not ashamed of her. But don't you think the family is a little d . . . daunting, to meet all at one go?'

She had shrugged. 'Daunting? No, of course not. How ridiculous!'

So the invitation had been given to Eve and surprisingly she had accepted.

'You don't have to come,' he had said, anxiously, 'if you don't want to. I can make an excuse.'

'Don't you dare!' she had said. 'It'll be great fun. I want to see how the other half live.'

Since their first meeting at New Year she had acquired a car, a rusting Deux Chevaux with windows that would not fasten properly and an exhaust that almost touched the ground. Jeremy sat in his bedroom, waiting for her to arrive, listening for her car to rattle up the drive, growing more nervous and certain that the evening would be a disaster.

Olivia Grenville could not remember when she had begun to despise her husband. It might even have been before they were married. Then the Cadver had belonged to her grandfather. Her parents had been killed in a bombing raid when they were in town to celebrate a wedding anniversary during her father's leave, and she had moved automatically to the Cadver to be with her grandfather. She was fifteen and left her boarding school with some relief. The death of her parents scarcely touched her. She felt she hardly knew them. Her grandfather had a Victorian attitude to the education of women and thought she would be better off at home. He arranged for a music teacher to come from Appleworth to teach her the piano but otherwise she was left to her own devices. The lack of a formal education never bothered her, though there were areas where she had no knowledge at all. She had a sketchy recollection of history and English literature, but of geography and science she knew nothing. Her ignorance did not trouble her in the slightest and she made no attempt to teach herself. She convinced herself that if she did not know a fact it was not worth knowing. What was most important, she felt, was common sense and breeding and both those she had in abundance. She had a disdain for people with qualifications and degrees, as if they had spent their lives in self-indulgence.

Her grandfather had suggested Marcus Grenville as a prospective husband. He had been the chairman of the selection committee that had chosen the young man as candidate for the Conservative Party to fight a by-election after the war. In an area like Appleworth it was inevitable that he would become the constituency Member of Parliament. The old man brought Marcus Grenville home for dinner and afterwards asked in his mischievous way what she had made of him.

'Well,' he had said teasing. 'Isn't he a fine young man? Haven't we chosen well?'

She had been non-committal. She had seen him for such a short time, she said. It was hard for her to tell.

'You'll have plenty of time to get to know him,' her grandfather had said. He obviously enjoyed the matchmaking immensely. 'I've invited him to shoot next weekend. I'd say he's prime minister material. Of course, he needs a wife.'

And so, almost like that, the thing had been arranged. Olivia had supposed that Marcus Grenville would do. The only passion in her life had been for the young music teacher who sat beside her, very close, on the piano stool and showed her how to position her hands, but her grandfather must have noticed the eagerness with which she waited for the weekly lessons because he had said suddenly one day that she was too old for such nonsense and she had never seen the young man again.

There was, she supposed, nothing to object to in Marcus Grenville. He was practising at the time as a barrister with a prestigious London firm. He was charming and handsome in a dark, rather heavy way and he always knew the right things to say. In his education it seemed there had been no gaps. He could discuss opera and architecture and the latest technology with a fluency that impressed her grandfather and made him chuckle with delight.

Perhaps it was his education and his intelligence that she came to despise first. She felt that in all this clever talk there was an element of showing off and that if she knew anything at all about the theories he propounded she would discover him as a fraud. His knowledge, she felt, was superficial, acquired like everything else he did, not through interest but through ambition. She was aware from the beginning that ambition was what had prompted him to ask her to marry him. It was the Cadver, the estate and the land, which attracted him. The prospect of owning it excited him so that when he walked up the drive to meet her he was flushed and happy with all the appearance of someone in love.

'He's besotted with you, Livvy,' her grandfather would say. 'Any fool can see that. You'll have to marry the man.'

'No,' she could have said. 'You're the fool.' But still she went along with it.

Why *did* she go along with it? she wondered now as she arranged the flowers on the long dining-room table. To please her grandfather, of course, but there had been more to it than that. She had thought that she would be able to *manage* Marcus; that in the things that really mattered to her – the running of the house and the estate – she would be in charge. It had been a shock to find that he could be stubborn, wilful, even stupid.

Yet, she thought as she finished the flowers and went upstairs to change, she had succeeded in most things in getting her way. She had lost over the reservoir, which at the time had mattered more than anything else. It had been a desecration of land which had been in the family for years. She could not expect Marcus to understand. He had no real responsibility for the place. He had claimed that he had done all he could to protect it, that they had taken the matter to court, that compulsory purchase meant just what it said, but she had been able to tell all along that his heart had not been in the fight. His fight, she knew, was about getting more compensation than he had the right to expect, not in saving the land. She could not bear it, but she supposed she would give him the benefit of the doubt. She would maintain the appearance that they were a united and supportive couple and keep her contempt to herself.

When Simon Barton came home from work in Appleworth, Joanna was still in the pottery and had made no attempt to prepare for the party at the Cadver. He was mildly irritated, as he was by much that she did. Grenville was her father, after all. Simon minded the dinner parties less than she did. He had little time for the other guests but the food was always good and Marcus Grenville knew more about wine than he did about natural history. Besides, Marcus was being especially pleasant to him at the moment. Simon was an environmental consultant and Marcus saw him as a free source of unbiased expertise. It was rather flattering to have one's opinion so assiduously sought. After working for some years for a conservation charity he had recently set up in business on his own, hiring his services to advise industries that had been forced to become more environmentally sensitive. He worked from a small but attractive office in Appleworth and needed all the contacts Marcus Grenville could make for him. The week before, he had been approached by a major oil company to do an environmental impact assessment along a west coast pipeline and he suspected that Marcus had recommended him to the firm. It was good for his business image to be linked with a man so prominent in the conservation world. He should, he thought, be gracious.

Joanna was sitting on one of the low wooden chairs that had been left behind when the school had closed, dressed in jeans and the old shirt of his which she wore as an overall. Her hair was short, rather spiky on the top. She was thirty-five but seemed not to have aged since they had married ten years before.

'Shouldn't we be getting ready?' he asked carefully. The dinner parties always made her tense, unsettled.

She looked at him, her face turned to the light so he could see the high cheekbones and fine, wide mouth, and he thought, with detachment, that she was quite lovely.

'I don't want to go,' she said. 'Why do we live so close to my bloody parents? Perhaps I should get rid of the pottery altogether and set up a hostel for teenage heroin addicts in the city. I'd be good at something like that.'

Simon showed no reaction. She often spoke of leaving the valley, of travelling to India, of living in Chelsea, or at least of doing something worthwhile with her life. He tried not to sound bored. He humoured her as he always did.

'You're a good potter,' he said. 'And you know you'd never leave the valley. You're miserable if you're away for a week.'

It was true. Something seemed to hold her at Crowford. He thought she would find it impossible to break away. At Easter they would open the shop and the visitors who came to the lake to picnic and the collectors who knew of her reputation would come to buy. The shelves that had been built across the large school room already held unglazed pots. This was her busiest time of year. She worked best in the winter and the spring when it was quiet.

He waited, knowing that if he tried to bully her she would have a tantrum and it would take hours to calm her. Despite what she said she was tied to the family and the Cadver as much as to the valley, and despite the protests she was always there, at the parties, to play at being Daddy's loving daughter. She stood up suddenly and moved to the deep white porcelain sink and began to wash her hands. There was dried clay on her cheek and in her hair.

'You'd better come and have a shower,' he said, 'before we go.'

'Yes,' she said. 'I suppose I should.' She seemed very tired.

They walked out into the yard. There was a view of the lake and the dark silhouette of Crowford Rigg against the starlit sky. She locked the door behind her and shivered. After the warmth of the pottery it seemed very cold. He took her elbow more like a nurse helping an elderly patient than a lover, and together they ran to the house. In the storm porch she waited, staring out over the reservoir, while he opened the door.

'Don't trust my father when he's giving favours,' she said suddenly. 'He always wants something in return.'

'Oh,' Simon said lightly. 'I think I can handle your father.'

'I thought that once,' she said. 'I know better now.'

They went inside and up the stairs in silence to prepare for the dinner party.

The Bartons were the last to arrive at the Cadver and Olivia was beginning to feel annoyed. Joanna had always been a problem. It was Marcus's fault of course. He had spoilt her because she was pretty. Jeremy, born ten years later, had been much more her child. Olivia was not entirely satisfied with the result – there was a weakness which displeased her – but at least he knew how to conduct himself. He knew that appearances mattered. Joanna had made life difficult for them all.

It made no difference to Olivia that tonight the only stranger to be impressed was Eve Theobald. Still, there was something shameful about Joanna and Simon being late and causing this awkwardness as they stood in the drawing room, holding drinks, waiting to go in to dine. Perhaps Eve was the only person not to notice it. She seemed perfectly at ease, talking to Jeremy, making him laugh out loud. She was quite unsuitable, Olivia had seen at once, dressed in a short black dress which scarcely covered her buttocks, over tight black leggings and shoes of the sort Olivia had worn on the moor when she went grouse shooting as a girl. At the same time there was something about her. She could see why Jeremy had been attracted to her. She had strength, confidence, the personality he lacked. Olivia had decided from the beginning that the girl was dangerous. All the more reason, then, she thought, to present the image of a united, impenetrable family. Let the girl see what she was taking on.

Marcus Grenville stood in front of the fire, looking at them. He was large, thick-lipped, soft.

'Where's Joanna?' he asked of nobody in particular. 'Where's my little girl?'

Olivia ignored the question and looked sideways towards Eve. What could she think of such an inappropriate description of a woman approaching middle age? Again, Eve seemed not to notice and it was Jeremy, standing closest to the window, who said he had heard a car.

'That's it, then,' Olivia said with satisfaction, almost to herself. 'Simon and Joanna are here.'

Because the others had been waiting for them, the entrance of the Bartons had a dramatic, theatrical quality. Eve could imagine them outside, touching up greasepaint, straightening costumes before facing their audience. And the effect, she had to admit, was quite stunning. She felt suddenly heavy, graceless, badly dressed. She had never before seen a woman as beautiful as Joanna Barton. She was thin and fine and was dressed in a lacy dress in 1920s style. She wore beads and long earrings. She came into the room and smiled and apologised that they were so late. It was Simon, she said. Now that he was working for himself he never knew when to stop. She went up to her mother and moved her mouth towards the older woman's cheek, taking care, Eve saw, that there was no actual contact between them.

Then she went to her father and smiled, while he put his arm around her and squeezed her and called her his little girl. It was not, after all, an inaccurate description, Eve thought. There was something remarkably childlike about her.

Simon Barton stood just inside the door, watching his wife's performance. He was short, sturdy, muscular. She caught his eye and turned away to talk again to Jeremy. Olivia called them all into the dining room to eat.

The interruption came when they were eating cheese. It seemed to Eve, who had been careful because she was driving, that they had all had a lot to drink. Even she felt a little light-headed, so the banging of the door in another room, the sound of raised voices, was only of mild interest. No one else took any notice. Perhaps, she thought, it would have been bad manners to comment. Then the dining-room door was flung open and it was impossible for the diners to pretend that everything was normal. A tall, large-boned woman with a shock of white hair stood just inside the room, followed by a flustered housekeeper.

'I want to talk to you!' the woman said. Eve saw that her boots had left muddy footprints across the pale carpet. She felt wonderfully entertained.

'Ursula!' Marcus Grenville said in his mellow satisfied voice. 'Whatever is the matter?' He patted Eve's hand reassuringly as if to say: don't worry. The old girl's mad as a hatter. But perfectly harmless.

Ursula Ottley took a deep breath and seemed determined at self control.

'You are a murderer,' she said. 'And a hypocrite.'

Grenville seemed about to interrupt but she continued, quite reasonably.

'You pretend to be interested in the countryside, but today on your land I found illegal poison, which had already killed a buzzard and two cats. I have the evidence and you will be prosecuted. I am here to tell you that I intend to give the matter as much publicity as the media are prepared to offer. You are not to be trusted with our countryside and I will make it my business to see that you are never given responsibility for it again.'

'Poison?' Grenville said. 'You've found poison on the estate? But that's impossible. I gave orders . . .'

She took no notice of him and turned sharply so the mud on her boot was ground into the carpet, then she left the house without a word.

Chapter Four

George Palmer-Jones had been invited to the conference at the Cadver because he had a reputation as an independent ornithologist. His name often appeared in scientific journals and he was considered a prominent member of the natural history establishment. He accepted the invitation because work had already taken him north and because his wife's aunt lived at Crowford. He suspected that nothing constructive would come of the conference. It would be perhaps a chance to meet old friends and it gave Molly the excuse to visit Ursula. He had met Marcus Grenville on other occasions – they had served together on the council of an environmental charity – and had not been impressed.

On Friday they had a meeting with a solicitor in York who sometimes gave them work and spent the night in a pub on the Durham Moors. Molly, disturbed by the phone call to Ursula, was restless and impatient, and almost persuaded George that they should drive on to Crowford on Friday evening.

'Are you mad?' he said. 'It would be midnight before we arrived. Besides, I want to look for blackcock on the moor before breakfast.'

So Molly had to wait until he had returned from bird-watching on Saturday morning, then they set off west, across the empty spaces of the north Pennines. Molly drove. George would be tempted to look for merlins or harriers at the same time as driving, and on such steep and narrow roads her nerves would not stand it.

They came to Appleworth soon after nine, just as the shops were opening, and it was already busy. The town had been built along the black peaty waters of the River Crow. There was a low bridge, only wide enough for single-lane traffic and streets of small squat grey houses. There was already one coach parked in the square. In the summer Appleworth would be filled with trippers. It had been used by a television company as the location of a long-running serial about a rural doctor's practice and now tourists flocked there to see its charms first hand.

The road to Crowford followed the river. Molly was reminded of adolescent trips to visit her aunt and uncle. There had been a station at Appleworth then and Ursula had collected her in a large and comfortable car.

'My parents never quite approved of Ursula,' she said suddenly. She remembered the whispered conversations at home before her aunt's wedding, and the shocked silences that descended whenever she entered the room.

'Oh?' he said. 'Why?' He suspected that Molly's parents had never quite approved of him.

'They thought she married beneath her,' Molly said. 'They thought it would never work out.'

'But it did?'

'Of course. Perhaps they were too wrapped up in each other. They seemed to have no time for anyone else. When Fred died Ursula was devastated.'

'How did she meet him?'

'She came with my mother and their parents to the Cadver for a shooting weekend. My grandfather was a friend of Olivia Grenville's grandfather. Ursula was quite young, eighteen or nineteen. Fred Ottway's parents were tenant farmers at Back Rigg and Fred worked there for them. The story of how they met has become quite famous in the family. Ursula was bored at the Cadver and walked out by herself. She bumped into Fred in the lane and they started talking. She invited him back to the Cadver for tea! Can you imagine what they thought when she turned up with one of the tenant farmers still in his working clothes? Fred tried to refuse but she had enchanted him. I don't think Olivia has ever forgiven her. She waited until she was twenty-one, then they married. By then Fred's father was dead and they moved into the farm. That was just before the War and she's been at Back Rigg ever since.'

'Isn't it too much for her now? She must be quite elderly.' George was not really interested. He was looking out at the hills, wishing he had a day to walk there. If there were golden eagles in the Lake District why not here, where there were fewer observers?

'She doesn't farm the land any more,' Molly said. 'The Estate's leased it to a neighbour. She's just got the house and a few chickens. And her cats.'

The road and the river were at the bottom of a steep-sided, twisting valley. There was little other traffic. They drove through a thicket of deciduous trees and past a huge Forestry Commission conifer plantation. Then there was a sharp bend and suddenly they were on the top of the dam with the lake spreading far to the west. To the east was a sharp drop and the regulated flow of the river trickling on down the valley.

'Can you stop for a few minutes?' George asked. 'The thing doesn't start until ten and I don't want to be early. Let's see if there's anything interesting on the reservoir before we go on.'

Molly waited patiently in the car while he took his tripod and telescope from the boot and began to scan the lake. She had never shared his obsession, had never properly understood it, but she knew that birdwatching was essential to him. Without it, the latent depression that sometimes troubled him would become overwhelming. The light was behind him so he had a good view of the lake, but when he straightened he seemed disappointed.

'Nothing much there,' he said. 'I suppose it's too high and the sides are too steep . . .' He spoke almost to himself.

Molly drove on across the dam, past the gothic towers built at the end of it and Keeper's Cottage to the main gate.

'You can drop me here,' he said. 'I'll walk.' Now that he was here he was regretting his decision to come and wanted to put off the moment when he would be trapped in a room with all that talk.

'No,' she said. 'I'll take you right to the house. It's miles.'

The drive was like a country lane, leading through woodland to open lawns and a formal garden. There was a view of a square eighteenth-century house with long windows and tall chimneys. A flight of impressive stone steps, almost the width of the house, led to the front door. Marcus Grenville stood there, welcoming another guest. He shook the man's hand and put his arm round his shoulder, the professional politician.

George hesitated by the car, wondering whether it would be worth taking the telescope and tripod with him. If this was a conference on the countryside there should be an opportunity to see something of what they were discussing. He decided against it; binoculars would be sufficient. Grenville saw the other guest into the house and bounded down the steps to greet them.

'George,' he said. 'My dear old friend. How kind of you to come!' He took George's hand and held on to it, beaming, as if he were some statesman waiting for all the photo-journalists to get their pictures. Molly had a sudden sense of tension and unease. Why was he trying so hard? Then she told herself that he was a politician and all politicians were desperate to please.

When she arrived at Back Rigg it was in full sunlight but still the house looked cold. Whenever Molly imagined the place it was in winter with banks of snow on the fells, the windows frosted and the sky as grey as the stone walls and the slate roof. The place had deteriorated since Molly had last been there for Fred's funeral four years before. She was shocked. The window frames were rotting and there were slates missing from the roof.

What sort of landlord is Grenville, allowing an old woman to live in a place like this? she thought, the sight adding to her prejudice about his politics and his personality. And then she felt guilty because it was so long since she had visited.

She knocked at the front door but there was no reply, so she made her way through the overgrown garden to the kitchen. The door was pushed to but not properly shut. Perhaps the wood was so warped by the damp that it was impossible to close it firmly. She knocked again, shivering because the back of the house was always in shadow and always cold. Still there was no reply. With some difficulty Molly pulled open the door and went inside. The room was warm but with none of the blazing, comforting heat she remembered from her childhood. She opened the range and saw that it was nearly out. There were just a few red embers at the bottom of the stove. She took logs from a pile in the corner and threw them in, then opened the flue to let the air get to them.

'Ursula!' she shouted, but without much hope of reply. Ursula would be out on the fells. She had always seen being confined indoors as a form of imprisonment. The Land Rover was still in the yard so she would not be far away. She would be looking out for Molly's car and soon she would return.

Molly was not shocked by the state of the kitchen. Her own, if marginally cleaner, was just as untidy. But she was disturbed by the lack of evidence that any cooking was done there. There were no fresh vegetables and the pans were dusty, obviously not recently used. Ursula had always been a good if haphazard cook and Molly hoped that now she was feeding herself properly. Molly began to open cupboards, thinking that she might make some soup, have something hot for when Ursula came back. The range was not yet warm enough for cooking so she lit a gas ring and put the kettle on it to make tea.

In the fridge there *was* an indication that Ursula had recently been shopping. There were tubs of margarine and packets of ready-wrapped cheese, a two-pint carton of milk, unopened. The milk bottles delivered by the milkman had obviously been emptied the day before – by those cats, Molly thought – and had surprisingly been washed out and set upside down to drain. In the fridge there was a meat pie, obviously homemade, with one portion removed. Molly was reassured by the pie – it showed after all that Ursula was looking after herself.

When the kettle had boiled Molly went out into the garden to look up at the hills, expecting to see Ursula's tall ungainly figure loping down towards the house, but there was only a youngish man whom she supposed must be a keeper. He was dressed in a khaki camouflage jacket and carrying a gun. Why do they all want to pretend to be soldiers? she thought. The sight of the figure, somehow sinister in his military outfit, added to her unease about Ursula. She left the garden and began to search the rest of the house.

The curtains of the drawing room were closed and the room was quite dark. She wondered why she had not noticed the drawn curtains when she came into the house. Perhaps the windows were so grimy outside that it was impossible to tell. She groped for a light switch just inside the door but could not find it and went instead to draw back the curtains. She walked slowly across the room and stumbled over a stool or low table, swearing under her breath at the pain to her ankle. The curtains were heavy velvet and lined and she had to tug at them to get enough light into the room to see.

Ursula was lying on a worn leather Chesterfield. She was dressed in her work clothes and still had her boots on. There was an open bottle of whisky on the mantelpiece but no glass. Her head had fallen so that it touched the floor. She looked like a child, Molly thought, who found it impossible to sit still, in the middle of some sort of gymnastic exercise. But Ursula Ottway was quite still. Her face was purple where the blood had drained to her head and her body was already stiff with rigor mortis.

George did not hear about Ursula's death until late afternoon. Molly, at Back Rigg, had been busy with the bureaucracy that follows sudden death, even the sudden death of an elderly lady. Besides, she had seen no need to interrupt George at the Cadver. She had no suspicions.

The conference proceeded much as he expected. There was a lot of rhetoric but few real assurances and no discussion about who would provide the money to pay for the policy changes they all decided were needed. George had learnt as a civil servant that without a firm budget any project was doomed. Some of the papers were worth hearing – the speaker on the EEC agricultural directive was especially interesting – and Marcus Grenville chaired the event with skill, though his introductions were too sycophantic for George's taste.

At one o'clock they stopped for lunch, which was spread out as a buffet in the large dining room. The food was excellent and the cost of the meal would probably have paid, George thought, for the maintenance of a small nature reserve for several months. While the others were still drinking coffee he went outside. He needed fresh air, a little exercise, a reminder too of what all the talk was about. Because of that he saw the policeman arrive and heard the exchange between him and Grenville on the door step.

The policeman appeared on foot from the back of the house. He must have come up the east drive and parked there. He was embarrassed, apologetic. Even from his seat out of sight on the terrace George could tell that. When he spoke to the housekeeper who opened the door his voice was loud and defensive.

'I'd like to speak to Mr Grenville,' he said.

'I'm sorry,' she said. 'Mr Grenville's busy with his guests.'

For a moment George thought he would leave it at that and arrange to come back later when it was more convenient but he stood his ground.

'It won't take a minute,' he said. 'I'll wait here for him, shall I?'

The door closed and there was silence, except for the sound of the policeman nervously pacing at the top of the steps. Then the door opened and George heard Marcus Grenville, breezy and polite, never forgetting that this was one of his voters.

'Yes?' he said. 'What is it, Constable? I can't give you much time, I'm afraid. I'm tied up all day.'

'I've been asked to come to talk to you, sir . . .' The policeman had obviously prepared a speech but now, faced with the man he had seen so often on the television, it was forgotten.

He began again: 'We had a phone call this morning from a member of the public making certain allegations.'

'What sort of allegations?' Grenville was less dismissive than George would have expected. He was on his guard.

'About the illegal use of poison on the estate, sir,' the policeman continued unhappily. 'Contrary to the Wildlife and Countryside Act 1981.'

'And who made these allegations?'

'I'm sorry, sir. I can't tell you that.'

'It's that bloody Ottway woman again,' Grenville said, forgetting for a moment that he was a politician. He controlled himself. 'That's all right, Constable. She's made similar allegations to me. Of course

44

as a responsible landowner I've looked into it. I take such matters very seriously. I spoke to my head keeper this morning about it and he assures me that no illegal poisons have been used at the Cadver. You know Vic Liddle. He's a careful man. I think you'll find that your informant is malicious.'

George waited until Grenville had gone back into the house before coming out from the shadow of the terrace and into the sunlight.

In the afternoon the conference split into discussion groups, each considering a different aspect of environmental policy. George's was looking at apparently green methods of energy production. It was a subject about which George felt strongly and he spoke forcefully. What was so green about an enormous windmill park on an area of outstanding natural beauty like the North York Moors? he demanded. And how could any conservationist approve the proposals for barrages on the country's most valuable estuaries? What was needed was a real energy conservation policy. The money and research should go into finding a way of saving energy, not producing more of it.

At the end of the session George felt depressed. He had talked too much and made a spectacle of himself. Besides, what did all this talking achieve? Perhaps the young people, the new environmentalists with their radical views and their insistence on action, were right.

At four o'clock there was tea and then most of the delegates began to drift away. Grenville stood at the door, shaking hands, thanking them effusively for their attendance. He seemed relieved to see them all go. George was at the end of the queue but still Grenville greeted him with professional enthusiasm.

'George!' he said. 'Thank you for your contribution. Invaluable!' He held on to George's hand until the room was empty and he could be sure they would not be overheard. 'George,' he said. 'I wonder if I could talk to you. Take up a little more of your time. It's a delicate matter. I'd be grateful for your assistance.'

George was about to say that Molly and Ursula would be

expecting him but found himself being guided towards Grenville's office, sat in a deep leather chair and being given a large Scotch.

'It's about your wife's aunt,' Grenville said. 'Mrs Ottway. She's one of my tenants.'

'Yes,' George said. He gave no indication that he had overheard the conversation between Grenville and the policeman.

'To put it bluntly, she's making a bloody nuisance of herself.'

'In what way?'

'She came here last night making accusations. Claimed someone had laid poison on the estate. Said it had killed a buzzard. And her cats.'

'Have your keepers been using poison?' George asked mildly.

'No!' Grenville said. 'Of course not.'

'It's not that uncommon, is it, even on the big estates. There was that prosecution last year of the keeper working for a minister in the Scottish Office. And aren't there moves to make landowners more responsible in law for their employees' actions?'

'George!' Grenville said. 'I know all about that. The Scottish affair made us all think. I'm not saying that at one time I wouldn't have turned a blind eye to the more . . . effective methods of predator control. I lease out the shooting on the hill to a syndicate. It's a valuable form of revenue. And there's always pressure to have good numbers of birds for them to shoot. But now I've got too much to lose. Imagine the publicity!'

'Yes,' George said. He felt inclined to believe the man. 'Of course.'

He drank some of the whisky and waited for Grenville to continue.

'George,' Grenville said. 'I know what sort of business you're in and I must say I admire your enterprise. Setting up on your own at your age takes courage.'

No, George thought. Not courage. Retirement made me feel old. His career as a civil servant in the Home Office had been stressful, frustrating but seldom boring. He had been concerned in his later years with police administration and training, and had enjoyed the demands of the work. Although he had looked forward to retirement as an opportunity to give all his energy to natural history, he found that he missed the challenge and stimulus of work. The inquiry agency had been founded almost by chance and still George only took the cases which interested him.

'I didn't set up on my own,' he said. 'Molly is an equal partner in the business.'

But Grenville was not listening. 'I want you to stop the old woman making these allegations,' he said. 'Find out what she's doing it for. What does she want? I know she's a relative of a sort but that might make it easier. I'm not asking you to do it for nothing. You're a businessman after all, even though it's a strange sort of business. I thought last night I'd be able to forget about it. She was pissed, you know. I thought she'd see sense in the morning. But she went to the police and told them her fairy stories. I can't have her going to the press. They don't need evidence to ruin a man's career, and I must tell you, George, that I'm very optimistic about my chances in the next Cabinet reshuffle. So long as nothing happens to balls it up. If the animal rights lot get to hear about these allegations I'm finished. It doesn't bear thinking about.'

'What would you like me to do if Ursula's allegations are true?' George asked quietly.

'True?' Grenville demanded. 'Of course they're not true. I've spoken to Liddle. He's given me his assurance and I trust him.'

'But if I have evidence,' George persisted. 'If Ursula shows me the buzzard and we find that it's been poisoned. What would you want me to do then?'

'Deal with it!' Grenville snapped. 'Discreetly. If I find Liddle's been using poison, I'll sack him. You can tell Mrs Ottway that.'

Chapter Five

When Vic came in for lunch on Saturday he was furious. Marie wanted to tell him that she had her own troubles, that for once in their marriage she needed his support, but even if she had found the courage he would have been too angry to listen to her.

'Do you know what bloody Grenville's accused me of now?' he demanded as he stormed into the kitchen, forgetting to remove his boots. 'He thinks I've been using poison on the estate.'

Marie had made a stew. She was standing by the stove stirring the pot. Cassie was sitting in an easy chair in the corner and shrank away from the violence in Vic's voice. Marie spoke quietly. Cassie needed calm. The girl picked up any tension in the house.

'What makes him think that?'

'Ursula Ottway went to the house last night and made a scene. She said we'd poisoned her cats.'

Marie said nothing.

'You don't seem surprised!' he said. He wanted her to be as outraged as he was, indignant on his behalf.

'No,' she said. 'I'm not surprised. Ursula came here last night on her way back from the Cadver. You were in the pub.'

'You didn't tell me,' he said. He felt betrayed. 'Why didn't you tell me?'

'Because,' she said, keeping her voice even and quiet but obviously angry all the same. 'Because I had other things on my mind. You're not my only responsibility.'

'What happened?' he demanded. 'What did the loony old bitch say?'

'That her cats were dead and she'd found a poisoned buzzard

on one of your gibbets. She said she didn't think it was like you. There'd not been poison used on the estate for years. She wondered if it could have been some mistake or if Grenville had put pressure on you to clear the hill of vermin. She was quite reasonable. I believed her. She didn't think it was killed by one of the shepherds because of the gibbet.'

'Which gibbet was it?' he demanded.

'By the stone wall behind Back Rigg.'

'I was there yesterday. There was nothing there then.'

'She said the bird was freshly dead.'

He paused, thinking. 'That's not my gibbet,' he said. 'It would be one of Danny Craven's.'

'Well,' Marie said. 'Perhaps Mr Grenville would do better having a word with him.'

'Why would Danny Craven do a thing like that?'

She shrugged. She seemed hardly interested. She wanted Vic to eat his dinner and go out again so she could restore Cassie to some sort of peace.

'To make mischief,' she said. 'To put you in the wrong. Who knows how his mind works? Now wash your hands and sit down so we can eat.'

But still he would not leave the subject of Ursula Ottway's visit to Keeper's Cottage alone.

'How long was she here?' he asked.

'I don't know. An hour, perhaps.'

'What were you doing?'

'Talking,' Marie said. 'We had a drink together and we talked. Then I gave her one of the pies I'd baked to take away.'

'But what did you talk about?' he demanded.

'All sorts of things. Not just about the estate ...'

This is it, she thought. I should tell him now. Why did she find it so easy to talk to Ursula when it was hard to confide in him?

But he washed his hands under the tap at the sink and sat at the table waiting to be served so the moment was lost. She ladled stew into bowls, leaving Cassie's on the windowsill so it would be cool when she was ready to feed her. Vic ate the meal in silence and went out again without a word. Marie did not think that there had ever before been such bad feeling between them.

She sat on the arm of Cassie's chair and fed the girl with a spoon. They said at the school that she could feed herself and usually Marie let her have a go. But today Marie needed the comfort of feeling she was needed, the closeness. She made soft, reassuring noises.

'What a good girl!' she said. 'Aren't you Mummy's good girl?'

Cassie ate the food without any of her usual fuss.

One of the estate worker's wives phoned Marie to tell her that Ursula Ottway was dead. She had no reason for phoning other than for the pleasure of passing on interesting news. There was the excitement of the gossip in her voice.

'One of her relatives found her this morning. Apparently she'd been dead all night. It was just as well the niece had arranged to visit, or she might have been there for days without anyone realising. Marie? Are you there? Did you hear what I said?'

'Yes,' Marie said. 'I heard.'

She replaced the phone while the woman was still in mid-sentence and began to cry. Ursula had been her last hope. Now there was no one to help her.

Marcus Grenville offered George a lift from the Cadver to Back Rigg but George said that he preferred to walk. He had accepted Grenville's offer of work because he was curious and because he found the indiscriminate use of poison detestable, but he had no sympathy for the man. He did not have to pretend to a friendship that did not exist.

When he arrived at Back Rigg the house was quiet and for a moment he thought it was empty. Molly was in the larder looking for something to turn into a meal and when she emerged into the kitchen, dusty and cobwebbed, he could tell immediately that something was wrong. She had been crying.

'Where's Ursula?' he asked.

In a muddled, disjointed way she told him what had happened.

'You should have phoned,' he said. 'I would have come.' But Molly had never needed him as he needed her.

'I can't help thinking that I could have done something,' she said, 'if we'd come last night as she'd wanted. Perhaps she wasn't feeling well then. I feel that we are, in a way, responsible.'

'That's nonsense,' George said, but he shared her unease.

'I'll have to stay on for a few days,' Molly said. 'There's no one else . . .'

'I thought there was a daughter.'

'Yes,' she said. 'Sally.' She had spent most of the day trying to track down Sally. In the end the conversation had been held over the crackling line of a car phone. The woman had expressed little grief and had been remarkably unhelpful.

'Will you come up?' Molly had asked.

'Of course. Just let me know when the funeral is.'

'But I thought you'd want to come and make the funeral arrangements.'

'Oh no!' Sally was more shocked by that than she had been by the news of her mother's death. 'I can't possibly spare the time. I'm due in Rome this afternoon. I'll leave all that to you.'

Molly described the conversation to George. He made no comment.

'Why did Ursula die?' he asked. 'Had she been ill?'

'I don't know. She never said anything to me, but then she wouldn't have done. The doctor talked about tests, a post-mortem.'

'Did they give you a time of death?'

'Not an accurate one. Some time in the early hours of the morning, the doctor said.'

'Was he sure?' George spoke sharply. 'It couldn't have been later?'

'No,' Molly said. 'Soon after midnight, the doctor said. It was half past ten in the morning when I found her and she'd been dead for hours then.'

Molly stood at the kitchen table, opening the tins of soup she had found in the larder. The kettle on the range boiled and she made tea.

George described his conversation with Grenville.

'He wants to hire us to find out if poisoned bait was used on the estate,' he said. 'But perhaps in the circumstances you'd prefer us to leave it alone.'

'No,' she said. 'I told you. I feel responsible. We should try to find out what happened.'

'Ursula claimed that the poison had killed a buzzard and her cats. Grenville had implied that she was deranged, senile, or making the whole thing up out of malice. You knew her better than me. Was that possible?'

'Not the malice,' Molly said. 'She was often aggressive but never mean. It would never have occurred to her to go to such elaborate lengths to hurt an enemy.'

'Was Grenville an enemy?'

'Oh,' Molly said. 'They never got on. She thought he was pompous and silly. But it was Olivia she disliked most. She thought Olivia despised Fred and could never forgive her for that.'

'What about her mental state?'

Molly shrugged. 'I haven't seen her since Fred's funeral. She's always been slightly eccentric, but not the sort you'd think to have delusions or hallucinations. What's the significance of the time of death?'

'Someone phoned the police to make a complaint about the poisoned buzzard. The policeman definitely said the call came through this morning. It can't have been Ursula. If there was an independent witness of the poisoning it can't all have been a figment of her imagination.'

'Unless the police made a mistake about the time.' Molly had no great faith in the police.

'Yes,' George said. 'That's always a possibility.'

'If her allegations were true what would she have done with the buzzard?' Molly asked.

'She would have wanted it analysed to test for the poison,' he said, 'and there would have been no possibility of getting that done last night. She would have frozen it to keep it fresh. Is there a freezer in the house?'

'Yes,' Molly said. 'It's in the scullery. I found it when I was looking for potatoes.'

They went together to look. The scullery was a damp, evil-smelling room with a twin-tub washing machine and an old-fashioned mangle. The freezer was scratched and rusty. George opened the lid and moved ancient packets of frozen peas and grey lumps of meat until he could see to the bottom.

'No,' he said. He was disappointed. He did not like to think of Ursula as having descended into lonely senility. 'There's nothing here.'

They returned to the warmth of the kitchen. That was it, then, George thought. There was no reason now for Marcus Grenville to hire them. Ursula's death had been a convenient coincidence and the landowner had no further cause for anxiety. It was Molly, beating eggs together in a bowl to make an omelette, who thought of the cats.

'Where are Belle and Lottie?'

He looked at her, as if she too was mad.

'The cats,' she said. 'Belle and Lottie were Ursula's cats. If Ursula was loopy and made the whole story up, why haven't the cats been under my feet all day whining for food? Why haven't they been sitting on that chair next to the Aga where they always sit? I haven't seen or heard them since I arrived.'

Then they began to search for the cats, as Ursula had searched for them the day before, and as it was not yet dark they found the newly dug grave in the middle of the daffodils.

Joanna Barton learned of Ursula's death from her mother and that in itself was unusual. It was Saturday evening and she had switched the phone through from the house to the pottery where she was working. Simon was out. He had disappeared the evening before as soon as they had left the Cadver.

'It's the pipeline project,' he had said. 'I'll book into that hotel on the Solway where we used to stay, then I can make an early start. You don't mind, do you?'

How could she mind? How could she deny him anything?

All the same, she protested. She liked his company. She felt really low at the moment and needed someone around.

'But it's the weekend! They can't expect you to work at the weekend.'

'It's a rushed job,' he had said. 'And I get a bonus if I finish on time.'

When the phone rang in the pottery she assumed it was Simon. He usually phoned her when he was working away, to tell her that he was fine. He assumed that she worried about him. He rarely gave her a phone number where she could contact him and she thought sometimes that he could have a quite separate life away from her, another woman, perhaps, even children. He was away from home so much.

But it was her mother on the end of the line and the contact was so surprising that at first she did not recognise the voice. Olivia usually communicated with her daughter through a third party. She would send Jeremy to the Old School House with a message, or the housekeeper would ring and relay the information that Mrs Grenville would like to see Joanna at the house.

'Mother,' Joanna said abruptly. 'What do you want?'

'It's about Ursula Ottway,' Olivia said. 'I suppose you've heard that she's dead.'

'No!' Joanna said. 'I didn't know.'

'I'm surprised,' Olivia said. 'I should have thought you'd see the undertaker going to the farm . . .'

How did you find out? Joanna wondered. How do you know everything that goes on in the valley when you're stuck in the Cadver? What spy brought you the information this time?

'No,' Joanna said shortly. 'I've been working.'

'I want to talk to you about Ursula Ottway. I don't suppose you saw her yesterday.'

'Of course I saw her yesterday. We all saw her. She came storming into the house in the middle of dinner.'

'Not then,' Olivia said sharply. 'Later. Did you see her later?'

Joanna was not surprised by the question. She had always known her mother was a witch.

'No,' she said. 'Of course not. Why should I?'

Olivia seemed satisfied by the answer.

'I don't know,' she said. 'She was such a strange woman, don't you think? It's a tragedy, of course, but I can't help thinking that it's all for the best.'

Joanna Barton replaced the telephone and returned to her work.

Jeremy Grenville spent the day in Appleworth with Eve. It was Saturday, after all, and he was entitled to a day off. His father would have liked him at the Cadver to meet the important guests at the conference but he knew that he would be intimidated by the occasion and would make a poor show of it. Even with Eve he was jumpy and on edge. That business with Ursula at dinner had unnerved him. Usually they spent the days in her flat in bed, the curtains drawn against the bright sunlight, with the sound of children playing in the street below. Normally he was quite relaxed there. He was reminded of childhood illnesses, when he was tucked up in bed during the day and even his mother was kind to him. But today he could not settle. He sat on the windowsill looking moodily down into the street.

'Whatever is the matter with you?' Eve demanded. 'You don't know anything about the poison on the hill, do you? You didn't tell the keepers to put it out?'

'No,' he said. 'Of course not. You know I wouldn't do a thing like that.' But he could tell all the same that she did not quite believe him.

His mother told him that Ursula was dead as soon as he arrived home. She was in the hall when he opened the door and he thought later that she must have been waiting for him.

'Mrs Ottway is dead,' she announced. 'I thought you would like to know.'

He felt ill, faint.

'What happened?' he said, stammering so badly that he almost choked. 'Was it an accident? Yesterday she seemed so well.'

'Oh!' Olivia said, as if the cause of death were insignificant, unimportant to her. 'As to that I can't say. Old age, I expect. I haven't been told.'

And she walked imperiously away to the kitchen to make sure that dinner was being prepared to her satisfaction.

George Palmer-Jones informed Marcus Grenville by telephone of Ursula Ottway's death, so Olivia was denied the pleasure of telling her husband. He came in to dinner when she and Jeremy were already seated, rubbing his hands, obviously pleased with himself.

'So,' he said. 'The old trout's gone at last, has she? Can't say I'm sorry. It'll solve quite a few of my problems.'

They ate the meal in silence and Ursula Ottway was not mentioned again.

In the East Lodge Danny Craven drank half a bottle of whisky and fell asleep, fully clothed, on the floor.

Chapter Six

Cassie Liddle slept badly on Saturday night and Marie had to go up to her several times. Cassie's bedroom was at the front of the house under the roof, with a sloping ceiling and a small bay window. Marie crouched by the girl's bed, stroking her forehead, and watched the moonlight come through the thin curtains. When Cassie finally slept she drew back the curtains and looked out over the lake, then up the valley towards Back Rigg. She saw that there was a light in one of the bedrooms at the Old School House and wondered why Joanna Barton was still awake. Any troubles Joanna had were surely of her own making. At last, when it was almost dawn, she went back to her room, to Vic, who was only pretending to sleep.

They woke late on Sunday morning but still they were all listless and overtired. Vic went out to work in the garden and from the kitchen Marie watched him. He was planting seeds in rows of obsessive straightness, pacing the distance between rows with his boot, marking the line with a piece of twine stretched taut between two sticks.

She had not told him about the letter from the school. She was not sure exactly what she was frightened of – and occasionally he looked up at her, hurt, because she seemed so wrapped up in herself. At eleven o'clock she dressed Cassie up in her coat and scarf and wheeled her out into the garden to give her some fresh air. Usually Cassie liked being out with Vic. She would watch him intently, pointing and clapping when he reached the end of a row. But today she huddled into her clothes and stared blankly ahead of her, so he might not have been there.

At midday Marie phoned her sister. They always spoke to each other at least once a week and the woman did not assume there was any special purpose to the call. She had married a teacher and moved south and she and Marie rarely saw each other. Besides the distance, she had never really got on with Vic. Marie had always been close to her sister and thought she might gain some strength from the call, but it only made things worse. Her sister's cheerful description of family life and holiday plans, the background noise of pop music and teenage voices made her want to cry. When Vic came in to wash his hands she was sitting at the table, quite still.

'What are we having for dinner, then?' he said, looking round for signs of cooking. Usually they had a traditional roast at Sunday lunchtime, and a pudding.

'Oh. I don't know. I hadn't thought.'

She jumped up and took the colander to go into the outhouse to fetch potatoes, but he stopped her.

'Are you all right, lass?' he said. 'You don't look well.'

She paused, and tried to form the words to tell him what was troubling her.

'No,' she said. 'I'm fine. Just tired.'

The knock at the front door came at two o'clock and it surprised Marie. Most of their visitors were people from the estate who came to the back and walked into the kitchen without waiting to be asked. She was washing up the lunch things and Vic was in the front room watching football on the television. She had put Cassie to bed for a nap. At first she went on with the washing up because she thought Vic would answer the door. It was more likely to be for him – it would be Jeremy Grenville, perhaps, with some query that would not wait until the morning.

Living in a tied cottage meant that there was no privacy, even on a Sunday. She waited, a saucepan in one hand, but there was no movement from the front room and the visitor knocked again, firmly and without impatience. She dried her hands on a teatowel and went to answer the door.

Through the open living room door she saw that Vic was asleep in his chair, his legs stretched in front of him, his mouth slightly open. The television was still on, but he had turned off the sound and footballers chased after the ball without commentary. He had lit a fire and the room was very hot. There was a half-empty mug of tea by his chair and the Sunday tabloids were spread over the floor. She shut the door, ashamed of the mess, not wanting any visitor to see.

The man who stood in the porch was tall, gaunt-faced, very serious. Even if it had not been Sunday Marie would never have mistaken him for a salesman or a Jehovah's Witness. He had too much authority and he dressed like a gentleman. She supposed he was one of Grenville's friends who had lost his way and was about to direct him to the Cadver when he spoke.

'Mrs Liddle,' he said. His voice was precise, middle-class, just what she would have expected. 'My name's George Palmer-Jones. I wonder if I might talk to you.'

She stood aside and let him in, and still she thought he was something to do with Grenville, a member of the syndicate, perhaps, wanting to see Vic about the shoot. She was sure Vic would know him.

'Come into the kitchen,' she said, 'and I'll tell my husband that you're here.'

'If it's convenient I'd like to speak to you both,' said the man as he took the chair she offered by the table.

That surprised her and for a moment she was frightened. What did this stranger want with them? Could it have anything to do with that other business?

'I'll tell Vic you're here,' she said again and hurried from the room.

She had to shake Vic to wake him and he was aggressive, still fuddled by sleep.

'What's the matter with you, woman?' On the television the football match continued and he stared, transfixed, at the silent, brightly coloured figures. He was hardly conscious.

'There's a gentleman to see you,' she said. She took his arm and pulled him to his feet. 'Look at the state of you. Tuck in that shirt.' She fussed about him as if he were a child.

'What gentleman?'

'I don't know. I've never seen him before. He wants to talk to us both.'

'Is he a copper? Someone from the police went to the house yesterday about the fairy stories of Mrs Ottway's. Grenville said he'd sorted it out.'

'I don't know,' she said, then she considered. 'Yes, he might be a policeman.'

The man was still sitting at the kitchen table. When they came into the room he stood up and held out his hand.

'It's very good of you to take the time to see me,' he said, and Marie decided that he could not be a policeman after all.

'What's all this about?' Vic demanded. He stood just inside the door, glaring. Marie hoped he would behave himself. He was always rude when he was worried.

'My name's George Palmer-Jones,' George repeated. 'My wife is Ursula Ottway's niece.'

There was a silence. Vic Liddle was in no mood to say anything pleasant about Ursula Ottway. He could not bring himself, even, to mutter the usual condolences. Marie, embarrassed by the silence, spoke in a rush.

'Of course,' she said. 'I should have recognised the name. She talked about you often enough. I liked her, you know. She was a kind woman. I was so sorry to hear that she'd died.'

'Would you mind if I ask some questions about her?'

'What for?' Liddle asked. 'She kept herself to herself. What else is there to know?'

I don't know, George thought. That's why I'm here. Not because Marcus Grenville asked me to work for him. I would want to find out anyway. Because Ursula's death was too sudden and too convenient. Because, like Molly, I feel responsible.

'There are some points we need to clear up,' he said, being deliberately vague. 'Things we don't understand. Her cats, for example . . .'

'What about her cats?' Vic was tempted to swear. He had better things to do on a Sunday afternoon. But something about the man and Marie's disapproval made him control his temper.

'They're dead,' George said simply.

'She told Grenville they'd died,' Vic said. 'It doesn't mean it was true. She talked a lot of rubbish. She was daft about those cats.'

'They're definitely dead,' George said. 'We found the grave last night.'

'What's that got to do with me?' Marie felt sorry for Vic. He was no match for the tall man with his quiet voice.

'I'd say it had rather a lot to do with you,' George said. 'If you've been using poison on the hill you'll be prosecuted, fined. And you'll lose your job.'

There was a shocked silence. They had not expected such plain speaking.

'You'll have to forgive my husband,' Marie said. 'He's upset. He's a good keeper and Mr Grenville doesn't give him the support he should.' She paused. 'We know what Ursula said at the Cadver, Mr Palmer-Jones, but Vic doesn't use poison on the estate. Not now. Mr Grenville doesn't allow it. Besides, keeping the hill clear of predators isn't his responsibility. He's had an under-keeper since February.'

'What's the under-keeper's name?' George wondered, with some irritation, why Grenville hadn't told him that there had been a recent addition to the keeping staff. Surely it wasn't a coincidence that the poisoning coincided almost exactly with the new man's arrival?

Still Vic did not speak and it was Marie who answered. 'Danny Craven,' she said. 'He lives in the Lodge by the east drive.'

'Craven wouldn't have put down poison,' Vic said uncomfortably. 'What reason would he have?'

'What's he like?' George asked. 'Reliable?'

Liddle shrugged. 'Grenville appointed him,' he said. 'I wouldn't have done.'

'Did he have any dealings with Ursula Ottway?' George asked.

'I shouldn't have thought so. She'd have been able to see him at work from her house but she'd have no reason to talk to him. And they'd hardly have met socially.'

'How did she get on with the other people in the valley generally?'

Liddle shook his head as if the question were beyond him and looked to Marie to answer.

'It's difficult to explain,' she said. George waited. 'She didn't fit in. Not really. It wasn't that she was snobby but if she hadn't married Fred she'd be more likely to mix with the Grenvilles and their friends at the Cadver. She talked to me sometimes about what she'd done when she was young. She went away to finishing school, you know, in Switzerland. The tenant farmers and estate workers didn't understand her. Not really. If she'd been a guest at the Cadver it would have been different ... And then the Grenvilles couldn't accept her, either. Fred was a tenant, almost an employee. They could hardly invite the pair of them round to dinner.'

She went on, stumbling over the words, trying to explain the ridiculous, delicately balanced class system that had left Ursula a lonely old woman.

'But you got on with her?' George said.

'I liked her. She wasn't always easy. She was used to being on her own. She didn't trust anyone and who could blame her? Grenville's been trying to get her out of Back Rigg since Fred died. He wants to do up the house and let it to people who come to shoot on the hill. We all knew that. Ursula was an embarrassment to him.'

'Well,' George said. 'She can't embarrass him now. When did you see her last?'

'Friday night,' Marie said. 'She called in here after making that scene at the Cadver. Vic was at the pub and I'd put Cassie to bed. We had a drink and a chat.'

'How did she seem then? Did she complain of being ill?'

'No,' Marie said. 'She'd had a fair amount to drink but she seemed well enough. She was upset, of course. We talked about her cats. She was very fond of them.'

'Did she say anything else?'

Marie shook her head. 'I talked about Cassie. Our girl. She's handicapped, brain damaged. It's always a worry. Ursula seemed to understand.'

'Yes,' George said. 'I see.'

Vic Liddle got to his feet. 'Is that it, then?' he said. 'We've told you all we know. I've things to be getting on with.'

'Just one more question,' George said. 'If Craven, or anyone else, had been using poison on the hill, where would he get hold of it?'

Liddle turned away impatiently and again Marie answered for him, knowing that to this man it was no use lying.

'From our shed,' she said. 'It's never locked and there's all sorts in there.'

'Perhaps we could look,' George suggested. 'Clear the matter up ...'

'Come on, Vic,' Marie said gently. 'It would get Grenville off your back and you've nothing to hide.'

Liddle muttered under his breath but he stood up. He trusted Marie's judgement in this as in most things. 'It won't do you any good. As the wife says, there's all sorts in there and not much of it labelled.'

'All the same, if you wouldn't mind.' George got to his feet and waited for Vic to lead the way. They trooped out into the sunshine.

George felt strangely at home in the yard. He had been brought up in rural Herefordshire and the pile of tools, the saw horse and the logs, the big dog half asleep, waiting for exercise, brought back memories of an uncle's house.

Vic opened the door of the shed to let in the light.

'Most of all this is from before my time,' he said, defensively. 'It's illegal to use these pole traps now.'

'Yes,' George said. 'I know.'

'I never liked them,' Vic said. 'It always seemed to me a cruel way to carry on.'

'What about phosdrin?' George said. 'Have you ever used that? Or alpha-chlorose?'

'When I started as an under-keeper my boss used phosdrin – mostly against rats – but I've not seen it on the estate for years.'

'You had some?' George said. 'Was it kept in a jar?'

'Aye. Once upon a time. But I've told you I've not seen it for ages.'

'You've never thrown it away?'

'No,' he said. 'I've never thrown it away.'

'So the jar should still be here,' George said cheerfully. He went into the shed, crouching to get in through the low door. Although he had seen pole traps and snares before, the rusting metal objects still offended him. But Liddle had been telling the truth when he said they had not been recently used. They were covered in dust and cobwebs. He clambered over them, ignoring Marie's protests that he would get his clothes dirty, to the shelf at the back of the outhouse.

'I wonder,' he said, 'if I might borrow a torch.'

'There's one in the kitchen,' Marie said quickly. 'I'll get it.'

'What are you, then?' Vic demanded, the hostility returning with his wife's absence. 'Some sort of conservationist?'

'Something like that.'

'Keepers care about the countryside too,' he said. 'We're not all monsters.'

'No,' George said. 'Of course not.'

Marie came back with the torch.

'If I shine it for you,' she said, 'you'll be able to use both hands.' She had begun to quite enjoy the adventure of Palmer-Jones's visit. It distracted her from her other worries. She looked out of place, rather comical, perched at the door of the outhouse. Vic crouched to stroke the dog's nose and pretended to have no interest in what was going on.

At first George just stood and looked. There were coloured bottles and rusting tins. The shelf and all the bottles seemed covered with dust. Then George saw a jam jar with a screw lid, tucked at the back behind a tin of wood preservative. The dust on the jar had been disturbed around the neck, and a ring in the dust on the shelf showed where it had been removed and replaced. George took a large handkerchief from his jacket pocket and lifted the jar by the screw top. He carried it out into the sunlight. In spidery writing on a paper label was written phosdrin. The jar was empty.

Vic and Marie stared at it. Neither spoke.

'I don't suppose you remember,' George said, 'if there was any left when you saw it last.'

'Of course not,' Vic said violently. 'How would we see it, hidden away there?'

'Yes,' George said. 'Quite.' Then, absentmindedly: 'You won't mind if I take this away with me? I'd like to get it analysed.'

'I suppose not,' Vic said, 'though you seem to be taking rather a lot on yourself. I don't know what Mr Grenville would say.'

'Oh,' George said. 'Perhaps I didn't explain. Mr Grenville asked me to find out if there was any truth in Ursula's allegations. I'm sure he wouldn't mind.'

'He didn't say anything about it to me.'

They stood, awkwardly, looking at each other.

'It seems a coincidence,' George said, 'that there should be a poisoning incident on the weekend when Mr Grenville was holding his conference to consider environmental policy. It's almost as if someone wanted to embarrass him deliberately. Is there anyone who dislikes him enough to do that?'

Liddle did not reply directly. He was very flushed. 'I've listened to enough,' he said angrily. 'You're all the same, you people from the city who come to the countryside and tell us how to carry on. I'm going to look at the birds.'

He whistled to his dog, expecting the usual immediate obedience, but the dog seemed excitable and did not respond. It bounded through the open door of the shed and pushed into the corner with its nose, its hind quarters moving violently from side to side. Liddle whistled to it again but it took no notice and he had to go into the shed to pull it out by its collar.

In the corner, hidden by a propped-up wheelbarrow, was a plastic bag. George had seen it but dismissed it as containing perhaps some rotting garden waste.

'What is that?' he said. 'Do you think I could see?'

Liddle brought it out, trying to restrain the dog with one hand, carrying the plastic bag with the other. He was giving his full attention to controlling the dog and it was George who saw the buzzard's claws extending from the neck of the bag. He took it from Liddle, trying to hold back his excitement. The bird's probably been there for years, he thought. But when he untied the string from the top of the bag he saw that the bird was too fresh to have been there for years and in the corner of the bag, damp but still legible, was a till receipt. It was an itemised, computerised list of all the articles bought. There were many tins of cat food recorded on the receipt and it was dated the Friday of Ursula's death.

Marie stared in horror at the creature. George lifted it from the bag and held it by the legs.

'You fool,' she said, almost hysterical. 'I thought you said you had nothing to do with that.'

'It's true,' Vic said. 'I didn't even know it was there.'

He moved some steps away from them as if he wanted to distance himself from all responsibility for it. The dog was quieter and lay panting at his feet.

'Look,' he said to them both. 'I'm telling the truth. You'll have to believe me.'

He turned quickly and walked away, followed by the dog. At the end of the garden he paused, as if he expected one of them to call him back, but they watched him go in silence.

Marie saw George out through the front door, formally shaking his hand to say goodbye.

'I'm sorry,' he said, 'to have been the cause of such upset.'

She shook her head to imply that it was not his fault.

'Will you be staying at Back Rigg?' she asked.

'At least until after the funeral.'

George walked briskly along the road away from Keeper's Cottage. He did not notice that the woman stood in the porch looking after him, as if making up her mind to catch him up. He was preoccupied, troubled. As he walked towards Back Rigg he went over the details of Ursula's last day and for the first time a seed of suspicion took root. Although he rejected the suspicion as fanciful it would not go away and by the time he arrived at the farm he was wondering how he would tell Molly that he believed Ursula Ottway had been poisoned.

Chapter Seven

It was Sunday lunchtime and Jeremy Grenville and Eve Theobald were in the bar of the Crowford Hotel. Jeremy had phoned her early in the morning to say he wanted to meet her and they had agreed to have a drink. The hotel was a curious place, run by a cheerful Midlands couple who had bought it several years before. Once, perhaps, it had been quite grand. It was on the opposite side of the lake from Back Rigg and there was a terrace with magnificent views. It had been built in the thirties, rather in the style of a provincial cinema with a curved bow front, and even now that the brick had worn and a garden had grown around the house it looked horribly out of place on the hill. The couple had arrived with great pretensions and little taste. It would be, they thought, 'classy'. Then they found that the greater part of their income came not from the respectable guests who stayed the night in the large underheated bedrooms but from the locals who drank in the public bar and from the day trippers who wanted fish and chips at lunchtime and cream teas on the terrace in the afternoon. Reluctantly they had adapted to meet these needs and in the summer the dining room had the air of a transport café, with plastic sauce bottles on plastic tablecloths, and the bedrooms were scarcely used.

The public bar was small and quite busy with men drinking pints of beer to wash down their Sunday lunch. Eve and Jeremy sat at a small table near the window.

Eve made the connection between Ursula Ottway's death and the poisoned buzzard and cats immediately.

'A bit of a coincidence, isn't it?' she said when Jeremy told her the old woman was dead. 'She made all those threats and now she can't do anything about them. Very convenient for your old man.'

'Don't say that,' Jeremy said. 'Not even as a joke. Someone will hear.' He turned to her angrily. 'I mean it. It's not funny.'

'Have the police been to see your father about it yet?'

'No. Of course not. Why should they?'

'Of course,' she said. 'Why should they? They're not going to know the details of Mrs Ottway's allegations on Friday night unless someone tells them. And everyone who was at the Cadver on Friday was family. They wouldn't tell. Except me, of course. I'm not family.'

She spoke in the hard, joking voice that always confused him. He could never tell exactly what she was thinking.

'Someone did contact the police,' Jeremy said uncertainly. 'Dad thinks it must have been Ursula. They came to the house on Saturday lunchtime. It was routine, they said. They had to follow it up. Dad convinced them there was no need for any more action.'

Eve smiled and he wondered if she knew more than she was telling.

'But they didn't know then,' she said, 'that the old lady was dead.'

'Do you really think that makes any difference?'

'It depends,' she said, 'how she died.'

'You must be mad,' he said, 'to talk like that.' But she seemed not to realise how upset he was and only smiled. They sat without speaking over their drinks, staring at the cold, hard sunlight reflected on the reservoir.

'Jeremy,' she said at last, 'there's something I want to ask –' But the loud Wolverhampton voice of the landlord was suddenly raised to interrupt her and like all the other customers in the bar they turned to watch.

'You've had enough,' the landlord said. 'I can't serve you with any more today. Go home and sleep it off.'

The man to whom he was speaking could hardly stand. He was tall, dark. From where she sat Eve could see little more than greasy hair, unfashionably long, curling over the collar of a green camouflage jacket. He was slouched against the bar, one hand around a small glass. Perhaps he slipped or tensed involuntarily because the glass suddenly shattered and there were shards of glass on the bar and the floor. The man's hand was bleeding but he seemed hardly to notice.

'That's it!' the landlord shouted. 'Get out! You're banned.'

He leaned across the bar and fished in the breast pocket of the camouflage jacket for a set of keys. 'You can walk,' he said. 'The fresh air will do you good. Besides, if I let you drive you'll finish up in the lake.'

'Go on then, Den. Give him his keys back. That'd do us all a favour,' someone in the crowd shouted and there was general laughter. Obviously there was little sympathy for the drunk. He swayed back on his heels, turned round and walked unsteadily across the room. Den, the landlord, came round the bar, followed him to the door and shut it behind him with great ceremony. There was a round of applause.

'He's not very popular,' Eve said. 'Who was it?' But before Jeremy could reply Den came up to their table. He was swinging the car keys on his finger, still making a show.

'I'll give these to you, Mr Grenville,' he said. 'You can let him have them back when he's sober.'

'Yes,' Jeremy said. It was obvious to Eve that he was embarrassed by the exchange. Already a hint of the stutter had returned. 'Yes, I'll do that.'

'It's not my place to say,' the landlord went on, aware that he had an audience, thinking that there was something brave about confronting Marcus Grenville's son, 'but I don't know how your father puts up with that Danny Craven.'

If he was hoping to provoke a response he was disappointed. Jeremy put the keys in his pocket and said nothing.

'Who was that man?' Eve said again. 'Danny Craven.'

'He's an under-keeper on the estate,' Jeremy said absently.

'No one seems to like him.'

'No,' Jeremy said. 'He's not a very pleasant chap.'

'So why *does* your father put up with him?'

'I don't know,' Jeremy said. 'I've wondered, but I don't know why my father does anything.'

'You're not very close,' she said. 'For father and son, working together.'

'Oh no,' he said. 'We've never been allowed to be close.'

She wanted to ask what he meant but he looked at his watch. 'Look,' he said. 'I'll have to go now. Simon and Jo have invited me for supper at the pottery and I've still work to do on the estate. Why don't you come too? They won't mind and you might enjoy it.'

But there was no conviction in his voice and she thought he was not even sure that he would enjoy it.

'No,' she said slowly. 'No thanks.' She felt, quite suddenly, that she had had enough of the Grenvilles for one weekend.

When Simon Barton married Joanna Grenville he was very much in love with her. His friends made sarcastic remarks about the marriage. They said he was selling out, that he was more interested in the big house and the money than the girl, but none of that was true. Not then. When they met he was a post-graduate student researching the breeding habits of merlins in the hills. It was 1975 and they were both twenty-one. He was serious, rather academic. The work at university had not come easily to him and he had realised from the beginning that if he were to get a good degree he would have to miss out on the round of parties and concerts which seemed so important to his friends. He was also a virgin.

When he met Joanna she was not living at the Cadver, but in Monk's Wood, a house further up the valley that had been left to one of her friends by an aunt. Monk's Wood had been her second home since she had left school, and Alex, the owner, had been her best friend since she was a toddler. When Simon was introduced to the place Alex was running it like a commune. There were usually at least six adults there. Some, like Joanna, were more or less regulars, others stayed for just a couple of weeks at a time. They were students pretending to be artists or musicians. Joanna had just left art school, though Alex was older than the rest and had children. The set-up seemed quite exotic to Simon and different from anything he had ever known.

He had met the group one night in a pub – it was spring and he was camping in the fells so that he could spend as much daylight as possible looking for merlin nests. They had been sitting in the garden in the dark, the children wrapped up in blankets and asleep. One of the regulars in the bar had called them 'bloody hippies', and because he, too, felt an outsider he had gone to join them. For some reason they had adopted him. They admired his work immensely, they said.

Of course the whole group was committed to the environment. They invited him to Monk's Wood for meals and when they found out he was camping said of course he must stay. They had room after all and it would be good to have someone explain the important issues. They told him proudly that they were all Friends of the Earth.

At first he did not notice Joanna. She was much quieter than all the others, shy, withdrawn, painfully thin. Alex with her long red hair and her loud clear voice was always the centre of attention. She had the authority of motherhood and seemed strong enough to look after them all. At first Simon thought he was in love with *her*. It was Alex who introduced him to cannabis and Nietzsche and took him into the big low bed with the Indian cotton cover and babies sleeping close by and made love to him. But Alex gave her favours to everyone and there was something demeaning in the universal benevolence. He thought they could never be on equal terms.

One day Joanna asked if she might go with him on to the hill. He always got up before the rest of them. He seemed to be the only one with regular work and was never sure how they survived. The dole, he supposed, or rich parents. Because he knew he would be out all day he usually cooked a big breakfast while the kitchen was quiet. Most of the residents were vegetarian and disapproved of his sausage and bacon so it was a furtive, almost shameful, operation. Joanna appeared at the door of the long, draughty room and he saw her as if for the first time.

71

'Can I come too?' she asked. Her hair was long then, fine and curly. She wore tight jeans, a T-shirt and no bra. She was as thin and shapeless as Alex's six-year-old daughter.

'I don't know,' he said. 'It's a long walk. Would you keep up?' He was frightened she would be a liability. Alex talked about her to him sometimes with concern and had once described her as neurotic.

'I'm stronger than I look,' she said. 'I've got boots.'

So he took her with him and was surprised that she knew the hills so well. She even made suggestions about where to look for nests.

'I used to live round here,' she said when he commented on her local knowledge. 'My dad brought me for walks in the hills when I was a kid.'

She said nothing more about her childhood and at that time he had never even heard her surname. He did not connect her with the Cadver Estate.

She took to accompanying him regularly on the walks. Sometimes she shared his breakfast but more often she was waiting for him in the untidy garden when he came out of the house. But though they spent whole days on the hills together he learnt little more about her.

She confided in him one evening when she was drunk. It had been somebody's birthday and there had been a special meal. They had broken into the homemade wine, though Alex said it wasn't really ready. They were in the living room, a strange place still mostly full of Alex's aunt's furniture, but with cushions added on the floor. Alex's latest boyfriend was playing the guitar. Most of them were smoking dope but Joanna refused it, and then she started talking to Simon.

'I never smoke,' she said. 'I was really heavily into heroin before I came here. It really cracked me up. That's why I had to drop out of college. My bloody family locked me up in a nursing home to sort me out.'

He was not sure what to say. She was sitting on the floor beside him.

'But it worked,' he said. 'It did sort you out?'

'Do you think so?' she said. She seemed pleased. 'Perhaps it did.' But she still seemed unhappy and lonely, and he put his arm around her to comfort her and she nestled up to him like a child needing reassurance.

'What will you do now?' he asked.

'I don't know,' she said. 'Go back to college, I suppose, if they'll have me.'

That night he thought she might go to bed with him. He walked with her up the stairs, still with his arm around her, and at the door of her room he kissed her. But she pulled away, tense and frightened, and he realised it would not be that easy. She became a challenge, and as the summer went on he grew obsessed with her.

At the end of August, just as he was preparing to return to the university, he asked her to marry him. He had decided that that was the only way to deal with the situation. He would never get her unless she felt secure. He had even discussed it with Alex, who had replied cautiously that the plan might work but that Jo had more problems than he realised and he might be taking on more than he'd bargained for.

'I love you,' he said to Joanna, 'and I want to marry you.' It was early one sunny morning and they were walking along the lane from the house. He had meant to tell her when they were up on the hill with the view of the lake in the distance, but he could not wait.

She turned to him. 'Are you sure?' she said.

'Of course.'

She seemed to be turning the matter over in her mind as if it were a business proposition.

'Well,' she said, repeating the words Alex had used earlier in the day. 'It might work. At least I wouldn't have to go back to my bloody family and I can hardly stay at Monk's Wood for the rest of my life. If you're sure you want to do it . . .'

'Yes,' he said. 'I'm sure.' Her cold weighing-up of the options disturbed him but he had no doubts. He thought he could save her from the troubles of her past. Her uncertainty made her even more attractive.

They married in the following spring. By then of course he knew exactly who she was. He had thought that Marcus Grenville might not consider him good enough and was excited by the prospect of having to fight for her, but the MP had welcomed him with open arms, relieved only it seemed to find someone willing to take her on. The wedding was a quiet affair. Simon's mother had expected something grand and for Simon the ceremony was an anti-climax. Only Joanna's immediate family and the residents of Monk's Wood sat on the bride's side of the church, and the reception afterwards was small, with everyone trying to be on their best behaviour.

They settled very quickly into respectable married life. Simon completed his MSc and Joanna finished her course at art school, but they no longer seemed like students. On their first wedding anniversary Marcus Grenville bought the Old School House for them. It seemed to Simon like a prize for perseverance. By then he had started to work as Conservation Officer for the Westmorland Wildlife Trust, but they would never have afforded a home of their own without Grenville's assistance. Joanna turned the school into a pottery and seemed happy enough.

There weren't any children but everyone said that was probably just as well. Joanna had never been strong and it would be criminal to interrupt such a promising career with a family. Their friends did not like to ask outright if they had taken a decision not to have children or if there was some medical problem. It was not the sort of thing you brought up out of the blue, and Simon and Joanna never discussed it. If the question had been asked Simon would have been unlikely to answer it with the truth: that they had no children because Joanna would not allow him to make love to her. He had thought when they were first married that her unease, her inability to respond to affection, was a temporary setback, a result of her previous problems. If he loved her, he thought, she would trust him enough to let herself go. But if anything the problem got worse and his sympathy wore thin. She refused to seek help. She seemed trapped in a pre-pubescent childhood, safer without the responsibilities and physical contact of adult life. In the end her frigidity was only tiresome and he stopped making the effort to get through to her. He told himself that she was sick and treated her kindly and dispassionately as if she were an invalid, and looked for sex elsewhere.

Simon arrived back from work on the Solway in time to cook Sunday dinner. He had said that he would be, and usually in the strange, businesslike way that they ordered their affairs he kept his promises. She was waiting for him and that surprised him. It was her busiest time of year. Later in the season there would be too many interruptions from trippers, interested buyers, and she liked to have the pottery stocked by Easter. Usually she worked all weekend but today she opened the door to him as soon as he had parked in the playground.

Oh God no, he thought. Not one of her scenes. Not today, to spoil it all.

'What is it?' he asked gently. 'Are you feeling ill?' Tenderness too was part of the bargain, like turning up on time.

'No,' she said, quite distracted. He could see that she had not brushed her hair. It was tousled as when she first got out of bed. 'Something terrible's happened.'

'Let me come in,' he said, 'and you can tell me all about it.' He spoke as if he expected some minor domestic disaster but he gripped the handle of his overnight case so tightly that his knuckles were white. 'Shall I make some coffee? Perhaps I should start on the supper?'

He set the case carefully in the hall, put his arm around her shoulder and moved her gently towards the kitchen.

'You don't understand,' she said. He had never seen her so upset. He stroked the hair away from her face as if she were a child, and was relieved that he felt none of the old desire. 'Ursula Ottway's dead.'

'So?' he said. 'I know you were fond of her, but she was an old lady. She was fit enough on Friday night so she must have gone quickly. She would have preferred it that way. To go out fighting.'

'You don't understand,' she said again. 'There were things she knew . . . things I never told anyone else . . .' She turned her head so she was looking directly into his eyes. 'I think my mother murdered her.'

'Where's Jo?' Jeremy asked.

'She's not very well. I sent her to lie down but she insisted on working. She's in the pottery.'

Jeremy did not know what to say. His sister's health had always been a matter of some curiosity to him and still he did not understand exactly what was wrong with her. As children there had been too great an age gap between them for them to have been close. He had been vaguely aware of his parents' concern for her, the suggestion that she was ill. He had been away at school during most of the times of crisis but had still picked up the fact that his sister was not suffering from a real illness like appendicitis. There was an element of moral judgement in his mother's attitude to Joanna. She had done something wrong. When he had suggested during one holiday that he might visit Jo in the nursing home his mother had refused immediately. It was not the place, she said, for an impressionable young boy. He felt that Joanna's frailty increased the pressure on him. Olivia implied that he was the family's last chance. If he messed things up too there would be no one to carry on her work. In one way he envied his sister. Olivia had given up on her and left her alone. But he saw that Joanna was unhappy and he treated her carefully, afraid that there might be some recurrence of the old trouble.

'Is something the matter?' he asked.

Simon began to peel the papery skin from a clove of garlic and paused before answering.

'The death of the old lady at Back Rigg seems to have upset her. She's got hold of some idea that she was murdered.'

'That ridiculous,' Jeremy said. 'No one's suggested that to me.'

Simon shrugged. 'Of course it's ridiculous, but you know what Jo's like . . .'

Again, Jeremy, who had never known what Jo was like, kept quiet.

'Perhaps you should have a word with her,' Simon went on. 'Explain that she can't go round making accusations like that. It might be very awkward. Especially for your father. She might listen to you.'

'No,' Jeremy said. 'I don't think so. She's never had a very high opinion of me.'

'All the same,' Simon insisted. 'I think you should have a go. I'll go and talk to her, see if I can persuade her to come in to dinner.'

He was halfway through the back door when there was a sharp knock at the front door. Jeremy walked from the kitchen into the hall and shouted up that he would go.

'It'll be a visitor wanting to know about the pottery,' Simon said. 'It's a bloody nuisance. Tell them it's not open until Easter.'

But when Jeremy opened the door he found a little elderly lady with cropped hair and schoolboy glasses who said that although she was sure the pottery was fascinating that was not why she was there. She told him that she was Ursula Ottway's niece and waited, blinking, on the door step to be let in.

Chapter Eight

When George returned to Back Rigg from Keeper's Cottage he spent some time on the telephone. During his time as a senior civil servant in the Home Office he had made a useful list of contacts. He had been respected in his work for his fairness and his integrity and he still had many friends in the criminal justice field.

The first person he spoke to was Jane Mason, consultant pathologist at a Yorkshire teaching hospital. She had given evidence to a committee he had chaired on the procedures following serious crime, then he had discovered that she was a keen birdwatcher and had bumped into her several times in Norfolk and on the Scilly Isles. She was a large, jolly woman, a spinster, something of a laughing-stock in ornithological circles for claiming a number of dubious records. She was what more competent birders called a 'stringer'. George put her claims down not to a deliberate attempt to deceive but to an over-optimistic attitude in the field – if she had not seen a bird clearly enough to make a positive identification she would persuade herself that it was the rarest of the range of possibilities. She was very proud of her friendship with George. He was well thought of, famous in the conservation world, and contact with him gave her a certain credibility.

She answered her telephone immediately and was delighted to hear from him.

'George! My dear boy! How can I help you?' She was younger than he was but she spoke to him as if he were a favourite nephew.

'Phosdrin poisoning,' he said. 'Have you ever come across it?'

'Not professionally,' she said. 'I've heard of it, of course. There was a documentary on the telly about a year ago. It's what keepers put down to kill off birds of prey.'

'Yes,' he said. 'But would it be capable of killing a person?'

'Oh yes,' she said. 'I should think so. I'm sure I've read about it in the literature. And I've heard anecdotal reports. There was a keeper who kept the filthy stuff in an old cider bottle. He came home pissed one night from the pub and drank it by mistake. There was only a little left in bottle but it killed him immediately. Served him bloody well right. Do you want me to check the details and phone you back?'

'That would be very kind, Jane. If it's not too much trouble.'

'Now, George. You know that nothing is too much trouble for you.' She giggled like a flirting adolescent and hung up.

While he waited for the pathologist to phone him back he sat in the drawing-room. The room was as cold as the freezer where he had put the dead buzzard on his return to Back Rigg. There was no fire in the grate and it had never occurred to Ursula and Fred that they might install central heating, so the kitchen was the only warm room in the house. But Molly was in the kitchen and he did not want to talk to Molly until he had all the facts straight.

Jane Mason phoned back remarkably quickly, having digested, apparently, all there was to know about the subject. George often marvelled that someone so obviously intelligent and professionally competent could make so many mistakes about birds.

'The active chemical in phosdrin is mevinphos,' she said. 'I've only a summary of each of the cases here but I can send you photocopies with more detailed histories if you need them.' She paused. 'It's powerful stuff, George. It's been known to kill a healthy adult within an hour.'

'Could it be easily masked?' he asked.

'Quite easily. It's an reddish orange liquid, and you need so little that it would be very hard to detect in, say, a glass of whisky or brandy.'

'Would a pathologist be able to tell that the poison had been used?' He held his breath as he waited for her to reply.

'Not purely on post-mortem appearances,' she said. 'You know the procedure as well as I do, George. This is like telling my grandmother to suck eggs. If there was no anatomical cause of death and no specific pathological abnormality the pathologist would ask the police to consider the possibility of poison. Then tests would be done at the Forensic Science Lab in Wetherby. That's very dramatic. They send the samples down by police car, sirens wailing.'

'Yes,' he said. 'Of course. Would the laboratory pick up the phosdrin? Even if they didn't know what they were looking for?'

'Eventually, though you wouldn't be very popular asking them to look. There are screening procedures that take ages if you haven't anything to go on. If you asked them specifically to look for phosdrin it would probably only take a morning to get the results back.'

'I see,' George said, giving nothing away. 'Yes. Thank you. You have been remarkably helpful.'

She would have gone on to tell him about her latest claimed rarity, but George disentangled himself from the conversation and replaced the receiver.

His next call was to another friend, a retired detective superintendent who had worked for most of his career in Carlisle. George asked as tactfully as he could whom he should contact at Appleworth Police Station to be sure of receiving a sympathetic and intelligent hearing.

'Come on, George!' the man said. 'Spit it out! You want to know which of them has more brain cells than the average chimpanzee.'

'Not exactly,' George said. 'It's a delicate matter. I wouldn't want the Appleworth officers to think that I'm trying to teach them their job, but I've had access to certain information that they'd not come across otherwise.'

'Benwell,' the man said. 'Dave Benwell. He's a young detective inspector. He's not flashy. Not one of those that has to show off in front of the men. But he's confident enough of his own ability not to resent being offered help. He's a grafter, too. Stubborn, once he gets his teeth into a case. Behind the scenes. You know the sort.'

'Where would I get in touch with him this afternoon?'

'I'll give him a ring if you like,' the Superintendent said. 'Put in a word for you. Find out if he's free. Important, is it?'

'Oh yes,' George said. 'Very important.' He paused and spoke almost to himself: 'I think it's a case of murder.'

When he finished his phone calls he went back to the kitchen where Molly was sitting by the Aga, waiting for him. She was reading a favourite John Le Carré spy novel but could not concentrate and when he came into the room she set it aside.

'What's going on?' she said. 'What is this about?' She was angry. They had been married for all these years and they were in this business together, yet still he felt he had to exclude her. She thought he was making a fool of himself, skulking in the scullery, shutting himself in the living room with the phone.

'I'm sorry,' he said. 'I know it seems absurd, but I'm not convinced that Ursula died of natural causes.'

'Why?' she said.

'It was too sudden,' he said. 'I know she was in her seventies but she was as strong as an ox. Besides, there are other facts that don't tie up.'

'What was it, then?' she said. 'Suicide because she couldn't stand life without the cats? Hardly likely.'

'No,' he said. 'Hardly likely. Besides, I found the buzzard this afternoon at Liddle's house. How would it get there? Someone must have been here on Friday night or before you got here on Saturday morning.'

'Murder, then?' She was not shocked. After thirty years as a social worker nothing, he thought, surprised her.

'I can't be certain,' he said. 'Not yet. I've spoken to Jane Mason. Apparently there are specific tests that can be used to find the poison. I have to talk to the police about it. They'll find it a lot easier to make a positive decision about the cause of death if they know what they're looking for.'

'You think she was poisoned, then,' Molly said. 'Like the bird and the cats?'

'I don't know yet.' He had a sudden stab of self doubt. Perhaps the whole theory was the product of an overheated imagination.

He was not looking forward to facing a bright young inspector with his ideas.

'But you think she might have been?'

He nodded.

'By the same person?'

'I don't know,' he said again. 'Marcus Grenville was the person with most to lose by her allegations, but it hardly seems likely . . .'

She was going to say that she would believe anything of a politician with the views of Marcus Grenville but stopped herself. George would accuse her of childishness. He thought her politics were naïve and simplistic.

'What will you do now?' she asked.

'I've made an appointment to see a police inspector at Appleworth to discuss it with him.'

'What do you want me to do?'

'Nothing,' he said. 'Wait here until I have some definite news.'

'No,' she said. 'I can't stay here with nothing to do.' She thought, If Ursula was murdered we should speak to the people at the Friday night dinner party. I'll go to the pottery. I knew Joanna quite well when she was younger. She and Ursula were close. She used to come to Back Rigg to play. I'll start there.

So when Jeremy Grenville opened the door of the Old-School House expecting a visitor wanting to buy pottery he met Molly Palmer-Jones insisting that she had to speak to Joanna.

'I don't know,' Jeremy said awkwardly, 'that she's up to seeing anyone.'

His presence there surprised her. She remembered him still as a boy.

'Oh,' she said. 'I think she'll see me.'

As he hesitated Simon joined them. He must have heard the exchange from the kitchen.

'Mrs Palmer-Jones,' he said. 'It *is* Mrs Palmer-Jones. Of course you must come in. We were just going to have a drink before dinner. You must join us.'

He led her into a small living room, decorated in dark reds and browns and lit richly by the evening sunshine.

'Perhaps you'd go to the pottery,' he shouted to Jeremy. 'Tell Jo that Mrs Palmer-Jones is here. Have a word with her.'

The significance of the last phrase was not lost on Jeremy. Calm her down, Simon was saying. Tell her to keep her ridiculous accusations to herself. Jeremy nodded to show that he understood, but thought that he was not up to the job.

Joanna was standing, softening a piece of clay by throwing it over and over again on to the wooden bench. Jeremy had expected a withdrawn depression but she seemed instead in almost hysterical good spirits. He wondered how Simon could live with the swings of mood, this wild elation, and thought he was some sort of saint.

'Hi!' she said. 'Is supper ready?'

'Almost, I should think. Simon's just pouring some drinks.'

'I brought mine with me,' she said, giggling. There was a half-empty bottle of white wine on the bench beside her. She was drinking it from a coffee mug. 'Do you want one?'

He shook his head.

'Dear Jeremy,' she said. 'Always such a *good* boy.'

'What is the matter?' he asked.

'Nothing,' she said. 'Nothing that a good boy like you would ever understand.'

'There's a visitor in the house,' he said.

'Who?' She stopped laughing immediately. 'Not my bloody mother?'

'No,' he said. 'Of course not. It's Ursula's niece.'

'Molly?' she said. 'Is Molly here?' He could not tell whether she was pleased or sorry.

'She wants to talk to you,' he said. 'Will you come?'

'Of course I'll come,' she said. She began to wipe her hands on her overall.

'You will be careful what you say.' Jeremy spoke carefully. 'You shouldn't make allegations you can't substantiate.'

'Oh, don't worry,' Joanna said. 'I'll behave myself. I've had years of practice.'

She took off her overall and followed him into the house, carrying the bottle of wine with her. In the kitchen she stopped to pour some into a glass and when they reached the living room she was almost composed.

Molly, sitting in a corner in a deep armchair, saw that Joanna was drunk and suspected that she was unhappy.

'I'm sorry to disturb you,' Molly said. 'But I'm staying at Back Rigg. You'll have heard that Ursula is dead?'

Joanna nodded.

Molly turned to the men. 'Perhaps you would leave us alone for a while. The three of us were very close, you know, at one time.' She thought for a moment that Simon would object, but eventually he muttered something about needing to prepare the dinner and left with Jeremy.

The women sat in silence.

'I'm sorry,' Joanna said. 'I loved her, you know.'

'When did you last see her?'

There was a pause. 'I don't know. Ages ago. I was really bad about visiting.'

'But you saw her on Friday night?'

'Friday night?' Was she playing for time?

'At the dinner party at the Cadver.'

'Oh then, of course.' Molly thought she sensed relief. 'But not to talk to. I've probably not talked to her properly since Fred died.'

'Why not?'

'I felt awkward. She'd never got on with my father. And I was afraid she might see me as the squire's daughter, playing Lady Bountiful. She would have hated that. As time went on it got more difficult so I just stayed away. But that business on Friday night really upset me. They were all saying that Ursula was barmy and had made the whole thing up but I knew that wasn't true. She might have been a lonely old woman but she wasn't insane.'

'Was she lonely enough to have committed suicide?'

Joanna shook her head. 'She was too much of a fighter,' she said. 'She wouldn't have done a thing like that.'

'We're not absolutely sure,' Molly said, 'that her death was an accident.'

'What do you mean?'

'There was no apparent cause of death. She hadn't been ill. There's a possibility that she might have been poisoned.'

Joanna's reaction appeared hysterical but Molly was not convinced by it. It was a performance. She wondered what possible reason lay behind it and thought that Joanna had always been cleverer than her family had realised.

'You think Daddy killed her!' Joanna cried. 'Because of the fuss she made on Friday night. What a scream! After all those speeches he's made about law and order. Did you know he always votes to bring back hanging?'

She paused, waiting for a reaction to the outburst. When none came she continued more reasonably: 'It won't do, you know. He couldn't have murdered Ursula. He wouldn't have had the guts.'

So, Molly thought, who could have done it? Who *would* have had the guts?

'You can see Back Rigg from here,' she said. 'Did you see Ursula again late on Friday night?'

'No,' Joanna said. 'I didn't see anything.'

'I wondered if you might have gone to Back Rigg yourself, later, to check that she was all right. It's the sort of thing you would have done when I first knew you.'

'Yes,' Joanna said. 'Well. I've changed since then.' She set the half-full glass of wine on the mantelpiece and stood looking through the window towards the farm.

The men came in. Simon was making every effort to be the perfect host, carrying bottles of wine and bowls of nuts and crisps, implying that in contrast Molly was being exceptionally rude not to see that they wanted to eat. Jeremy was silent and nervous. When Joanna saw them she became witty and lively again, turning the question of Ursula's death into a trivial game. She seemed to be teasing them. Molly was confused by her tone.

'Guess what?' she said. 'Mrs Palmer-Jones thinks Ursula might have been murdered. Isn't it exciting?'

'I'm not sure,' Simon said, 'that it's wise to make that sort of accusation without proof.'

'Oh!' Molly said mildly, becoming a harmless old woman who

would be frightened to offend anyone. 'I'm not making an accusation. But there are some questions surrounding my aunt's case. It'll be cleared up at the postmortem. I feel guilty in the way one often does when someone close dies. I feel that I should have offered more support, visited more often.' She leaned forward confidentially. 'I'm anxious, you see, that she might have committed suicide.'

That seemed to reassure him. It provided an excuse for her questions, her concern. She had done nothing for her aunt when she was alive but now she wanted to ease her guilt by showing she cared after Ursula's death.

Simon treated her graciously, poured more wine and answered her questions freely while making it clear that he found them foolish. It was just the impression Molly had hoped to create. Even Jeremy seemed to relax.

'These unfortunate allegations Ursula made on Friday night,' Molly said. 'I suppose there's no possibility that they could be true?'

'No possibility at all,' Simon said. 'Mr Grenville's made it clear that he would sack immediately any keeper who used poison. He asked my advice when there was unfavourable publicity about predator control on other estates a couple of years ago. He lets the moor to a syndicate and of course it's in his interest to have good quality shooting but it's not something he'd jeopardise his political career for.'

'No,' Molly said. 'Of course not. I see.' She turned to Jeremy. 'You have responsibility for the everyday management of the estate,' she said. 'You would know, I suppose, if one of the keepers was using poison.'

'Yes,' Jeremy said. 'I think I would. I took a course in estate management after my degree. We had a series of lectures from the RSPB's investigations officer about the consequences of using poison. It's something I've always taken very seriously.' There was hardly a trace of the stammer. What could there be to fear from this old lady? 'Besides, there are only two keepers on the estate and we work together very closely.' But as he spoke he remembered Danny

Craven, drunk in the Crowford Hotel, and thought that he could have been up to anything.

Molly accepted another glass of wine and turned her attention back to Simon Barton. 'I've already asked Joanna,' she said. 'I wonder if you saw anyone going to Back Rigg late on Friday night. You can see the track from here.'

'No,' Simon said. 'I wasn't even here late on Friday night. I was working in Scotland on Saturday and as soon as we left the Cadver I drove north. I spent the night in a hotel in Galloway so I could make an early start. My company's preparing the environmental impact assessment for a new west coast pipeline.'

Molly allowed him to continue, wondering why he was giving her so many details in reply to a simple question. She looked at Joanna but the woman's face was blank.

'And you, Mr Grenville?' she asked. 'Did you see my aunt after the dinner party on Friday night?'

'I did see her, actually,' Jeremy said. 'She was coming out of Keeper's Cottage. I was going past in a car. We didn't speak.'

'Where were you going?' Molly asked and she seemed so harmless and good natured that no one dreamt of accusing her of interference or suggested that she should mind her own business.

'Nowhere,' Jeremy said. 'Not really. Only to the end of the valley. Eve, my girlfriend, had been at the Cadver for dinner. We'd had no opportunity to be alone. I drove with her to the dam and walked back alone. I saw Mrs Ottway coming out of Vic Liddle's cottage on the way out.'

'Did you see anyone on your way back?'

'No,' he said. 'No one.'

Molly sat back in the chair and they stared at her, waiting for her to go. Simon stood up and walked to the window beside Joanna, but Molly made no move.

'When I arrived at Back Rigg yesterday there was someone on the hill behind the house,' she said. 'A young man, dressed in one of those army surplus jackets. It wasn't Mr Liddle. I'd recognise him.'

'That would be Danny Craven,' Joanna said. 'He's the new under-keeper.'

'Ah,' Molly said. 'Yes. I see.'

Then she did stand up. She took the quilted jacket from the back of her chair and put it on, sensing their impatience to get rid of her but refusing to hurry, allowing the tension to build.

Jeremy opened the door for her and waited for her to leave the room.

'And your father?' she said. 'Will he be driving back to London tonight?'

It was more appropriate than any of the other questions she had asked – a common politeness – but for the first time Jeremy showed anger.

'No,' he said sharply. 'Father hasn't any urgent business in Westminster for the next few days so he's decided to stay here until after the Easter recess.'

She paused, registering disapproval of his irritability. Then: 'It's such a beautiful estate,' she said mildly. 'I'm not surprised he's taking the opportunity to spend more time here.'

She beamed at them all and left.

In the Cadver Marcus and Olivia Grenville took tea in the drawing room. There were scones and a gingerbread and Marcus ate hungrily.

'There will be rumours about Ursula Ottway's death,' Olivia said. 'You must be careful what you say. It's a nuisance that girl of Jeremy's was here on Friday night. If it were just the family there would be no need to mention the incident at all.'

She sat, very upright, on a chair by the window. Her hair was pulled back from her face and pinned up in an old-fashioned, elaborate style. Marcus, sitting by the fire, reached for another slice of buttered gingerbread and thought how like her grandfather she was becoming. In the way she looked, of course, not in her personality. The old man had some warmth and humour about him.

'Don't worry about that,' Marcus said. 'I've got someone looking into that poisoning business. Someone discreet. George Palmer-Jones.

He's an ornithologist. Very well respected. If the press get hold of the poisoning story now I can show I've taken steps to deal with the matter. Not that there should be any problem with the old girl dying like that.'

She turned to him slowly, back and neck straight despite the weight of hair on her head.

'Marcus,' she said, conversationally. 'You are such a fool.'

Chapter Nine

The police station where George met Inspector Dave Benwell was new. It had been built on the edge of the town, close to the main road to Carlisle and the M6, part of a small trading estate. Immediately opposite was the supermarket where Ursula had been shopping on Friday afternoon. From the outside it could have been a hightech electronics factory. It was the communications centre for the north-west and there were impressive aerials on the roof and a carpark with a line of patrol cars.

George was as impressed by Dave Benwell as the superintendent had said he would be. He was blond and amiable, completely unflappable. Most policemen seemed to work under continuous stress but Benwell was unusually well adjusted. He brought no personal angst or prejudices to the job. If he was ambitious, it did not show and he did not let it affect his judgement. George never learned anything about Benwell's family – the policeman once mentioned having to get back to the wife and kids but gave no details of either. Perhaps they provided the stability that allowed him to be so relaxed.

Benwell had a desk in a large open-plan office and saw George there. Otherwise the room was empty. He wore jeans and an open-necked shirt. George thought at first that the clothes were making a statement and apologised for disturbing the man on a Sunday afternoon, then realised that there had been no intention to make him feel uncomfortable.

'That's all right,' Benwell said. 'I'm on duty anyway. And I'm hardly rushed off my feet.' He moved a pile of papers from a chair so George could sit down. 'What's all this about, anyway?'

George had expected to find the interview awkward and embarrassing. He was conscious of his age, his background, his lack of any practical policing. He had presumed the detective would be cynical and defensive, resentful of an outsider questioning the handling of the case. In fact, Benwell was remarkably easy to talk to and George found it a relief to share his worry about Ursula's death. He explained briefly the background to the case. Benwell listened, leaning back in his chair, his eyes half closed, so George wondered if he was taking it in, but when he asked a question to clarify the story he seemed to have grasped immediately the most important facts.

When George finished Benwell leaned forward. 'There'll be a post-mortem anyway,' the policeman said. 'The pathologist couldn't find an obvious cause of death. But I thought it would be quite straightforward. She was an old lady.'

'Will you ask the pathologist to look for phosdrin? That's the only poison keepers inject into hens' eggs.' George said tentatively. 'He'd not be able to tell without sending samples to the lab, but then apparently it would be easy to detect.'

'Sure,' Benwell said. 'I'll speak to him first thing tomorrow.' He stretched. The sunlight streamed into the room through the large windows. There was a view of hills and they could hear the distant rumble of traffic on the main road to the Lake District. 'If she was poisoned how do you think it was administered?'

'In alcohol,' George said. 'She'd been drinking heavily all evening. We found an empty whisky bottle in her house. I've brought that with me. If there's no trace of phosdrin in the bottle there's a possibility that it was put directly into the glass.'

'Did you bring that to be tested?' The detective smiled.

'No,' George said. 'There was no point. It had been washed.'

'Do you think that's significant?'

'Not necessarily. Ursula might have washed it herself before the poison took effect. There was a second glass. That could be important, though she wasn't houseproud. It could have been left on the draining board from a previous occasion.'

There was a pause. George thought the detective was trying to find the words to tell him tactfully to get lost. 'You're convinced, aren't you,' Benwell said, 'that she was murdered?'

'Yes,' George said. 'I'm not sure why. It's so convenient, I suppose, that she's gone.'

'It won't be an easy investigation,' Benwell said. 'Grenville's a powerful man. I take it that Marcus Grenville *is* your chief suspect?'

'I don't know.' George was shocked, a little disturbed that the detective had pushed the thing to its logical conclusion. 'I hadn't gone that far.' He had a sudden fear that he would provoke a terrible disaster, an unstoppable chain of events. 'I'm not making any accusations, you know,' he said in panic. He thought again that he was a fool, a vacillating old man without the courage of his convictions.

'If it wasn't Marcus Grenville,' Benwell said, 'who else could it be?'

'One of the keepers, perhaps. I found the buzzard in Liddle's shed. It must have been taken from Back Rigg on the night of Ursula's death, so he's obviously implicated.'

But I believed him, George thought. I believed his shock and surprise when the buzzard was found.

'After Grenville the keepers would have the most to lose if Ursula made her allegations public,' he continued. 'There's been a lot of publicity about the use of poison on big estates lately. Grenville would want to dissociate himself with the practice even if he's turned a blind eye in the past. If one of the keepers was involved he would almost certainly lose his job.' He paused, uncertain of his ground. 'Perhaps I shouldn't have gone to see Liddle this afternoon,' he said. 'I didn't want to pre-empt your investigation, but it seemed important to find out if he had access to phosdrin. The buzzard was a bonus.'

'And he did have access to the poison?'

'Apparently. The jar's empty, but it's impossible to tell when it was last used. In the past it was put down to kill rats.'

'Why would anyone want to kill a buzzard?'

George was surprised. He had supposed Benwell was a local

man. But perhaps he could only maintain his confident detachment because he was an outsider.

'Buzzards and other birds of prey are supposed to take young grouse,' he said, 'though in fact their impact is nowhere near as great as some keepers seem to think. I suppose it must be annoying if you've kept moorland to a high standard and raised a lot of young birds to think that they're lost to predators. In the past keepers have been put under a lot of pressure by landowners to keep the prey population down. Now that it's illegal they're in an impossible situation – if they're caught using poison they get the sack and if there aren't as many grouse as expected they're blamed for not keeping the vermin under control. On lots of estates the message seems to be "do what you have to but make sure you don't get caught".'

'And on the Cadver?' Benwell asked. 'Is that the message there?'

'No,' George said. 'I really don't think so. Marcus Grenville is an ambitious man and he wants high office. His only hope is to get into government through his environmental interest. If it became public knowledge that he wasn't as clean – or as green – as his PR people would like us all to believe, he would lose his last chance. I don't believe he'd be prepared to take the risk.'

The phone rang on Benwell's desk and there was a short and incomprehensible conversation. The policeman replaced the receiver then looked at George, expecting him to continue.

'I've been thinking,' George said, 'that there might still be poisoned bait on the hill. It might be worth a look.'

'Would you be able to do that?' Benwell said. 'A stroll on the hill behind Back Rigg shouldn't attract too much attention. Not if you're staying in the house.'

'Of course I could do it,' George said, 'if you want me involved. I thought you might prefer me to keep out of your way. I've not official standing any more.'

There was another pause. Somewhere in the building a door banged shut. The room was very hot. Benwell chose his words carefully. He wanted to make his position quite clear.

'Look,' he said. 'You might be right about Mrs Ottway but at the moment the whole thing is too ... politically sensitive for me to wade in without proper proof. As you say, the rumour could easily wreck Marcus Grenville's career. I've got to wait for the post-mortem results before I take any action. You do see that?'

George nodded. He was disappointed but he had already achieved more than he had expected.

'But you're not working under the same constraints,' Benwell went on. 'You've been employed by Grenville, given permission to investigate the poisoning incidents. I know of your reputation – we all read your papers on interviewing techniques during training – and if you can dig up any information before I can begin the formal investigation I'd be grateful.' He hesitated again. 'But perhaps you have other commitments,' he said. 'Perhaps you feel you deserve some peace in your retirement.'

'No,' said George. He felt absurdly flattered. 'No. I'll be pleased to help.'

'Had you intended to stay at the farm for a while anyway?'

'Yes,' George said. 'At least until after the funeral. There's a daughter but she wants to leave the arrangements to us.'

'She couldn't have had anything to do with this business?'

'No,' George said. 'I hardly think so.'

'So,' Benwell said. 'If you're right we're looking for someone in the valley – someone involved in the Cadver Estate.' He scribbled on a piece of card. 'This is my home number,' he said. 'If I'm not in someone will take a message. And I'll be in touch as soon as I've got the results from the pathologist.' He stood up. 'I'd better get back to the wife and kids,' he said. 'They'll be wondering what I look like,' and he led George through the quiet, sun-drenched building to the cars.

When George got back to the farm it was dusk. He had driven through Appleworth past a roadside chapel, caught in the last of the sunlight, where old ladies in hats were gathering for the evening service. The trippers were gone and the town was quiet. George felt the exhilaration that always came at the beginning of an investigation, and the old guilt that he should gain such satisfaction from another person's misfortune, especially someone he had liked as much as Ursula. When he was at the Home Office he had worked closely with the police. He had felt the same excitement then at the beginning of a challenging case, but it had been possible to justify it as necessary to the work. Now he was afraid that he was just playing at cops and robbers. It was a dilemma he thought he would never resolve. He could not give it up – it was as addictive as birdwatching. Molly seemed to have no moral qualms abut their inquiry agency. She had spent her career as a social worker, she said, and was used to interfering in other people's business.

When he arrived at Back Rigg Molly was waiting for him and there was a smell of cooking. The kitchen was warm and welcoming. There was a light on. She was standing by the Aga, making gravy in a black meat tray, stirring it with a wooden spoon. The heat had steamed up her spectacles and when he came into the room she took them off and wiped them on her rather grubby jersey.

'It's chicken,' she said. 'It'll soon be ready.'

'You haven't been at one of Ursula's hens with a cleaver?' he said. 'We're not that desperate.'

'Don't be silly,' she said. 'I found it at the bottom of the freezer and took it out last night.' She produced a bottle of whisky from the dresser. 'I found this too at the back of the larder. It's quite safe. It was sealed.'

George poured himself a glass and topped up hers.

'I went to the pottery this afternoon,' Molly said. 'Jeremy Grenville was there.'

'What did you make of them all?' He always valued her opinion. She saw through bravado and pretence and picked up tensions that he missed.

She laid the spoon against the rim of the tray and turned seriously to face him.

'I'm worried about Joanna,' she said. 'I don't know the others well enough to tell but I think she's going through some sort of crisis. She was always vulnerable, a bit neurotic. Hardly surprising considering her background. She never got on with her mother and by the time I knew her the relationship had pretty well broken down. I don't think it was Joanna's fault. I don't know Olivia well but she seems incapable of warmth. Joanna adored her father but of course he was hardly ever there – there was always business in Westminster and he travelled a lot. She was one of those thin, nervy children given to temper tantrums, rather spiky, always in trouble. She never got the knack of protecting herself from being hurt.'

George listened patiently. Molly tended to talk as if she were preparing a report for the juvenile court but the information was useful all the same.

'I remember that there was something of a scandal when she was at college,' Molly went on. 'The story went that she took a heroin overdose. Certainly she was very ill. Olivia and Marcus hadn't realised before that she was having problems. She was shipped off to some private clinic to get sorted out. The family claimed that she had some mysterious illness, though it was pretty clear to most people that she was an addict. It's impossible to keep that sort of thing quiet. The Grenvilles seemed to be embarrassed by the whole affair. They never seemed to show any concern for Joanna.'

'Do you think she might be taking drugs now?'

'I don't know,' Molly said. 'She was rather excitable this afternoon, but I think she had been drinking.' She paused. 'I'd thought she was much more settled recently. Not happy, exactly, but settled. She's been married to Simon for ten years. The pottery seems to be very successful. She's making quite a name for herself. She's even established reasonable relationships with her mother and father. She's still quite neurotic – always following the latest diet fad, worrying endlessly about her health – but there are lots of middle-class women with the same sort of self-obsession.'

'So what's the cause of the present crisis?' George said. 'Do you think she can have been involved in Ursula's death?'

'No,' she said. 'I don't think so. They were very close at one time. She used to come here a lot when she was a child. I wish I could persuade her to talk to me.'

When the meal was over George was restless. He wanted to move the investigation on but Sunday night was hardly a convenient time to make uninvited visits to Grenville and his family and it was too dark to begin his search of the hill.

'I suppose,' he said, 'we should sort through Ursula's things.'

'What do you mean?'

'Grenville will want the house back eventually and if Sally only comes up for the funeral she'll not have time to do it.'

'You want to search through Ursula's things,' Molly said, 'to find some reason why she died.'

'Yes,' he said. 'There's that too.'

He did not know what he was looking for. He knew he would find it impossible to sit still all evening.

The task was less demanding than they had expected. Upstairs one of the bedrooms was quite empty, the floorboards bare, the windows uncurtained. In another tiny room at the back of the house, where Molly had slept as a girl, there was just a bed, with blankets folded under a threadbare candlewick quilt and an empty white wood cupboard. Molly stood by the window and looked out at the hill. She remembered the novelty of her stays at Back Rigg. There had been an informality quite different from the restrictions of her conventional county family. Ursula had encouraged her when she was at school and celebrated with her when she reached university. Her aunt's outspoken views on politics, farming, the welfare state had made her consider her own opinions. Though they often disagreed violently they shared a commitment to the independence of women and that had brought them together.

Molly drew the thin curtains and followed George into the room where they were sleeping. There the furniture was equally sparse. There was a high solid bed on a dusty square of carpet and a huge mahogany wardrobe. George opened it and found two men's suits with big lapels and wide trousers.

'That was Fred's best suit,' Molly said. 'Don't you remember? He wore it to my father's funeral.'

They moved on quickly to Ursula's room. It was untidy, the bed roughly made. A hot-water bottle full of cold water lay on the floor and there were clothes on a bent-wood chair by the window.

'What was Ursula wearing when you found her?' George asked.

'Brown corduroy trousers and a handknitted green jersey.'

'Would that be the sort of thing she would usually wear?'

'Yes,' Molly said. 'I can't remember her wearing anything other than trousers on the farm.'

'I would have thought she might have changed into something more respectable before going to see Marcus Grenville,' she said.

'Oh,' said Molly, 'that would never have occurred to her.'

George felt in the pockets of a jacket thrown over the back of the chair. They were empty.

'Shall we make three piles?' Molly said. 'One for rubbish, one for Oxfam and one for the stuff Sally might want to keep?'

But George had hoped to achieve something more significant than sorting through jumble.

'Later,' he said. 'Let's look downstairs and see if there's anything there first.'

He felt strangely that there was a time limit to his involvement with the case. Once the pathologist had completed the postmortem and the test results were returned from the lab he would be forced to leave it all to the police. He wondered why it was so important for him to succeed. Was it, as Molly sometimes said, despicable male pride? Or the need to prove to himself that although he had retired he was still competent? He was ashamed of his need for recognition. There was something squalid in this scrabbling through a dead woman's clothes to get ahead of the police.

He wished he could be as relaxed and secure in his own abilities as Molly. But fear of failure and a relentless curiosity drove him on. He switched off the light in Ursula's bedroom and they walked together down the stairs.

The living room was freezing. There was already a sheen of frost over the window pane and Molly grumbled, monotonously and under her breath, that this was all a waste of time. She had no hope of persuading George to give up.

The room was dusty but ordered, obviously scarcely used. There was a book case with a glass door full of unread Dickens and Thackeray, and large and uncomfortable furniture. Why had she died here? George wondered. What had she been doing? Surely she would have spent the evening in the kitchen where at least it was warm. Had she been trying to reach the phone? Why, then, had she been found lying on the sofa?

'When did Ursula use this room?' he asked.

'Whenever she had visitors,' Molly said. 'She thought the state of the kitchen would offend people.'

'So if she had a visitor on Friday night she would have brought them in here,' George said. 'It's another confirmation of our theory.'

He prowled around the room, opening sideboard drawers to find nothing but a tray of tarnished silver and a pile of old photographs. He ran his hand between the cushions on the sofa and brought out ten pence in small change and a pensioner's bus pass in Fred Ottway's name. Frustrated, he stopped in front of a watercolour drawing of a house, built of local stone with tall gables, surrounded by trees.

'Where's that?' he asked.

'It's called Monk's Wood. The only close friend Ursula ever had in the valley used to live there. She was a widow called Kathleen Prime, a lovely woman. She did the painting herself. She died fifteen or sixteen years ago.'

'Who lives there now?'

'Her great-niece, Alex,' Molly paused. 'Joanna went to stay there, I think after she'd been ill.'

She might have added more detailed information but George had moved on to the small room which Ursula had called the office. It contained a kitchen stool and a huge roll-top desk. George opened the desk and looked at the mound of paper inside with a perverse satisfaction. Here, at last, there was something to get his teeth into. Molly was horrified by the thought of the task and said she would go to the kitchen to make tea. When she brought him a mug, and another glass of whisky, he had scarcely made any impact on the chaos.

'There are receipts for the sale of lambs going back to 1969,' he said, almost in admiration. He hardly looked up at her and left the tea undrunk on the windowsill, while he set in an orderly pile

Sally's school reports and some uncompleted football pools. Ursula, it seemed, threw nothing away.

It was more than an hour before Molly saw him again. She had suggested that they bring all the paper into the kitchen where they could sort through it together, but he said he preferred to do it alone. He could concentrate better. He put on his overcoat and stood at the desk and all she heard was the rustle of paper and an occasional whistle of astonishment.

'Well,' she said when he emerged finally and came into the kitchen stamping his feet. 'Was it worth it?'

'Oh yes,' he said smugly. He was pale with the cold and stood with his back to the Aga, his hands against the oven door. 'I think so.'

'Well?' she repeated.

'Marcus Grenville's been trying to get Ursula out of Back Rigg since Fred died,' George said.

'I know,' Molly said. 'It was common knowledge. He wanted the house as a sort of holiday home for the syndicate who shoot on the hill. There's no suitable accommodation for them on the estate and he was afraid it might make them look elsewhere. He'd miss the income they generate. Apparently, he even suggested putting them up at the Cadver but Olivia wouldn't have it.'

'Did you know that recently Ursula had been to see a solicitor to fight her case?'

'No,' Molly said. 'She hadn't told me that.'

'There's a copy of a letter that the solicitor sent to Marcus last week. Listen: "My client feels that she is being put under pressure to return the tenancy of Back Rigg farmhouse to the estate. She instructs me to inform you that she considers your frequent visits and telephone calls as harassment and if you do not behave towards her in a more reasonable manner she will pursue the matter through the court."'

'How could she do that?' Molly said. 'She had no money.'

'Yes she had!' George said. 'She was an extremely-wealthy woman. She must have inherited a fortune from her family years ago. She never touched it. There are brokers' reports going back for years.

She and Fred lived off the farm while she had investments worth tens of thousands of pounds.' He paused. 'But this is even more interesting. It's the draft of a letter to her solicitor, asking him to look into the possibility of buying Back Rigg from the estate. Apparently as tenant she'd have first option if it came up for sale. Marcus Grenville wouldn't like that at all. Where would he put his shooting parties then? This is the only house big enough on the estate.'

'Couldn't he build?'

George shook his head. 'He'd never get planning permission. Not even with his influence. This is the heart of the National Park.'

'So this provides Marcus Grenville with another reason for wanting Ursula out of the way.'

George poured himself more whisky. 'It gives us another suspect too,' he said. 'Sally. It's unlikely, of course, but it would be interesting to find out if she knew how rich her mother was.'

'I'm sure she didn't,' Molly said. 'I don't want to be uncharitable, but Sally's always been mercenary. She'd be here by now going through the papers by herself if she thought there was something in it for her.'

George gathered up the loose letters into a file. A black and white photograph floated on to the table. Molly picked it up. A tall, handsome woman in a floral print dress looked at her.

'This is Ursula,' she said, 'as she was when I first knew her.'

She began to cry.

Chapter Ten

When Danny Craven woke up he was lying fully clothed on the settee in the Lodge. It was dark. He awoke suddenly, like a child disturbed from a nightmare, and for a moment he did not know where he was. He thought he was a boy again in the cottage down the valley, in the room he had shared with his sister. Then his eyes grew accustomed to the dark and he saw that the window was in the wrong place and he could make out the shadows of the heavy old furniture. He shut his eyes and turned his head into the cushion in an attempt to recreate again the illusion of childhood happiness but the moment was gone and gratefully he sank back into a drunken sleep.

When he awoke again it was light and Vic Liddle was banging on the door wanting to know what he had done with the van. Craven sat up carefully. His head throbbed in two distinct places just behind his eyes. He thought he might be sick. Ignoring Liddle's increasing anger he went into the kitchen, splashed water on to his face, then drank half a pint of milk straight from the bottle.

What a bloody state to get into, he thought, but he did not blame himself for the hangover. It was all Grenville's fault, he thought. If Grenville wasn't such a bastard he wouldn't be here, alone, with drink as his only comfort.

He returned to the living room and opened the door to Vic Liddle, then stood, blinking in the sudden light. He still held the milk bottle in one hand.

'Bloody hell, man,' Vic Liddle said. 'What's the matter with you?'

'What do you think?' Craven said. 'You'd better come in.'

He leaned against the door frame and realised he was still a little drunk. When he had finished in the hotel he had continued drinking at home. He could not remember much about it. He had never been able to take his drink. When they were teenagers his sister had been able to keep up with him pint for pint. He sensed Liddle staring at him and turned away, back into the house.

'Suit yourself,' he said.

'What do you mean "suit yourself"?' Liddle was so angry he could hardly speak. 'This is Monday morning. You've a job to do.'

'Look,' Craven said. 'I'm not doing anything until I've had some tea. You can come in and have some too or not, just as you like. It's all the same to me.'

He left the door open and went back into the room. He drew back the curtains and carried an empty whisky bottle and glass into the kitchen. Liddle followed him, attracted despite himself by such depravity.

'Bloody hell,' he said again. 'It stinks like a brewery in here.' He opened the window wide and a cold breeze blew and made Craven shiver. 'What set all this off, then?' Liddle asked.

There was real interest in the question and for a moment Craven was tempted to tell him. He longed for sympathy. It's the anniversary of my sister's death, he wanted to say. It happened two years ago. But he had not come this far to give his plan away at the first kind word and he just shrugged.

'You know what it's like,' he said. 'Some days there doesn't seem anything else to do.'

He filled the kettle from the tap and looked in the cupboard for something he could turn into breakfast. The effort was too much and he sat heavily on a stool by the plastic table.

'It's not worth it if you ask me,' Liddle said. He looked disapprovingly, without comprehension, at the chaos in the house, the piles of dirty washing, the unwashed dishes. 'You need to sort yourself out, lad.'

Craven set the milk bottle on the table with a bang. 'Look,' he said. 'You don't understand what it's like. How could you, all cosy and cared for in Keeper's Cottage? You don't know what it's like on your own so don't give me all that crap!'

He was shaking and a nerve under his eye began to twitch uncontrollably. He got up suddenly and put tea-bags into mugs. The man's a nervous wreck, Liddle thought, then he looked at the slouching figure, unshaven, dirty, and his irritation returned.

'We've all got problems,' he said shortly. 'Families bring problems of their own.'

'Oh!' Craven said. 'For Christ's sake. If you're going to start preaching you can piss off.'

But he poured boiling water into each of the mugs, pressed the teabags with a spoon until the liquid was brown then scooped the bags into the sink.

'Help yourself to milk,' he said. The bottle he had been drinking from was still on the table. He reached into a cupboard for a bag of sugar.

'I'm here because I wanted to talk to you,' Liddle said, suddenly conciliatory.

'If it's about the van it's at the pub. I was over the limit so I walked home. I'll get it later.'

'No,' Liddle said. 'It's not that.' Reluctantly he poured milk into his tea. He hesitated.

'Go on!' Craven said aggressively. 'What is it? What else am I supposed to have done now? Get on with it.'

'Nothing,' Liddle said. 'So far as I know you've done nothing. At least that's what I'll say. Someone was at my house yesterday afternoon, snooping. It's possible that he'll come to see you too. I wanted to warn you.'

'Who would that be, then? The poll tax inspector?'

'For God's sake, man!' Liddle lost his temper. 'This is serious. If this goes wrong we could both lose our jobs and the chance of ever being employed as keepers again. We've got to decide on a story and stick to it.'

Craven looked up at him. He smiled as if he were suddenly pleased with himself and Liddle wondered if was being deliberately provocative.

'All right, then,' Craven said. 'I'm listening. Who was this mysterious snooper?'

'His name's Palmer-Jones,' Liddle said. 'He's staying at Back Rigg. His wife was Ursula Ottway's niece. He claimed he just wanted to ask a few questions, but he took away a jar that'd had phosdrin in it. It was empty, though I'd swear that the last time I went into the shed I noticed it was half full.' He looked at Craven. 'Not that I told him that.'

'I don't understand,' Craven said, 'what this has to do with me.' He smiled again. Liddle tried to control his temper.

'I want to know,' Liddle said, 'if you've been using poison on the moors. Since you've been here it's been your responsibility, controlling the vermin. I've been a young keeper myself. I know what it's like to put in all that work then see those bloody birds flying over the hill. It's soul-destroying. But if you've been using poisoned bait up behind Back Rigg I have to know.'

He paused. Craven made no response. 'You might as well tell me,' Liddle said. 'I found the buzzard. I know we've had our differences but that was a mean sort of trick.'

'What was a mean trick?' Craven said. 'What are you accusing me of now?'

Liddle took no notice. 'I'd like to know,' he said, 'how you got the thing back from Mrs Ottway.'

'What the hell are you talking about?' Craven stood up and was shouting.

'Palmer-Jones found the corpse of a buzzard in my outhouse while he was looking for poison. You're not telling me you didn't know it was there.'

'No,' Craven said. 'I didn't know it was there.' He paused. 'Why's this Palmer-Jones so interested, anyway?'

'Because he thinks Mrs Ottway was poisoned,' Liddle said. 'That's why I'm so bloody worried and I have to know what's been going on up there. Don't you see? If you've been injecting hens' eggs with phosdrin she might have picked one up thinking her hens had been laying away. She'd just have to fancy an omelette and she'd be dead. I don't know the legal position but that seems to me a sort of manslaughter.'

'Yes,' Craven said, no longer joking. 'There are all sorts of ways of killing a person.'

'Well?' Liddle demanded, his impatience returning. 'Will you tell me what you've been playing at up on the hill?'

There was a hesitation and Vic thought that for once he was going to get a straight answer. But Craven only shrugged. 'Nothing,' he said. 'I've been playing at nothing. Why should I? What do I care what happens to Marcus Grenville's grouse? I don't pay him thousands of pounds for a weekend's shooting.'

He paused again. 'But I'll tell you something,' he said. 'When I last saw that jar of phosdrin it was half full too.'

Vic Liddle left the Lodge soon after and went back to Keeper's Cottage for breakfast. The conversation with Craven had left him dissatisfied and unhappy. He felt suddenly that he was quite alone. Even Marie had become moody. She seemed not to care that things looked so bad for him. He thought vaguely that it was probably her age. He had heard that the change of life affected women in strange ways. His mother had complained of hot flushes and palpitations it seemed for years. His father had been a martyr to them. All the same, he thought, Marie could have picked a better time to go moody on him.

Outside the kitchen there was the smell of bacon. The ambulance had not arrived to take Cassie back to school and he waited at the back door, wondering if he could find an excuse to go away. He hated the fraught ten minutes of leave-taking, Cassie distressed and shaking as if she were being sent from home for the first time, Marie fighting back tears. Something always seemed to get left behind and there was the farce of chasing up the garden path before the ambulance drove away. It wasn't a dignified way to carry on. But Marie saw him and called him in to breakfast.

'Where have you been?' she said. 'It'll be burnt to nothing.'

'I've been at the Lodge,' he said, 'talking to Craven.'

'What did he have to say for himself?' She cracked an egg into a frying pan. He watched suspiciously as it spread and sizzled.

'Where did you get that?' he asked.

'From Mrs Ottway. Like I always did. I'll have to find somewhere else to buy eggs now.'

He took the shell from the table and studied it carefully, then sat back, satisfied that it had not been tampered with. Cassie, all ready in her coat and hat, watched him.

'Well,' Marie said again. 'What did Craven have to say for himself?'

'Nothing much,' he said. 'He claimed to have nothing to do with the poison on the hill.'

'Did you believe him?'

'I don't know. He's a strange man. But, as he says, what reason could he have?'

She set the plate in front of him and he started to eat. Cassie began to whimper and he turned angrily and glared at her.

'What's the matter with her this morning?'

'You know what's the matter with her,' Marie said angrily. 'She's always upset when she has to go back.'

She crouched beside the girl's chair and hugged her, stroking her hair. 'That's all right, love,' she said. 'That's all right.'

'You shouldn't spoil her,' he said savagely. 'You only make things worse. You've made her dependent on you.'

As soon as he had spoken he regretted the words. It wasn't Marie's fault that there was all that trouble at work. He knew it was irrational to vent his anger on her.

'I'm sorry,' he said. 'I didn't mean it. You know how Craven gets on my nerves.' But to his horror Marie had already started to cry.

When Molly awoke, George was already up and out of the house. She presumed he was on the hill looking for poisoned bait. He had brought her tea, perhaps even tried to wake her, but the mug stood now on the bedside table, the tea cold, the milk turned into a greasy film on top. The room was filled with bright morning sunlight which shone through the smeared glass of the window. She got out of bed and went to run a bath. The bathroom was gloomy with peeling wallpaper and a damp patch on the ceiling. When she turned on the taps the water choked and gurgled in the pipes and came out in a scalding rush. She lay in the bath until the water was almost cold, remembering Ursula, wishing she had made more effort as an adult to know her better.

When Molly went downstairs George was still on the hill. She felt childishly resentful of his absence. They were supposed to be partners but still he took the lead in the investigation, only feeding her information when he thought she was ready for it. He's not always right, she thought spitefully, remembering small victories, the times when he had made important mistakes. She knew he did not mean to exclude her – he had worked alone for so many years that it was a habit – but still it rankled that she had to prove her worth.

Perhaps he's missed something, she thought as she went into the office where the piles of paper still stood on the desk, but she knew he was far more thorough than she could ever be. She looked around the tiny room hoping for some lead that would provide an excuse for not checking George's work. Hanging on the wall above the desk was a calendar, donated by a fertiliser company. There was a small space by each date, with just enough room to write in appointments. Ursula, it seemed, had hardly had a full social diary. The whole of March was empty except for one entry in the week before her death. Alex, it said. 4.00 p.m.

Molly remembered immediately who Alex was. Alex was Kathleen Prime's great-niece who had inherited Monk's Wood. Molly had met her a couple of times when the old lady was still alive, but knew her most by reputation. Kathleen loved to tell stories about her fiery nature, her ability to shock her parents.

'She takes after me,' the old lady had often said. 'My spirit must just have missed a generation.'

It had surprised no one when Kathleen left Monk's Wood to Alex in her will.

Why had Ursula arranged to see Alex during the week before her death? Molly wondered. Had she gone to Monk's Wood? Perhaps it was a regular social contact, replacing the visits to Kathleen Prime. If so she would hardly have noted it on the calendar.

Perhaps she was clutching at straws, Molly thought, in her attempt to justify her position as George's partner, but she really believed the visit might be significant.

When Danny Craven left the Lodge he did not go immediately to fetch the van from the pub. He would not be bullied by someone like Vic Liddle. It could wait until later, until the pub was open and he could have a pint in the bar after the walk. He went instead straight on to the hill, thinking that the fresh air would clear his head. He had plenty to consider. The whole thing had seemed so simple when he had planned it. Now there were complications and he wondered if he should give up. On the hill, he thought he would come to a decision more easily. The weather was bright, with a strong wind from the south-west which blew shadows of clouds across the heather and straight into his face.

As he approached the land behind Back Rigg he saw a tall, elderly man walking backwards and forwards across the hill, his head stooped and a stick in his head to clear the long grass. The man must have caught sight of him against the horizon because he stood up and waited as if he expected Craven to approach him. Perhaps that was what he wanted. If so he was disappointed because while he was still too far away to speak Craven raised his hand in friendly greeting and turned away to walk back to the road.

So, Craven thought. Perhaps things were still going according to plan after all.

George, who had expected confrontation, questions about what he was doing there, watched him go. He considered chasing after the man, but he was young and fit and could easily outpace George if he wanted to.

When he reached the road, Craven walked down the hill to Keeper's Cottage to collect a spare set of van keys from Vic Liddle. His arrival coincided with the ambulance and Liddle was so preoccupied in seeing the girl off that he handed over the keys without a fuss. With a new sense of optimism Craven walked on over the dam and around the lake to the Crowford Hotel.

The landlord must have seen him coming up the drive because he was waiting for him at the door.

'The bar's not open yet,' he said sharply, expecting trouble. 'And your van's round the back where you left it.'

Craven said nothing. He waited until the landlord went away, then walked round the hotel and into the lobby where there was a public telephone. The room was empty and he could use it without being overheard.

Chapter Eleven

George Palmer-Jones spent all afternoon at Back Rigg waiting to hear from Dave Benwell. By now there should be some post-mortem results. The search of the hill had been unproductive. Either Ursula had found all that there was to find or someone else had gone before him to clear the last traces of evidence.

Molly said nothing about Ursula's meeting with Alex. George was irritable and bad-tempered and there was an element of wanting to pay him back. She was also afraid that he would appropriate the information for his own use. She would follow the matter further herself and surprise him with a new discovery.

Throughout the afternoon George found the tension of waiting unbearable. The sunshine had gone and the south-west wind brought heavy clouds across the lake, and rain. At four-thirty he could stand the waiting no longer and phoned Dave Benwell at Appleworth Police Station. He was told that Benwell was out. Perhaps someone else could help him? George replaced the receiver without answering. At five o'clock the telephone went, ringing loudly through the house, startling Molly who was almost asleep in front of the Aga.

George ran to the living room to take the call.

'Yes,' he said. 'Palmer-Jones.'

He had been so convinced that Dave Benwell would be on the other end of the line that the rich, imperious voice of Marcus Grenville came as a shock.

'George!' he said. The word had the resonance of a back-bencher struggling to be heard in the chamber of the House of Commons. 'George, Olivia and I would like to invite you both to dinner.'

'That's very kind,' George said. He wanted the conversation to be over quickly in case Benwell was trying to get through to him. 'When would you like us to come?'

'Tonight,' Grenville said, surprised, it seemed, that George had not guessed the urgency of the summons. 'We'd like you to come tonight.'

'I'm afraid that's impossible. I'm expecting an important phone call this evening.'

'Nothing that can't wait, I'm sure,' Grenville spoke with complete confidence and George thought: that's what money and an estate in the country gives you. It's such confidence that makes the idea of a classless Britain a mockery.

'I'm sorry,' George said. 'I must stay here to wait for my call.'

'Nonsense!' Grenville said, trying to make a joke of it but irritated all the same because he was not getting his own way immediately. Then, more seriously: 'Something's come up, George. It's something I need to ask your advice about. A professional matter. I wouldn't impose on you if it wasn't important.'

George was intrigued and flattered despite himself, and agreed to go to the Cadver. As he replaced the receiver he thought Grenville would have seen his resistance as a gesture and was ashamed of his weakness. But when he returned to the kitchen to tell Molly about the summons she said it was probably just as well for them to go out. If Benwell had not phoned by seven-thirty he was unlikely to call that evening and she could not put up with George's irritation all night. Then she began to panic about what she would wear.

They drove to the Cadver, though George would have preferred to walk. It was bad enough, Molly said, that the only respectable dress she had with her was the old one that she had bought twenty years before to wear when she was accompanying her clients to court. It would be worse to arrive breathless and covered in mud.

Marcus Grenville opened the door to them and showed them into a comfortable room with leather armchairs and a fire. There was no sign of Olivia and he did not mention her.

'Now,' he said, standing with his back to the fire, rubbing his hands together nervously. 'What will you both have to drink?'

Molly sensed that he was frightened. Was it guilt? she wondered, or an ambitious man's anxiety that his plans for advancement were in danger?

'There'll just be the four of us tonight,' Grenville went on. 'Jeremy's out with that girlfriend of his. Probably as well in the circumstances . . .'

He poured drinks and made polite conversation about the pictures in the room and the weather. Molly thought: I suppose all politicians have the skill to make trivial small talk while their minds are engaged elsewhere.

'What circumstances?' George asked and Grenville stopped suddenly and even blushed a little.

'Let's talk business later, shall we?' he said in a tone of faint rebuke. 'After we've eaten.' George had the impression that he had broken a rule of etiquette.

Then there was an awkward silence broken only by the entrance of Olivia, elegant and stately in a plain black dress. She stood in the doorway, looking them over, then called them in to dinner.

Throughout the meal, which was good in a solid English, rather overcooked way, Marcus Grenville took responsibility for the conversation. He talked first, with admiration, about Joanna.

'She's making a real reputation now with her pottery,' he said. 'There was an exhibition in London last year – I dragged half the Cabinet to see it. And she's making a tidy little income. I should know – I invested in her myself.'

He went on to speak in the same glowing terms of Simon Barton's consultancy. 'That's the way conservation should go in the future. There should be more private enterprise to inject some cash and energy into the environmental movement.'

George muttered that there had been more than enough energy in the conservation field – it was cash they were short of. But Grenville seemed not to be listening and had already changed the subject to Jeremy. He leaned earnestly across the table towards George. 'It's quite a responsibility, you know, for someone of his age to run an estate like this but I trust him implicitly – implicitly. I wouldn't dream of interfering!'

Then he told old jokes about opposition politicians which took them through pudding and up to coffee.

During the meal Olivia had maintained an almost contemptuous silence. She thinks Grenville is making a fool of himself, Molly thought. She thinks the whole evening is a mistake.

George was hating every minute of it. The afternoon of waiting for the policeman's phone call had made him tense and he was finding it increasingly difficult to pretend an interest in Grenville's conversation. It was an insult, demeaning. Was he some sort of peasant to be called to the big house and forced to sit through such drivel? With the arrival of the coffee he could contain his impatience no longer.

'What *is* all this about, Grenville?' he demanded. 'Why have you asked to see me? You know I'm a busy man.'

Grenville was suddenly sheepish and embarrassed. 'Of course,' he said. 'Of course. Silly of me. Why don't we take our coffee into the study so we don't disturb the ladies?'

'Nonsense, Marcus!' It was as if Olivia had spoken for the first time and they stared at her, astonished by the sharpness of her voice. 'We have no secrets and I'm sure Mr Palmer-Jones has none from his wife. We might even ...' the sarcasm was terrible '... have some contribution to make.'

Molly turned to Olivia and smiled at her. It was the last thing she would have expected. Grenville faltered for a moment and smiled awkwardly.

'Of course,' he said. 'I didn't mean...'

Then his habitual confidence took over and in his old blustering style he began to explain what was worrying him.

'I had a phone call today,' he said, 'from an old friend. Good chap. Editor of the local rag. Staunch party member. One of the most useful men in the Appleworth Association.' He paused, sipped brandy and continued. 'Late this morning there was a phone call to the news desk of the paper. My friend didn't take the call himself. One of the reporters answered it. The caller was making certain ... allegations about Ursula Ottway's death.' He paused again. 'Claimed it was murder.'

'Was the caller a man or a woman?' George asked.

'A man.'

'The paper must get a lot of malicious allegations,' George said, 'with a celebrity like you on the patch.'

Marcus Grenville seemed not to recognise the sarcasm. 'I suppose so,' he said. 'But this was different. The caller seemed to know an awful lot about the affair. Got the interpretation all wrong, of course. He implied that I'd killed Ursula because she'd found out we were using poison on the estate. How could he know about that scene of Friday night? My friend put the reporter off – said they couldn't make anything of an uncorroborated, anonymous call like that, but the journalist was interested and wanted to follow it up. You can't blame him. I suppose it looks like a good story.'

'And you're afraid he'll persuade his editor to let him investigate the accuracy of the allegations.'

'No, not that. Not old Henry. He wouldn't publish anything to cause me embarrassment. But I'm worried the mischief maker might have tried another paper, somewhere not so scrupulous. It wouldn't take much – a melodramatic headline, a few innuendos calculated to make the reader think the worst – to turn me into a murderer overnight. And the national press would pick it up in no time.'

'Have you any idea who might be behind the rumours?' George asked the question quietly. It was followed by a silence. Marcus and Olivia looked at each other. There was a battle of wills. Olivia, inevitably, triumphed.

'I think it was Craven,' she said. 'I've never liked him. I don't know why Marcus continues to employ him.'

Molly was surprised by the intensity of the malice in Olivia's voice. Surely it was beneath her dignity to concern herself so deeply with a junior employee. The outburst disturbed Grenville too.

'Look here,' he said gruffly. 'Don't be too hasty. We shouldn't make allegations either without proof. I know Craven's not an easy chap to get on with but I've always found him quite straight, you know. I don't think he'd play that sort of trick.'

He was flushed and uncomfortable. He fumbled for a handkerchief and wiped his forehead.

'I don't understand,' George said, 'what motive Craven would have. Has there been an incident on the estate, Mrs Grenville, which has made you suspect him, or any problem with his work?' He turned to Grenville. 'You've not threatened to sack him?'

'No,' Grenville said. 'There's been nothing like that. He can be insolent, bad tempered. That's why Olivia has taken against him. But he's a good worker and this estate needs two keepers.'

'All the same . . .' Olivia said spitefully, 'I think if Mr Palmer-Jones is looking into this problem for us he should be aware of our suspicions.'

There was a pause. '*Your* suspicions,' Grenville said. 'Your *imagined* suspicions.'

It was a public rebuke and Molly felt embarrassed for her but Olivia gave no response. She sat, quite still and upright at the end of the polished table, silent, commanding their attention.

'I've been wondering,' Grenville said suddenly, 'if Jeremy's girlfriend can have had anything to do with it.'

'Would she have reason to wish you harm?' George asked mildly. 'It would be in her interest, surely, to get on with her boyfriend's parents.'

'Oh, I don't think she's got anything against me personally,' Grenville said. 'I've only met the girl once. She was pleasant enough, I suppose, if you like the type. I prefer something a bit more feminine in a woman. No, I think she might have her own reasons for wanting bad publicity for the estate.' He paused. 'She's one of those animal rights activists. They're mad as hatters, of course, the lot of them. Jeremy met her when she came to the Cadver with a bunch of hunt saboteurs at New Year. In the old days you could have set the dogs on them, but he did the right thing and talked to them. They don't understand the importance of field sports in the countryside. They'd be up on the moor, if we let them, coming between the shooters and the grouse.'

'And you think that because she disapproves of the hunting and shooting on the estate she would make up stories to the press?'

'I don't know what to think,' Grenville said. 'But she was here on Friday night when Ursula made that scene. I suppose that has some relevance. They're sentimental, those animal rights people. Robin-strokers, I call them. The thought of two little pussy cats poisoned might have provoked her into action.'

'Ursula didn't call the police on Saturday morning to tell them about the poisoning,' George said. 'She was already dead by then. Presumably the calls to the police and the newspapers were, made by the same person.'

'There you are, then,' Grenville said. 'That just shows the extent to which they'll go. I want you to talk to the girl, George. Frighten her. Get her to tell you what's going on.'

'It seems a surprising relationship,' Molly said, almost to herself. 'A young woman with views like that and the manager of a big estate. It seems doomed to failure.'

'Perhaps she's leading him on,' Marcus said. 'Perhaps she's only going out with him so she can get close to us and cause us trouble.'

'You mean she's some sort of spy?' Olivia was dismissive. 'I hardly think that's likely.'

George shrugged. 'I don't know,' he said. 'The animal rights supporters go to extreme lengths. There have been bombs, you remember, in supermarkets and in a scientist's car, but in those situations the organisation admitted responsibility. It's possible, I suppose, that they're building up to some sort of campaign and the phone calls to the papers were a first step. Marcus might have been chosen because he's a public figure. And any rumours of cruelty on the estate would make him a natural target. If pole traps were being used, for example. Or poison. . .'

The statement hung like a question and Marcus Grenville reacted immediately. 'I've already told you, George. There's nothing like that going on here.'

'Besides,' Molly said. 'Didn't you say that the caller to the newspaper office was a man?'

'That means nothing,' George said. 'The activists work in small groups. One of the other members of the group could have made the call.'

'Rather melodramatic, don't you think?' Olivia said. 'Not the sort of thing you'd expect in Crowford.'

'All the same, we'll look into it,' George said. 'If that's what Marcus wants.'

'Yes,' Grenville said, uncertainly. 'Yes, I'd like you to look into it.' Molly had the sense that the evening had not gone as he had planned.

A candle that had been lighting the table was blown out by a breeze. Olivia stood up. The room seemed suddenly cold. She led them into the drawing room where they all sat close to the fire and talked about Molly's parents and Olivia's grandfather. The talk of weekend house parties and balls took them into a different world and it was as if the previous conversation had never taken place.

They left the Cadver early. It was only ten o'clock but Grenville had retreated into an uncharacteristic silence, clutching his brandy glass and staring at the flames. Olivia, talking about the elegant society events of her youth, became more animated, but Molly could sense George's boredom and decided they should leave before it was obvious to the others. Olivia stood at the head of the steps which led from the front door to the drive to wave them off. Grenville, who had grown more awkward in their company as the evening progressed, had muttered his apologies and said there was work to do before bed time. It seemed not to matter that no one believed him.

'What did you make of all that, then?' Molly asked as George drove up the road to Back Rigg. The rain of the early evening was over and there was a full moon, covered occasionally by brown clouds. The air was still damp and chilly. 'I got the impression that Grenville was trying to protect Danny Craven. What reason could he have? There's surely no shortage of competent keepers.'

'I don't know.' The effort of being polite to the Grenvilles had made him uncommunicative. He turned up the track towards the farm.

They saw that there was a light in the house before they noticed the car parked beside the Land Rover. It was faint and Molly decided it was the kitchen light, only visible from the front through an open connecting door.

'Perhaps it's Sally,' she said. 'Perhaps she's found time to come up after all.' She was pleased by the idea that the woman still had enough affection for her mother to prompt her into making the effort.

But George had recognised the car. 'No,' he said. 'I don't think it's Sally. I think it's the police.'

Dave Benwell was sitting by the kitchen table, reading one of Ursula's copies of *Farmers Weekly*. When they came into the room he folded the paper and stood up.

'The door was open,' he said. 'I didn't think you'd mind me waiting.' He gave the impression that he would happily have waited all night.

'No,' George said. 'Of course not. Is there any news?'

He found that he was intensely nervous. It was like waiting to hear an exam result. It was a purely selfish anxiety. At that moment he had no thought for Ursula. He was concerned only to find out if his instinct had been right or if he had made some terrible error of judgement.

Benwell returned to his seat. Molly watched him, suspiciously. She knew how vulnerable George was.

'We had the preliminary report from the pathologist this evening,' the policeman said. 'I thought you'd be interested. This is almost on my way home so I called in.'

'Well?' George demanded, almost rude in his impatience. 'Did they find anything?'

'Phosdrin,' Benwell said. 'They found traces of mevinphos in the samples sent to the lab.'

And George could have hugged him.

'So it was murder,' he said, giving nothing of his relief away.

'That's why I'm here,' Benwell said, 'to discuss the alternatives. My boss asked me to come. We have to be sure of our facts, he says, before we make a fuss.'

Molly's suspicion grew. He's a coward, she thought. A yes man.

'Because Marcus Grenville is involved?' she snapped.

Benwell nodded awkwardly. 'I suppose there's not a possibility that it could have been an accident?' he said. 'You say this stuff is sometimes injected into hens, eggs. She kept hens, didn't she? I heard them as I came round the house. Isn't there a chance that she found eggs on the hill and thought they were safe to eat?'

He looked unhappily at George. Bear with me, he was saying. I have to ask.

'No, Inspector,' George said. 'That's impossible.' He took a clear plastic bag from a shelf on the dresser and showed Benwell the handkerchief and fragments of shell inside. 'She must have found these on the hill at the same time as the buzzard,' he said. 'They were in her coat pocket. She recognised their significance enough to collect them. If she'd found an intact egg out there do you really think she would have eaten it?'

'No,' Benwell said. 'I didn't realise.' Then, defensively: 'You do see why I had to ask?'

'What else do you have to ask, Inspector?' Molly said brutally. 'You want to know, I suppose, whether she might have committed suicide?'

'Yes,' he said. 'I have to ask that too. She was depressed. She'd been drinking heavily. I have to look into the possibility.'

'No,' Molly said. 'Ursula didn't kill herself. She wouldn't have done. Not like this. Not in the middle of a fight with Grenville. She was never one for giving up. Besides, how could she have done? It's possible, I suppose, that she took a bottle of poison from the outhouse at Keeper's Cottage when she was there late on Friday night, but unthinkable, don't you think, that she put it back later and then returned here to die?'

'Yes,' Benwell said. 'You're quite right. That's impossible.' He looked at them, calm and serious. 'So,' he said. 'It's murder.'

Molly had expected that then the policeman would leave, that the impersonal ritual of a police investigation would begin and that they would have no further part to play in the affair. She had expected that she would have to deal with George's sense of frustration and helplessness as he watched the inquiry develop without him. But the policeman remained where he was at Ursula's table. It seemed that he was in no hurry to return to his family, that he had, in fact, all the time in the world. He accepted her offer of tea and when at last he began to speak it became clear that this was a council of war and that although the laborious business of police investigation would proceed elsewhere they were in no way to be excluded. George's lethargy and bad temper left him. He passed on, in a logical, methodical way, so that he might almost be reading from a previously prepared paper, all the information they had gained.

He told Benwell that Ursula was a rich woman, that Grenville was frightened of Danny Craven, and about the anonymous phone call to the local newspaper. Then they decided between them a strategy for action, a plan of campaign. When Benwell finally left Back Rigg it was gone midnight and the rain had returned.

In the Cadver Grenville sat in his office until midnight, worrying. He thought he had managed things badly. Olivia's attitude throughout the evening had disturbed him and he was wondering if his impulse to involve Palmer-Jones had been mistaken. He should have thought the thing through more carefully, right from the beginning when Craven first contacted him. The approach to George at the conference had been the result of panic; at Whitehall George had the reputation of being a careful handler. In his work for the Home Office he had been seen to deal discreetly with the most troublesome of problems: disputes between senior police officers, even occasionally, it was rumoured, with embarrassments in the security services, and there had never been the hint of scandal. Marcus had seen his presence at the conference as fortunate, but thought now that he had acted precipitate.

Then, as the evening wore on, Grenville wondered if he should have told George more. Laid all the facts on the table, as it were. Come clean. But he thought that even George's loyalty had a limit and that it would be safer to tell him only what he needed to know. He had always thought that his political judgement was sound and it upset him now to think he had made such a mess of things.

Chapter Twelve

Molly went to Monk's Wood in the morning. She did not phone Alex to warn her of the visit. She did not want to make too much of it. It would be a courtesy call, an elderly woman informing an acquaintance of the death of a family friend. Perhaps Alex would be out. Her children would be quite grown up by now and it was probable that she would be at work. In that case Molly would leave a note and call back later. Monk's Wood was close enough to Back Rigg to make a visit on impulse quite plausible.

George had woken optimistic, ravenous, full of energy. He had driven early to Appleworth to buy sausage and bacon and Molly had cooked a huge breakfast.

'Why do you want to go there?' he demanded when she told him she was going to Monk's Wood.

'I think Ursula was there in the week before her death. Alex was a close friend of Joanna's. She might know something. . .'

George seemed hardly to hear. He was wrapped up in his own ideas.

The breakfast delayed her and she started later than she had intended. She took the road that led away from the dam, in the opposite direction to Appleworth. It climbed steeply away from the lake into the hills. She saw no other cars. She had a map but as she drove she remembered the times when she had come with Ursula to visit Kathleen Prime, and she only missed a turn once. The distance was shorter than she remembered – five miles, perhaps – and then she came down into the hamlet, for which there was no place sign and whose name she could not recall. There was a line of grey single-storey cottages and a pub, patronised, she supposed, by the residents of the cottages, serious walkers and people from Appleworth looking for adventure. She remembered the place quite vividly. Nothing had changed since she was last there. A plump woman in an apron was shaking a door mat in the garden of one of the cottages and stared at her as she drove slowly past.

Beyond the pub was a NO THROUGH ROAD sign and the lane was narrower. There was grass growing in the middle of the road and she worried that she might not get through. Perhaps she should have brought her aunt's Land Rover. On either side of the lane the hill rose steeply. Through the open window she heard lambs' cries. George would have been looking out for ring ouzel and the first wheatear. She drove past a farm and had to brake as the dogs chased out in front of her and then she was at Monk's Wood.

After the bare hill and the severe blocks of Forestry Commission plantation, it seemed almost miraculous. In the lee of the hill sheltered from the north wind there were several acres of mixed deciduous woodland. The leaves were in bud. There was hawthorn blossom, wood anemone, primrose. It was too early for the bluebells, which Molly remembered from earlier visits. The wood was surrounded by a crumbling stone wall which showed some signs of repair and on each side of the lane was a gate post, though the gate that must once have marked the boundary to Monk's Wood land had long since disappeared. Molly drove on through the trees to the house, a Victorian construction of steep gables and high chimneys which had mellowed to become pleasing.

On the lawn in front of the house stood a young woman with long red hair. She turned and Molly saw that she was holding a baby. The image had a dream-like quality because Alex had stood in exactly the same way to say goodbye to them on Molly's last visit to Kathleen Prime. But that had been twenty years ago and by now Alex would be a middle-aged woman.

The girl must have heard the car but she took no notice and that added to Molly's sense of unreality. Like a character in a children's fantasy she felt she had gone-back in time and helpless and unseen was watching history run before her. The girl walked with the baby into the house.

Molly parked the car and walked across the lawn into a large porch with wooden seats on each side and two pairs of wellingtons on the stone floor. The girl had gone on into the house, but Molly waited in the porch and looked for a doorbell. Through the open inner door she heard:

'It's no good, Mother. I don't think I can go through with this.'

Someone, surely Alex, said: 'Nonsense, darling. Don't be so melodramatic!'

Molly gave up her search for the doorbell and banged hard on the glass of the porch. Alex appeared in the hall from a room at the back of the house. Even in middle age she was a striking woman, tall and well proportioned. Her hair was still long, plaited and pinned to her head.

'Yes?' she said. Then there must have been some trace of recognition. 'I'm sorry. . .'

'It's Molly, Molly Palmer-Jones. My aunt, Ursula Ottway, was a friend of Miss Prime's.'

'That's right!' Alex said. 'I remember now. You used to come with Ursula to visit her.'

'I don't want to disturb you . . .' Molly said, but she walked from the porch into the hall. 'My husband and I are staying at Back Rigg for a few days and I thought I'd just take the chance . . . I wondered if you'd heard that Ursula was dead.'

'No,' Alex said. 'I didn't know. I see Simon and Joanna quite regularly but recently we've not been in touch . . .' She paused. 'I'm so sorry,' she said. 'I liked Ursula very much. She and Kath were such friends. I hadn't realised she was ill.'

There was a silence. Perhaps she expected that, having passed on the news, Molly would leave, but she made no move to go.

'Come on into the kitchen,' Alex said at last. 'My daughter's here with the baby. I was going to make coffee.'

It was clear that Monk's Wood was no longer in communal occupation. Alex had stamped her style on the place and there was a peace and an order which would have been impossible if it were still shared by assorted strangers. The girl from the garden was standing by the window. She had unusually flat features, which gave her face the look of a rag doll.

'This is Rowan,' Alex said. 'And William, my grandson. He's nine months old but Rowan doesn't trust me to look after him while she's working away.'

'Mother, that's not true. It's just that I've never left him before for more than a few hours. I can't imagine five days without him.'

But she smiled and Molly saw that her hesitation was a matter of form, a gesture to show her mother how much she would miss the baby. She was excited at the prospect of the trip, so absorbed that she had no curiosity about the visitor.

'Rowan's an actress,' Alex said. 'She's going to tour *Much Ado* in the Hebrides.'

'Not the Hebrides, Mother. The Shetlands. You are hopeless!'

She smiled again and put the baby into a large wooden playpen.

'I'll have to go now,' she said. 'I arranged to meet Charlie at one.'

She bent to kiss William's forehead, hugged her mother and fled. They heard the sound of a car outside.

'I'm sorry,' Molly said. 'I interrupted your goodbyes. I hadn't realised. . .'

'Don't worry. Rowan would prefer it like that. She doesn't like a fuss.'

Alex filled a filter machine with water and spooned coffee into the brown plastic cone. If she resented Molly's intrusion she was too polite to show it.

'The last time I saw Rowan she was hardly older than William,' Molly said. 'It was after Kathleen's funeral.'

'And I was just divorced with two kids under five.'

'You must be very settled at Monk's Wood after all these years.'

'Yes,' Alex said. 'I love it here. I still can't believe how fortunate I am to own the place.' She was moving around the room, pouring sugar into a bowl, finding mugs, then stopped and looked directly at Molly. 'I felt terribly guilty, you know, when I found out it was mine. It seemed wicked to keep a place like this all to myself.'

'Is that why you had all the other people to stay?'

'Yes,' Alex said. 'It was partly guilt. And I needed the company. The divorce had made me frightened of being lonely. Besides, it was such a romantic idea to set up a commune. It was part of a philosophy we all believed in.'

'Did it work?' Molly was genuinely interested.

'For a while. For a while it was really successful. It's become trendy to mock that sort of idea now but I don't have any regrets. It was fun.' She laughed. 'We even had a colony of wigwams in the woods one summer. And I made such good friends during that time.'

'Like Joanna Barton,' Molly said. 'She lived here, didn't she?'

'Joanna was my friend before she came to Monk's Wood. She'd had a bad time. Her family didn't want her at the Cadver.'

'I remember there were a lot of rumours,' Molly said.

'Oh,' Alex said bitterly. 'There were a lot of rumours. Most of them encouraged by the Grenvilles.'

'Why would they do that?'

'Because they didn't want anyone to find out the truth.' Alex stood up abruptly, obviously angry with herself for giving so much away.

'So the drugs, the sudden illness. All that was untrue? Is that what you mean?'

'No,' Alex said and returned to her seat. 'I don't mean that.'

They sat looking at each other. Outside there was bird-song, bright and sharp as it always is in the spring after a winter of silence. The baby was lying on the floor of the playpen, his thumb in his mouth, almost asleep.

'Why do you want to know?' Alex's words were loud and aggressive. She had realised quite suddenly that this was no ritual social call to exchange memories of a woman they had both admired.

'Ursula was poisoned,' Molly said. 'The police think it was murder.'

'Why would anyone want to murder Ursula?' Shock had made her angry. She thought Molly had taken advantage of her hospitality and deceived her.

'She could be awkward,' Molly said. 'She asked difficult questions, too.'

'So that's why you're here? Because you think Joanna killed your aunt?'

'No,' Molly said. 'Not that. It's not as specific as that. The police will investigate, of course. They'll ask questions in Crowford, check statements and technical details. But they won't understand what the people involved were really like. They never met Ursula – how could they know the effect she had on people? Then they're scared of Marcus Grenville's influence and won't ask for personal details about his family unless they're convinced it's relevant. That's what this is all about. That's why I'm here. It's nothing to do with revenge and nothing much to do with justice. I just want to understand and' – she stopped, thinking how pompous she sounded. It would serve her right if Alex laughed at her and sent her packing. But Alex seemed to be taking the words seriously.

'I don't see how it would help,' she said with some regret, 'to bring up all that stuff about Joanna's past. You should ask her.'

'So talk about the present!' Molly cried, relieved that at least Alex was prepared to listen to her. 'You're still a friend of Joanna's. Tell me what's going on now. I met her on Sunday and she seemed under a terrible strain. Is she happy?'

Alex shrugged. 'I don't think Joanna has ever been that. Not consistently. She wasn't brought up to be. She adored her father but he was never there. Her mother was cold, repressive. She had always been frightened of Olivia. She never, somehow, got the hang of being *happy*.'

'But things must be different now. She has a stable marriage and a successful career. Can't she forget what happened to her before she came to live at Monk's Wood?'

'No,' Alex said. 'How can she forget when she's living so close to them all? She and Simon should have moved away when they got married. Here she's always reminded of failure.'

'I wish you would tell me what this is all about!' It was a cry of frustration. Alex was apologetic.

'I'm sorry,' she said. 'I can't tell you the details. It wouldn't be right. It's not only my promise to Joanna. There are other complications . . .' She looked away. 'Look,' she said. 'I can tell you this much. She was taking heroin when she was at college, but it wasn't only that that screwed her up. She had an affair with a married man, one of her lecturers. I don't know, perhaps with him she was really happy. She never got over it. He promised her the earth then deserted her when she needed him.'

'I see,' Molly said. 'Thank you for telling me.'

'I think that's why she married Simon,' Alex said. 'He was safe, unimaginative. She thought she would find some sort of peace with him.'

'But it didn't work?'

'He was crazy about her,' Alex said. 'For years he tried to give her what she needed, but she was too tied up in the past. In the end I think he gave up.'

'But they're still married?' Molly said. 'There's never been any question of divorce?'

'No,' Alex said quietly. 'There's never been any question of divorce. The present arrangement suits them both too well. Simon enjoys being Marcus Grenville's son-in-law, especially since he's started up in business by himself. He likes to have an attractive wife to take to business dinners and conferences. And Joanna enjoys the security of the relationship. It gives her the freedom to work. She knows Simon will make no demands on her as long as she entertains his colleagues and is pleasant to his clients. It's not my idea of marriage but it seems to work for them.'

In the playpen the little boy snuffled in his sleep and turned over. Alex stood up and brought the coffee jug to the table. Without asking she refilled Molly's mug.

'And you?' Molly asked. 'Did you ever marry again?'

Alex looked at the baby. 'No,' she said. 'There have been men, of course, over the years. Some of the relationships have been stable enough. But when the commune drifted apart I got used to being here on my own, just me and the children. It was selfish, I suppose, but I never wanted to share it. I'm a teacher by training and I work as a supply if something comes up that I fancy. That way I don't get stuck in a rut. I have a feeling, you know, that marriage would bore me.'

Molly drank from the mug. 'Have you seen Ursula recently?' she asked. Alex seemed surprised as if the old woman had the gift of second sight.

'About a fortnight ago.'

'Did she come here?'

'Yes, she turned up out of the blue, like you. She said she had plenty of eggs and thought I might like some but that was an excuse. She wanted to talk about Joanna too.'

'Why? What had happened?'

'Nothing much. Ursula and Jo were quite close at one time and I think Ursula still worried about her. She never really got on with her daughter. Perhaps in some way Jo took her place. She'd been to see Jo and had found her upset, crying. She was worried, so she came to see if I knew what had upset her or if I could help.'

'And could you?'

'I thought I had an idea what might lie behind it.'

'So you confided in Ursula?'

'Yes. I confided in her. In a moment of weakness. It didn't seem so much like a betrayal of trust. Ursula was like a stepmother to Jo. It was as if they'd adopted each other. Anyway she had guessed most of it.'

'But you won't tell *me!*'

Why do I mind so much? Molly thought. Am I jealous of Ursula's intimacy with Joanna? Or am I worried that I'm losing my powers of persuasion?

'In the circumstances,' Alex said, 'don't you think it's just as well? Ursula's knowledge doesn't seem to have done her a lot of good.'

Molly looked at her in astonished silence, realising immediately the implication of what had been said. Alex stood abruptly and began to unpack the bag that Rowan had left with the baby, setting brightly coloured objects, a pelican bib, feeding dish, cup with a spout, on the table in a row.

It was clear that she would answer no more questions about Joanna and Ursula.

'You're busy,' Molly said. 'I'll leave you now.' She thought there was nothing more constructive to be learned.

'Just a minute,' Alex said. 'I'll walk with you to the car.' Molly thought she would be a good mother – calm, relaxed, unfussy. And a good friend. She turned away from the table towards Molly, suddenly troubled.

'You mustn't think Jo killed Ursula,' she said. 'I'm not saying that at all.'

She led Molly through the kitchen door into the garden. They were at the side of the house, sheltered from the wind, and the sun felt warm. Molly made a trivial remark about spring having come at last.

'Yes,' Alex said. 'I was at the Solway at the weekend and it was still quite wintry there.'

She led Molly along a gravel path to the front of the house and her car. It was not until she had reached the pub, and was waiting for a mail bus to drop its passengers and turn in the small carpark, that Molly remembered that Simon Barton too had been at the Solway at the weekend. The fact seemed to take on a new significance.

Eve Theobald had a disturbing day. There was a case conference about a child of whom she was especially fond, who was being moved at the parents' request to a private residential home. She argued against the decision as strongly as she could but her opinion had no weight. She was only a teacher and the family had the right to send the child wherever they thought fit.

Then there was the phone call, which came at break time, just as she was sitting down in the staff room with her coffee, so she thought the caller must have taken the trouble to find out when she would be free. The voice was undemanding but persistent. He did not want to frighten her but he was determined to get his own way.

'My name's Palmer-Jones,' he said, after he had apologised for disturbing her. 'I'm staying at Back Rigg. My wife was Ursula Ottway's niece.'

'I'm sorry,' she said. 'I don't understand how I can help you.' She thought he was a crank and was about to replace the phone.

'Ursula was murdered,' he said. 'Poisoned. The police haven't been yet to take a statement? They want to interview everyone who was at the Cadver on Friday night.'

'No,' she said. 'No one's been here.'

'I'm working for Marcus Grenville,' he said, so she distrusted him immediately. 'I'd like to talk to you. Perhaps I can buy you lunch.'

'I'll tell the police the truth about what happened on Friday night!' she said. 'I'm not the sort Marcus Grenville can bribe to keep quiet.'

'Of course not,' he said, genuinely shocked. 'There was no question of that.'

Then she thought she had offended him and agreed to meet him in a pub in Appleworth. She would get a free lunch out of it and, besides, she was curious.

The policeman arrived just as she had returned to her class. He was in plain clothes and at first she thought he was a parent. He was quite untroubled by the children and usually strangers were frightened by the noise, the uncoordinated limbs, the dribbling.

'I'm sorry,' she said. 'I can't leave my class. You'll have to come back later.'

'That's all right,' he said. 'It won't take long. If you don't mind we can talk here.'

So they sat together in the corner where she read to the children and encouraged them to join in songs and counting games, and she told him about Ursula Ottway's outburst on Friday night, breaking off occasionally when one of the children needed her attention.

'I had a phone call this morning from someone called Palmer-Jones,' she said, just as the inspector was leaving. 'He says he's working for Marcus Grenville. He's asked me to meet him. Would you have any objection to that?'

The inspector paused, opened the door into the corridor. 'No, Miss Theobald,' he said. 'No objection at all.' He smiled easily as if at some private joke.

She got to the pub early but still Palmer-Jones was there before her, sitting at a table in the gloomy dining room. He stood up when she came in, obviously quite certain of her identity. She supposed that Marcus Grenville had described her to him and again felt resentful. When she had taken on Jeremy she had not expected this fuss, this intrusion in her private life.

He asked her what she would like to drink and she ordered a pint of bitter, defiantly, knowing she would regret it when she had to cope with the kids in the afternoon. Then she chose the most expensive meal on the menu. She expected him to ask the same questions as the inspector, to go over again the scene on Friday night, her perception of Ursula's state of mind and the reaction of the Grenville family. Instead he asked about her.

'I understand that you're an active member of the Appleworth Animal Rights Group,' he said.

She shrugged. 'Not so active any more.'

'Oh?' he said. 'Why?' It was not polite conversation.

She tried to make light of it, but she wanted him to understand too. 'I've grown out of all that. It was fun at first – the sense of outrage, the idea that your action could make some real change – but I realised it was all bullshit, all talk.'

'It had nothing to do, then, with your relationship with Jeremy Grenville?'

'No,' she said. 'Why should it?' She was going to add that she would let no man tell her what to do, then realised that it sounded trite. She sensed that the man at the other side of the table would see through bullshit too.

'But your sympathies still lie with the animal rights movement? You still disapprove of field sports?'

'Of course,' she said. 'Anyone with any sensitivity disapproves of field sports.'

'It must have been rather difficult for you on Friday night, then, while Ursula was making her allegations. You must have been tempted to support her?'

'Yes,' she said. 'I was tempted to support her. But I didn't have the guts. They're an intimidating lot, the Grenvilles.'

'So you didn't say anything at the time?'

'No,' she said. 'I was their guest. Jeremy was introducing me to them all for the first time. I didn't want to let him down.'

'What about later?' he said. 'Did you mention the incident to anyone later?'

'Who do you mean?' she asked. He could not tell whether the questions had surprised her or if she was stalling for time.

'Well, Jeremy, for instance. I suppose you talked to him about it. When you gave him a lift to the end of the valley? You did give him a lift to the end of the valley?'

'Yes,' she said. 'Of course.'

'And you talked about Ursula Ottway and the buzzard?'

'I asked him if he knew anything about it. He said of course he didn't and that his father must have given instructions to the keepers behind his back.'

'Did he tell you what he was going to do about it?'

'No,' she said sadly. 'He sounded quite helpless. I've told you, Marcus Grenville is an intimidating man.'

There was a pause while an elderly waitress brought plates and dishes.

'Did you mention the incident to anyone else?' George asked. 'Did you tell one of the Animal Rights Group, perhaps? It would be useful ammunition, wouldn't it, in their fight to stop shooting on the Cadver Estate? It would be hard to resist, I should have thought, the opportunity to pass on information like that.'

'I considered it,' she said. 'Using poison to control birds of prey isn't only illegal, it's barbarous. I should have told someone in the group.'

'But you didn't?'

'No,' she said. 'I didn't. I care too much for Jeremy. I forgot about my principles because I wanted to protect him.'

Then he looked at her with sympathy. 'It's always a difficult choice to make,' he said, and he began to talk about nature conservation and the compromises he'd had to make in his career. When the meal was over she was sorry that she had to go. He gave her a card, and wrote the Back Rigg phone number on the back. She promised to contact him if ever the need arose, though she told him, quite definitely, that she did not see why it should.

Chapter Thirteen

As George drove out of Appleworth, copies of the evening edition of a Carlisle daily newspaper were being set up on a stand outside a newsagent shop. A small balding man was struggling to fasten an advertising board on to the shop window but the gusty wind kept blowing it down. The man was wheezing, obviously asthmatic, and George wondered if he should stop to offer help, but as he pulled in to the side of the road the man fixed the board into position and disappeared into the shop.

'WHO KILLED URSULA OTTWAY?' screamed the large bold writing on the poster. 'Local MP implicated. Read tonight's *Chronicle*.'

George bought a copy of the paper and sat in the car to read it. The story was on the front page. The journalism was as sensational as any of the London tabloids, but what facts the piece contained were largely accurate. Ursula Ottway was portrayed as a sweet old woman who loved birds and animals. She had discovered the 'mutilated corpses' of her pets on the hill and had threatened to make the affair public. The next day she had been found dead 'and we understand from police sources that her death is being treated as suspicious'. The reader was left to draw his own conclusion, but the headline left him in no doubt as to the *Chronicle's* opinion that Marcus Grenville was at least in part responsible.

George felt a sympathy for Grenville. To deny the allegations implied in the *Chronicle* would only lead to more publicity. All his efforts to distance himself from Ursula's death had been in vain. George wondered how the newspaper had got hold of the story. Benwell had said that the police had been instructed to be discreet.

Perhaps there had been a particularly persistent reporter? Or had there been another anonymous phone call to the newspaper that was obviously not particularly favourable to Marcus Grenville? If so, who was the informant? Some political rival? That seemed unlikely. It would be two years at least before the next election, and the facts in the article were too close to the truth to be discovered by an outsider. Perhaps Eve Theobald was lying and had passed on information to the Animal Rights Group after all. Or perhaps there was someone more closely connected to Grenville who hated him and wanted to ruin his reputation.

When he returned to Back Rigg Molly was making soup and the kitchen was steaming. There was a smell of lentils and vegetables.

'How did you get on with Eve Theobald?' she asked.

'I don't know,' he said. 'She's a clever young woman. If she had anything to hide it would be hard to tell. Perhaps you should have spoken to her. You might have got more out of her.'

Molly looked at him suspiciously. Was this some gesture to appease her?

'Had Ursula been to Monk's Wood recently?' he asked.

'Yes,' Molly said. 'She went because she was worried about Joanna. Alex wouldn't tell me what it was about, but she admitted that she did confide in Ursula. It all seems to have started about fifteen years ago.'

'You always said Joanna was neurotic,' he said. 'Perhaps it was something trivial that she's blown out of proportion.'

'Perhaps,' Molly said. 'But Alex seemed to take it seriously too.'

'Could it be anything to do with Marcus Grenville?' he said. He put the newspaper on the table and told her to read it. 'Could Joanna have informed in some attempt to pay him back?'

She shook her head uncertainly. She had always been told that Joanna adored her father.

'There's something else,' she said. 'I think Simon Barton and Alex might be having an affair.'

'Did she tell you that?'

'No,' Molly said. 'But I think she told Ursula. Simon Barton wouldn't want it to be general knowledge. Marcus Grenville might stop passing lucrative contracts in his direction.'

'How did you find out about the affair?'

'They were both on the Solway at the weekend.'

'That's hardly conclusive.'

'No,' she said. 'But it's an interesting coincidence.'

Dave Benwell came after they had finished the washing up when they were drinking coffee. It was eight o'clock, dark. The wind was so strong and noisy, rattling the windows in the frames and through the badly fitting door, that they did not hear his car on the track. He came round the house to the kitchen and knocked on the window, almost unrecognisable with his anorak hood pulled low on his forehead, a strange face pressed against the glass. George pushed the door against the wind and let him in.

'I thought you might be curious,' Benwell said, 'to know what's been happening.' He took off his coat and accepted a coffee. They had no sense of urgency.

'Have you seen the evening paper?' George asked. 'I'd guess the story was given by the same person who phoned the police about the poisoning. Have you talked to the editor?'

Benwell nodded. 'It's not been terribly useful,' he said. 'The editor claims they had an anonymous call from a man. They sent a reporter in Crowford to check the facts, then decided to publish. Do you think it's important?'

'It would be interesting to know who dislikes Grenville so intensely,' George said.

'Yes,' Benwell said. 'Well, I might have some idea about that. I followed up what you said about there being something odd about Grenville's relationship with Danny Craven. I got someone from the Somerset force, an old friend, to make some inquiries on the estate where Craven worked on Exmoor. My mate took a retired keeper to the pub at lunchtime, bought him a few drinks and came up with some interesting information. I've spent most of the afternoon on the phone.'

'Well?' Molly demanded. 'What did you find out?'

Benwell leaned forward over the table. 'Craven worked on the estate for ten years,' he said. 'He went there straight from school. He was a bit wild at first, they said. Cocky, you know, but not unpleasant. He was a good worker and he steadied down as he got older. He seems to have settled well, to have fitted in as much as outsiders can in a place like that. There was even some talk of romance with a local girl.

'Then, two years ago his sister committed suicide and they say he never got over it. He was very close to her, apparently. The people on the estate knew her quite well – she used to go and stay with him for weekends and holidays. Very attractive, she was, according to the old keeper. A dark-eyed beauty, he called her. After her death it seems Craven went to pieces. There were long drinking bouts and he became unreliable at work. He seemed, they said, to be in a world of his own, always angry. He blamed some man for leading her on, a married man. It was an obsession. His colleagues were sympathetic at first but the head keeper was pleased when he got a job up here. It saved the boss from having to sack him.'

'Are you saying that the married man was Grenville?' George asked slowly.

'I don't know,' Benwell said. 'But it might fit. There was certainly a previous connection between them. The Cravens were brought up here in Crowford. Their father worked for Grenville.'

'What else have you found out about Craven's sister?' Molly asked. She was intrigued and moved by the story.

Benwell continued as if there had been no interruption: 'The sister's name was Kathryn. Known as Kate. She left home at eighteen and got a place in a business school in London. Became a sort of super secretary. We know she worked for a while as personal assistant to an editor in a publishing house. The keeper my friend talked to thought she'd changed jobs several times but he couldn't give any details.'

'You'll have checked if Kate Craven ever worked for Marcus Grenville,' George said.

'Of course,' Benwell smiled wryly. 'He's had the same secretary for years. She's sixty-two and about to retire.'

'But Kate might have met him socially,' George said thoughtfully, 'or through work in another context. Have you traced exactly where she did work?'

'Not yet. We'll find out eventually, of course, through the social security system, but by the time I got the information from Somerset all the civil servants had gone home. I've set someone to look into it first thing in the morning. There is a quicker way of finding out, though – I've traced her mother. Apparently the father died a while ago but the mother lives in one of those old people's bungalows on the edge of Appleworth. The warden knows we're coming but we'll have to be quick. They go to bed early.'

'You want me to come too?' George was pleased but hesitant.

'Why not? It's only an informal inquiry. You might pick up something I miss.'

George thought that Benwell would miss very little but he stood up and went to fetch his coat. At the door he hesitated and turned to Molly: 'Will you be all right on your own?'

She was already resentful. It was her fault, of course. She should be more assertive, put her views forward. But how typical that they should think that she had no useful contribution to make, that George had made no mention of her theory that Alex and Simon Barton had spent Friday night together. This patronising concern was the final insult.

'Of course I'll be all right on my own,' she said. 'You-boys run away and play.'

They were let into Mrs Craven's bungalow by a middle-aged woman in lilac Crimplene trousers and a fluffy lilac cardigan.

'Here you are, dear!' she called, in the bright, unnatural voice of those who care for the elderly, a voice that George thought would lead him to commit murder if he were subjected to it for more than a day. 'Here are the visitors I was telling you about!'

She led them into a warm sitting room, too small for the furniture crammed inside. She was obviously curious and was about to settle into one of the chairs herself when Benwell thanked her and told her they wouldn't need to trouble her any more.

'Stupid woman,' said a small vigorous woman in the high-backed chair near the fire. 'I can't abide her. Always fussing.'

The warden, still within earshot, blushed and departed.

'Would you like tea?' the old woman said. 'I'm here because of the arthritis but I'm not helpless. I can make you tea if you want it.'

No, Benwell said. They did not want tea.

'What *do* you want, then?' She was fierce, a fighter. No one would make a fool of *her*. 'Has Daniel got himself into some sort of trouble? I knew it was bound to happen one day.'

'Why do you say that, Mrs Craven?'

'He's always had a short fuse,' she said dismissively. There was no indication that she had any affection for her son. 'Not that I see much of him. He only lives down the road but he doesn't bother to come here.'

'It's not about Daniel,' Benwell said. 'We want to talk to you about your daughter Kate.'

'She's dead,' Mrs Craven said. 'I can't tell you anything about her. What's it got to do with you, anyway?'

'I'm a policeman,' Benwell said. 'We've been asked to look again at the circumstances surrounding her death.'

'Well, you're wasting your time, Mr Policeman,' she said. 'Kate killed herself. There's never been any doubt about that.'

'We realise that, Mrs Craven,' Benwell said calmly. 'But we'd like your help all the same. Perhaps it's painful for you to talk about it all over again. Shall I bring the warden back to look after you?'

'Don't you dare!' she said. 'If I say anything in front of that witch it'll be all round the town before I've had my breakfast.'

'Was there a lot of gossip at the time?'

'No,' she said. 'It all happened in London. We buried her here, of course, but no one knew the details. I let folks think it was an accident.'

'Did they believe that?'

'They could believe what they liked,' she said. George could imagine her at the graveside, uncompromising and friendless. Had she been as hard in her attitude to Kate and Danny when they were children? Was that why they had both left home as soon as they could?

'Why did Kathryn kill herself, Mrs Craven?' Benwell asked gently.

The old woman turned her head away from them and for the first time there was a sense of pain and vulnerability.

'She got herself into trouble,' she said. She spoke so quietly that they could hardly hear her, then she turned back to face them and she was as loud and fierce as before. 'She should have come home!' she cried. 'If I'd known I'd have helped her, whatever she decided to do with the baby. Why didn't she come home?'

Was it, George thought, because Marcus Grenville was here?

'We need a list of the jobs she had after leaving the business school,' Benwell said. 'Would you be able to help us with that?'

She took a handkerchief from under a cushion on her chair and blew her nose.

'When she came out of college Kate started with a publisher,' Mrs Craven said. 'She was happy there. Then it was taken over by a big American firm and her boss left and she didn't fancy it any more.'

'Where did she work then?'

'A bank,' she said. 'Some sort of bank. In the City.'

'A merchant bank?' George suggested.

The old lady nodded. 'She didn't stay there long. Only a few months. She was always a restless sort of girl. She thought it would be more exciting, I suppose, to work in the House of Commons.'

There was a brief silence but no other indication that she had said anything of significance.

'Is that where she was working when she died?' Benwell asked calmly.

'Yes. She was personal secretary to Geoffrey Lomax. She loved it, she said. I don't understand what came over her.' Mrs Craven pulled out the handkerchief again and began to dab at her eyes.

George looked at Benwell. Geoffrey Lomax was a Conservative Member of Parliament. Benwell appeared to change the subject.

'Did Kate have a regular boyfriend?' Benwell asked. 'Or do you think the pregnancy was the result of a casual affair?'

'I don't know,' Mrs Craven said. 'She never talked to me about it. I didn't even know she was expecting. We never seemed able to talk about that sort of thing. My husband and I were getting on, you know, when we had the children. Perhaps it was a mistake . . . There never seemed enough time to give them. Jim was working on the estate and I helped Mrs Grenville in the kitchen. We'd never have managed to send Kate down to London without what I earned. We did what we thought was best, but now I'm not sure. . .'

None of us is sure, George thought, but he knew reassurance was impossible. She blamed herself for Kate's death.

'Was there any special friend?' Benwell asked. 'Someone she might have confided in about the identity of the baby's father?'

'Only Daniel,' the woman said. All the fight seemed to have gone out of her. She was very small in the big chair. 'Kate was always close to Daniel. Perhaps they were too wrapped up in each other. Neither of them seemed very good at making friends of their own.'

'So you think Daniel might know who was the father of Kate's baby?'

'I'm sure he did,' she said. 'But he would never tell me.'

And George thought that even after her daughter's death she was excluded from her children's secrets.

She was reluctant then to let them go. She wanted to talk about Kate, show photos of the four of them standing outside their cottage, smiling, to prove perhaps that there had been a time when they were a real family. Eventually they had to interrupt. They stood up, feeling brutal and heartless, and left her sitting in the small room, staring at the fire.

'I know Geoffrey Lomax,' George said. 'He was a junior minister in the Home Office while I was there. He couldn't have been the father of Kate Craven's child.'

'Why not?'

'He had a vasectomy after his sixth child was born,' George said. 'He tried to keep it secret but the staff found out. There was, as you can imagine, a lot of ribald comment. Westminster had a lot in common with a boys' public school – the humour is almost identical.'

'How well do you know Lomax?'

'As well as anyone can know an MP. They're all performers.'

'Would he trust you, do you think?'

'Yes,' George said. 'We always had a good working relationship.'

'Will you talk to him?' Benwell said. 'Find out if there was any connection between Kate Craven and Marcus Grenville. If I send in a policeman he'll tell us nothing. After the Cecil Parkinson affair they're bound to be sensitive about this sort of publicity. Talk to him off the record and tell him we'll keep it quiet if we possibly can.'

So, early the next morning, George took the train to London.

Chapter Fourteen

Wednesday, the day George took the train to London, was still, airless, mild. The wind had dropped and the lake was smooth, the reflections along the bank perfect. Molly was glad to have Back Rigg to herself. She and George had always led busy and independent lives. She had returned to work when her children were younger before it was the fashionable thing to do, despite being accused of cruelty, neglect, greed. Of course the children had survived, Molly thought. She was really rather proud of them. And what a hypocrisy it was to protest that a mother's place was in the home and then banish your offspring to a draughty and barbaric boarding school.

Now, after forty years of leading separate lives, they were working and living together, almost constantly in each other's company. It hardly seemed to bother George. There were times when Molly thought he treated her as a personal assistant and only got cross when she did not live up to the standards of the magnificently efficient women who had performed that function at work. But she was used to being her own boss, to taking her own decisions, and the process of consultation, of considering George's opinion, of finding herself often persuaded round to his point of view, irritated and belittled her.

He had asked her if she would need the car and had suggested that she should drive him to the station. He could get a taxi back to Crowford in the evening if it was late. But she told him to keep the car. If she needed to go out she would use Ursula's Land Rover. She got up late and enjoyed the luxury of breakfasting alone, of making the coffee the way *she* liked it, of reading at the table. She let the hens from the hen house into the wire mesh run and fed them and collected the eggs. And all the time she was thinking of Ursula and Joanna Barton, trying to make sense of it all.

On the way back to the house she heard the repeated sound of a car horn from the road by the lake and went to the front of the house to see what was going on. It was the mobile library from Appleworth announcing its presence in Crowford. She remembered that there were several books in the study that should be returned. She fetched them and made her way down the track to the van.

Joanna awoke late and Simon had already left for work. That seemed to happen all the time now. Sometimes she thought she could sleep all day. She made coffee and carried the mug with her to the pottery but found it impossible to settle to work, and after ten minutes wandered back to the house. The decision to phone Alex was made on impulse and immediately she wondered why she had not thought of it before. Of course she should speak to old Alex, the most together person she knew. Alex would tell her what to do.

'Hi!' she said. 'Look, I haven't seen you for ages. I was wondering if I could come to Monk's Wood. I'll take you to the pub and buy you lunch.'

There was a pause. 'I'm sorry,' Alex said. 'I'm really tied up this week. Rowan's away on tour and I've got the baby.'

Well, sod you, Joanna thought. So much for friendship. Then it occurred to her that Alex might have a man in her life again and was disposed to generosity.

'That's OK,' she said. 'I'll give you a ring in a few weeks. You can tell me all about it.'

'Yes,' Alex said. 'Right.' And Joanna was surprised by the relief in her voice.

The arrival of the library van came as a welcome distraction.

Vic Liddle came back to Keeper's Cottage for coffee at ten o'clock. He had shot three rabbits and stood by the sink to skin them, deftly sliding his knife between the flesh and the fur.

'What shall I do with these?' he asked. He had to repeat the question because Marie, polishing silver at the other end of the table, seemed not to hear. She looked up.

'Leave one out,' she said. 'I'll make a stew for tonight. The others can go into the freezer.'

He held the rabbits by their back legs and slid them into a polythene bag, then rinsed his hands under the tap.

'That policeman was around again today,' he said. 'That Inspector. Mr Grenville called me into the estate office to speak to him.'

This time she responded immediately.

'What did he want?'

'I don't know. I couldn't make sense of it. The questions didn't seem to lead anywhere. Then he wanted to know about Craven. How did Craven get on with Mr Grenville? he said. I told him that if he had any sense Craven would see he had a lot to be grateful for. I never wanted him as under-keeper. If it wasn't for Mr Grenville he wouldn't have a bloody job.'

Marie listened but her mind was elsewhere.

'Have you seen that Mr Palmer-Jones today?' she asked suddenly.

Vic shook his head. 'No. Someone said that he'd taken the early train for London.'

'Is he coming back?'

'I shouldn't think so. Mrs Ottway was no real relation to him, was she? I expect he's got better things to do.'

There was a silence and to fill it he began to talk about the weather. It was really stuffy out, he said. There wasn't a breath of air. If it stayed as calm as this they would have a go at burning that last strip of heather on the hill tomorrow. He'd go and see Craven in the afternoon, make sure everything was ready.

'Isn't it late for burning?' she said and he was pleased because she seemed to be taking an interest again in his work.

'It's a bit late, maybe,' he said. 'But we've got an extension into April this year. It's quite legal. It'd be a shame not to get it all done.' He was thinking of the chart on the living room wall, the satisfaction of following it exactly.

'But there'll be birds nesting in the heather by now,' she said. 'Won't there?'

'I suppose there might be,' he said. 'But no grouse. Nothing worth saving.'

He went out, not sensing her distress, and she was left with an image of charred fledglings and adult birds who would never feed young. Only the arrival of the library van outside the house raised her to action. She fetched her books from the bedroom and thought she'd get a nice Catherine Cookson to take her mind off things.

When Molly got to the van there was a queue. People must have come from all over the valley to change their books. She stood in line behind Joanna Barton. The younger woman looked thin, tired, tense and for a moment she seemed not to recognise Molly.

'Hello,' she said. 'I was coming to see you later. I wanted to know when Ursula's funeral will be.'

She was dressed in denim jeans and a long brown sweater that reached almost to her knees. She clutched a pile of library books against her body.

'We don't know yet,' Molly said. 'When the police release the body. Probably early next week.'

The queue moved forward as an elderly woman hauled herself up the steep step into the van, but Joanna stayed where she was, so they stood a little apart.

'What's going on?' she asked abruptly. 'An inspector from Appleworth came to see us yesterday to take a statement about what we were doing on Friday night. He was very polite and answered all our questions, but you couldn't really learn anything from what he said.' She paused. 'Do *you* know who killed Ursula?'

'No,' Molly said calmly. 'Not yet.'

'But you think you will?'

'Oh yes,' Molly said. 'The police have a very good clear-up rate, you know, for murder.'

'Good,' Joanna said violently. 'Good.' She looked moodily across the lake.

'Did you ever know Kate Craven?' Molly asked. 'She grew up in the valley.'

'Daniel Craven's sister?' The question seemed to surprise, but not to bother her. 'Yes, I knew her. She was younger than me, of course, but I met her at parties or in the pub when she came back from London to see her parents. She was fun.'

'Were you surprised when she killed herself?'

'Yes. I'd have thought she had so much going for her. At least she'd had the guts to break away from this place. That's more than I ever had. I could never understand what made her so depressed.'

'She was pregnant,' Molly said. 'Perhaps you never knew that.'

This time there was a reaction. 'No,' Joanna said. She faltered then regained control. 'I never knew that. Poor Kate.' She turned away.

The queue moved forward again and this time Joanna walked on to join it. Molly began to ask about Simon.

'It's a brave move,' she said. 'Setting up in business by himself. Does he enjoy it?'

'Yes,' Joanna said. 'He seems to. He works very hard at it. I hope it works out for him.' She spoke in a curiously flat voice as if she were speaking to a stranger.

'He said he was staying on the Solway on Friday night,' Molly said. 'Does he go away a lot?'

'Yes. He has to. Especially since he got the contract for the pipeline.'

'Aren't you ever tempted to go with him? The Solway's beautiful, isn't it, in the spring?'

Joanna looked at Molly with the same flat, impersonal stare.

'What are all these questions about?' she said. 'One of the reasons I like you so much is that you don't usually go in for polite conversation.'

Marie Liddle, ahead of them in the queue, climbed into the van and handed her books to a pretty young librarian. Joanna and Molly were left alone on the road.

'I suppose you've found out that Simon spent Friday night with another woman,' Joanna said impassively.

Molly said nothing.

'Look,' she said. 'I know Simon's got another woman. I know he takes her with him when he's away on business. And I don't blame him, all right? So there's no possible motive for murder there.'

'Do you know who she is?' Molly asked.

Joanna seemed surprised. She thought Molly was above such curiosity. 'No,' she said. 'Of course not. And I don't bloody care.'

In the library van the elderly woman had had her books stamped out and was hovering on the step, frightened of falling. Molly and Joanna took an arm each and helped her down.

'You can go in next,' Joanna said. 'I'm not in a hurry. I've nothing better to do.' And she walked right away from the van and sat on the grass at the side of the lake. Molly felt she had let her down.

She handed in Ursula's books to the librarian and explained that there was no need to return the tickets. Marie Liddle was browsing close to the door and Molly was about to speak to her, to ask about Vic, when the younger woman turned abruptly to the librarian, said she couldn't find anything she wanted and left the van.

'That's a pity,' the librarian said to Molly. 'There's a lot of new stock on today. Still, you can't hope to please everyone.'

Molly stood at the door and watched while Marie walked across the grass to where Joanna was sitting. Her high-heeled sandals made the progress precarious, rather comical, but Molly did not feel like laughing. There was something desperate about the woman. Joanna stood up as she approached and started to walk away but Marie caught her arm. Molly could not hear what the gamekeeper's wife said, but Joanna's reply was clear and angry.

'Piss off,' she said. 'And leave me alone. For once my bloody family's right. It's best for everyone. I'd have thought you'd be pleased. I've made up my mind and I'm not going to change it now.'

She pulled herself free from Marie's grip and walked away up the road to the school house. Molly, still standing in the van, had found the encounter extremely interesting. She listened to the librarian muttering in a shocked voice about bad language and thought what puritans the young had become.

Daniel Craven waited all morning to be summoned to see the

policeman. Everyone on the estate knew that the inspector was in the office taking statements. After the newspaper articles the place was buzzing with rumour and gossip. There were reporters camped out by the east gate, just by the Lodge. They had been there when he woke in the morning. He could hear them laughing and through the kitchen window saw them standing in a conspiratorial group, drinking coffee from a shared flask. Later a van from the independent television company parked beside them and children waiting for the school bus banged on the window to get the autograph of the reporter they had seen on the six o'clock local news. Craven was tempted to go out to them, to say 'I can give you a story'. For a day he would be more famous than Marcus Grenville and his picture would be in all the papers. But he was frightened and confused and when the reporters crowded round him as he left the Lodge he shook his head and told them he had nothing to say.

As the morning went on his nerves became more frayed. Why hadn't the inspector asked to see him? What made him different from all the other employees on the estate? In the beginning he had his story prepared and was almost confident, but as lunchtime approached and still he had not been summoned to the office he became frightened. He imagined some sort of net closing in around him. He felt like running away.

At twelve o'clock when Vic Liddle went back to Keeper's Cottage for his dinner Craven took the van up the lane to the Crowford Hotel. The landlord scowled at him but served him all the same.

'What's going on at the Cadver, then?' Den asked, his curiosity overcoming his disapproval of Craven. 'Has Marcus Grenville come out yet to speak to those reporters?'

'I don't know,' Craven said. 'It's none of my business.' Then the irony of the situation struck him and he ordered another pint. He had never thought he would be in a position to stand up for Marcus Grenville.

He drank three pints of bitter very quickly and when the landlord asked if he wanted to order something to eat he shook his head. He needed the alcohol to steady his nerves. He was convinced that this afternoon the inspector would want to speak to him. If he didn't keep his cool he would be under arrest by teatime.

At one o'clock exactly he left the hotel.

'You could tell those fellows camped out at your place that I'm here,' Den said hopefully. 'They might fancy a pint by now.'

Craven said nothing. On the way down the hill he was strangely clear headed and his driving was flawless. He went immediately to the estate office and knocked on the door, his speech prepared: You haven't asked to see me yet but I think I might be able to help you.

But the voice that told him to come in was Vic Liddle's, and he wanted to talk not about poisoned buzzards or dotty old ladies but about burning the heather on the hill the following day.

'Where's the policeman, then?' Craven said, as casually as he could manage. 'Doesn't he want to see me?'

'He went ages ago,' Liddle said. 'Before I went for my dinner. He said he'd not be back. He reckoned he'd got everything he wanted. Why? Didn't he speak to you?' Bloody incompetents, he thought. You'd think they'd make sure they'd speak to Craven of all people. What chance did they have of sorting out what had happened?

At first Craven felt faint with relief. That was it, then. All his anxiety was over. He had been a fool to think he would be found out. Then he considered the matter more carefully, his mind racing. Why had he been excluded from the interviews? He was a keeper. It was his specific responsibility to deal with the vermin on the hill. He had known about the poison in Vic Liddle's shed. The fact that the policeman had ignored him was suddenly sinister.

'Didn't the inspector want to see me?' he insisted. Perhaps there had been a breakdown in communication. Perhaps the summons had been issued but not received.

Liddle looked up. His head was full of plans for the next day. He was irritated by the interruption.

'Look,' he said, 'if he'd wanted to see you he'd have asked for you. He had a list of everyone on the estate.'

'Oh well,' Craven said lamely. 'I suppose that's all right, then.'

But he remained unconvinced and all day he waited for the policeman to return.

Olivia Grenville stood in the large kitchen at the back of the Cadver. It was a gloomy, poorly lit room with huge larders and little in the way of modern convenience. Her housekeeper had taken a day's holiday and the daily woman who usually covered for her had been struck by some mysterious illness. All these facts conspired to add to Olivia's unease. She felt, as she had done when the valley was flooded to make the reservoir, that the world was disintegrating around her. It was not her place to be in the kitchen. Neither should she have to suffer the indignity of having her husband's photograph in the tabloid newspapers and a gang of reporters camping out by the main gate. She would not tolerate it. Marcus must be forced to sort it out. The morality of the situation did not concern her in the least. She had always known that appearances were what mattered.

She began, reluctantly, to prepare a simple lunch for the family. As she shredded lettuce into a colander she thought dispassionately that life would be so much easier if Marcus was dead.

Jeremy Grenville had been the first person summoned to give a statement to Inspector Benwell. In many ways the interview had been easier than he had expected. Waiting outside the estate office, trying to compose himself, he imagined himself in school again, having committed some unexplained misdemeanour. But the policeman had been far more human than the headmaster, far more reasonable. He had ignored Jeremy's stutter, waiting patiently for his answers. So eventually Jeremy had relaxed and had begun to speak quite fluently.

'On Friday night Miss Theobald took you as far as the dam, then you walked home,' Benwell said.

'Yes,' said Jeremy. 'It gave us a chance to be alone. And I find family dinner parties a bit difficult, a strain, you know. I felt I needed some fresh air.' He stopped, wondering if he was talking too much.

'While you were in the car did you and Miss Theobald discuss Mrs Ottway's disruption at the dinner party?'

Jeremy hesitated. 'I don't know,' he said. 'I can't remember.'

'Surely you *would* have talked about it?' Benwell insisted. 'It's not every day that an old woman accuses an MP of breaking the law. Or perhaps Miss Theobald was too polite to mention it?'

'No,' Jeremy said. 'Politeness has never been one of Eve's virtues.'

'So how did she react to the incident?'

'I think she was probably amused, entertained.'

'Doesn't that strike you as rather strange?' Benwell asked. 'She's a member of an animal rights organisation. Wouldn't you expect her to be shocked, outraged, even?'

'I didn't think about it,' Jeremy said. 'She's not particularly militant, you know. Not like some of them. Neither of us took the thing seriously. There was no proof then that any of Ursula's allegations were true.'

'No,' Benwell said. 'Quite. But now there is proof. Do you have anything to say about that?'

Jeremy shook his head uncomfortably.

'When you walked back from the dam,' Benwell said, 'you wouldn't have had to go past Back Rigg?'

'No,' Jeremy said. 'I came up the east drive and went straight to bed.'

'Did you meet anyone on the road?'

'No,' Jeremy said. 'No one.'

Then Benwell had smiled, quite unexpectedly, and said that the interview was over.

Jeremy would have liked to avoid lunchtime at home. He wondered if it might be possible to go to Appleworth to see Eve. He needed to talk to her. But when he made some excuse his mother insisted that he should be there and in her presence he reverted as always to the compliant school boy.

'These are difficult times,' Olivia said. She had emerged from the kitchen and was laying the dining-room table. 'We must present a united front. You, after all, must consider yourself at least in part responsible for what has happened.'

'Why?' The stammer had returned. He was shocked, pale.

'Someone must have leaked this story to the newspapers. Someone with a grudge against the estate. Your father thinks that it might have been your friend, Miss Theobald.'

'No!' he said. 'Father's wrong. Eve wouldn't do a thing like that.'

But as he spoke he thought that one of Eve's attractions was her recklessness and he could never be quite sure what she would do.

Olivia paused, surprised by his outburst. 'All the same,' she said. 'I'd prefer it if you didn't see her again. At least for a while.'

He said nothing and they sat in silence, waiting for his father to join them at the table.

Marcus Grenville had spent most of the morning in his office on the telephone to party advisers in Westminster. He knew that they would sacrifice him immediately if they thought it was in the party's interests, and he wanted to head off disaster. He had seen it done before to colleagues who caused embarrassment. Rumours would be started, off the record interviews would be given to lobby correspondents, coded messages would be passed to the initiated:

'Quite a sound man, Grenville, in his own way,' they would say, 'but he's never been, you know, one of *us*. All that business about the environment, for instance. Jolly important, of course, but not something you'd consider as mainstream policy. We wouldn't be at all surprised if he didn't decide to stand down at the next election. To allow him to contribute to the conservation debate outside parliament.'

So the assumption that he was about to leave would make his position untenable and he would be forced to resign.

He spent the first part of the morning mobilising support, calling in old favours. Confidently he assured his friends that the story would have blown over by the weekend, that in fact he was doing them a favour by distracting attention from the economy. By midday he thought he had achieved a reasonable power base and that he had gained, at least, a few days' grace. There would be no question of his being forced to resign immediately.

When he came in to lunch he was ebullient, sweating a little after the effort of the morning's work. He was prepared to be optimistic. It was all publicity, he said as he sat down to the meal. All part of the rough and tumble of parliamentary life. At least the punters would know who he was.

Chapter Fifteen

When Molly realised what lay at the bottom of Joanna Barton's unhappiness she wondered how she could have been so blind that she had not seen it before. She was surprised at the Grenvilles' skill in keeping the thing secret. Ursula had known, of course, had surely guessed even before Alex had confirmed it to her. But she was unsure about Simon Barton. She still was not sure what part he had played in it all.

The explanation came to her as she was walking back from the library van. The spiteful exchange between Joanna and Marie Liddle had puzzled her. What could the women have in common? At first she had thought it might have something to do with Vic Liddle's work. Had he been moonlighting, perhaps, for one of Simon Barton's clients? Then she began to go over all the information she had gained since their arrival at Back Rigg, trying to tie it in with the memories she had of Joanna as a girl. She thought of Joanna's friendship with Kate Craven. Then she remembered Alex, taking her grandchild into her arms at Monk's Wood, waving her daughter away to work. She remembered a letter received from Ursula many years before in which she was informed of Joanna's mysterious illness and the fact that the Liddles had decided to adopt a brain-damaged child. That both events had happened at the same time now took on a special significance. Quite suddenly all the facts fell into place and she was astonished by her stupidity.

At the farm she began, absentmindedly, to tidy Ursula's garden. As she pushed the mower over the straggling grass and pulled weeds from the overgrown borders, she made her plans. George would not be back from London until almost midnight. That gave her the evening to make sure of her facts before presenting the case to him. She was determined that he would not ignore her again. After an hour she decided that she was making no impression on the chaos of the garden and went into the house to wash and change into something more respectable. After a brief search of the obvious places she found the keys to Ursula's Land Rover in the kitchen on a hook next to the sink. At three o'clock she began to drive jerkily down the track towards Appleworth.

She found the special school without any problems, directed to it by a traffic warden from the town centre. It was a pleasant, modern building right at the edge of the town, beyond a small council housing estate. There were views of the fells and no shelter from the westerly wind. In the winter the children would have to be tough to play outside. The place seemed deserted. The children had all gone – either to their homes or to the hostel where the more severely handicapped were cared for. But it was not yet four o'clock and Molly thought that the teachers must still be inside. She parked the Land Rover opposite the main gate and waited, patiently, almost dozing.

After a quarter of an hour a group of teachers walked across the playground. They were all women and several were young enough to fit the description of Eve Theobald. For a moment Molly panicked. She wound down the window so she could hear what they were saying but that gave no clue to their identity.

'We're thinking about Turkey this year,' one said. 'It's supposed to be brilliant value. And really hot. It wouldn't be a real holiday without the sun.'

'I couldn't fancy the food,' said another. 'John always says there's nothing to beat Tenby. At least it's not all garlic and olive oil.'

They had come out of the gates and begun walking along the pavement to their cars when another young woman left the school and hurried across the yard towards them. She was wearing black stretch leggings and a long black T-shirt and carried a large wicker basket. One of the group discussing holidays shouted back to the newcomer.

'Bye, Eve! See you tomorrow!'

Then they all dispersed and the young woman in black was left to shut the gate and padlock it. Molly climbed out of the Land Rover.

'Excuse me!' she said. The woman turned and waited to be asked the time or the way into the town centre.

'I believe you're Eve Theobald,' Molly said. 'You've met my husband, George Palmer-Jones.'

'I told him everything yesterday,' Eve said aggressively. 'All that stuff in the papers had nothing to do with me.'

'No,' Molly said. 'I'm sure it didn't ... Perhaps I could give you a lift home.'

She thought Eve would refuse. She seemed frightened, jumpy, uncertain. Molly wondered how George could have failed to pick up the woman's tension.

'It's probably nothing to do with my aunt's death,' Molly said easily. 'There's a problem ... Not very important, probably, but I think you could help me to clear it up.'

She already had the passenger door open and watched with satisfaction as Eve climbed inside.

'If you just tell me where you live,' Molly said and in a brittle, staccato voice the woman gave directions to her flat. Molly pulled up on the pavement in the narrow street.

'Do you want to come in?' Eve said without warmth or enthusiasm.

'Well now,' Molly said, 'that would be very nice.'

The flat was small, untidy. The walls were covered with posters of rock stars and animals near to extinction.

'What's it about?' Eve demanded. She did not suggest making Molly tea.

'It's about one of the children who attend your school.'

Eve, looked suspiciously at Molly, as if she did not believe her, as if it were some sort of trap.

'I can't tell you anything about the pupils,' Eve said. 'If it's to do with the school you should come back tomorrow and talk to the head teacher. Now why don't you tell me what this is really all about?'

Molly ignored her. 'Just one question,' she said. 'Cassie Liddle. That's not her real name, is it?'

Eve stared at her, then shook her head. She seemed disproportionately relieved, Molly thought, that the question was not more personal.

'Do you know her real name?'

Eve shook her head again. 'Not her surname,' she said. 'It was an informal fostering arrangement approved by social services. Her first name is really Cassandra but she took the surname of her foster parents.'

In her relief she had become quite helpful, and was going to say more when she realised how unprofessional she was being.

'Look,' she said. 'I shouldn't be telling you this. The personal histories of the pupils are supposed to be confidential. I don't know what all this is about but I think you'd better go now.'

Molly left the flat slowly and happily. She had got what she came for.

At four o'clock Simon Barton had a phone call to his office from a landowner in Scotland who had been given his name by Marcus Grenville. The landowner said he was considering peat extraction but he was worried about the publicity. There had been such a fuss about it recently with that chap David Bellamy comparing it to the destruction of the rain forest. But really, it was the only way he could see of keeping his head above water. Perhaps Simon could put together a package, find a way of appeasing the conservationists but still allow him to make some sort of profit. What did he think? Simon arranged to visit the landowner the following week and tried not to think that he had spent his previous career trying to preserve the uplands.

He was still on the phone when his secretary, Felicity, came in to tell him that there was someone to see him. Felicity was tall and blond with a figure like a Barbie doll. He had thought when he appointed Felicity that he might fall in love with her, but she was too admiring and young. He'd had enough of innocence at home.

'I'm sorry,' Felicity said to Molly Palmer-Jones, who was waiting in reception. 'Mr Barton's rather busy just now. Perhaps you'd like to make an appointment to come back another day?'

'I don't think so,' Molly said firmly. 'I'll just wait until he's free.' She sat in the easy chair next to the large pot plant, reading a magazine and humming, irritatingly, to herself. At last Felicity told her, with a tired smile, that Mr Barton would see her.

Simon Barton regarded the small elderly woman who sat in his office with some amusement.

'What is all this about, Mrs Palmer-Jones?' he asked. He was thinking of the trip to the Highlands to advise his new client on peat extraction, thinking that the journey would be much more pleasant if he had company.

Molly expressed embarrassment, made it clear that she was intimidated by the splendour of the office. Really, she said, perhaps she shouldn't have disturbed him. Of course it wasn't of any importance. But as she was in Appleworth anyway. . .

Simon waited for her to come to the point, his mind still on other things.

'It's about Joanna,' Molly said. 'Well, I suppose it's about you and Joanna really.'

'What about Joanna?' he said, as one might ask about a difficult child.

'It's your wedding anniversary soon, isn't it?' Molly said. 'I know Ursula always used to remember it. She was so fond of Joanna and I'd like to give her something too. Nothing special, of course. Just a card or a small gift. To keep the tradition.'

If he was surprised that she could think of such things so soon after her aunt's death he did not show it. Perhaps, he thought, there were old ladies for whom a forgotten birthday or anniversary was a crime.

'Yes,' he said. 'Our anniversary's next week. It's very kind of you to think of us.'

'And how many years is it now?' she said, gossipy, tactless.

'Thirteen,' he said. 'We'll have been married thirteen years on Wednesday.'

Cassie Liddle is fifteen, Molly thought. She had such a hazy recollection of that time that she'd had to check.

'And had you known each other long when you married?' she asked, hoping that he saw her as a romantic old fool. 'I seem to remember it was something of a whirlwind engagement.'

'Not long,' he said. 'Less than a year.'

'Well,' she said. 'I always say if you know your own mind that doesn't matter.'

'No,' he said. 'Perhaps not.'

'You won't mention this to Joanna, will you?' she said. 'I'd like the present to be a surprise.'

'Whatever you say,' he said, obviously bored.

She stood up, gathering the plastic carrier bag of groceries she had brought to make the story that she was in Appleworth for shopping more plausible. At the door she stopped.

'This must be a difficult time for you,' she said. 'You're so closely linked to Marcus Grenville that all the adverse publicity must be bad for business.'

'Felicity will probably have gone by now,' he said. 'You won't mind seeing yourself out.'

Molly was untroubled by his rudeness. He had given her the information she needed.

As he had said, the room where Felicity worked was empty and her typewriter was covered. Molly opened and closed the outer door so he would think that she had left the building, then, without any idea what she was looking for, began to search the drawers of the desk. There was little of interest and she was about to leave when she heard Simon Barton's voice in the other room. He was speaking on the telephone.

'Hi,' he said. 'How would you like a weekend in the Highlands? I've got to go for work.'

There was a pause.

'Go on. You'd enjoy it. Besides, I want you to come . . . All right. Think about it. Give me a ring next week.'

He stopped again and then spoke so softly that Molly could hardly hear.

'Bye, Alex,' he said. 'And take care.'

When Molly got to Keeper's Cottage Marie Liddle was in the kitchen preparing the evening meal. She was jointing a rabbit and the slimy grey flesh slid over the melamine chopping board. The footsteps in the yard and the knock on the back door surprised her. She rinsed her hands under the tap and opened the door.

'I'm sorry to disturb you,' Molly said. 'I wouldn't come at this time if it wasn't important.'

'Come in,' Marie said. 'You won't mind if I carry on with this. Vic'll be in soon and somehow I'm all behind today.'

There were onions and carrots frying in a pan on the stove. She shook flour over the rabbit pieces and added them to the pot. Molly sat at the kitchen table and waited until she had Marie's full attention. The woman's depression surprised her. In other circumstances she would have expected the keeper's wife to be enjoying the drama of the reporters at the Cadver gate, imagined her on the phone to her friends, passing on the news. Now she was listless and tired, hardly interested in what her visitor might have to say.

In the pan the meat sizzled and Marie moved it around with a wooden spoon to stop it burning. She took an empty milk bottle from the windowsill and filled it with water which she poured over the rabbit. She folded a teatowel in two and lifted the pan into the oven. Then she turned to Molly.

'I'm sorry,' she said. 'Would you like some tea?'

Molly shook her head. 'I'm here about Cassie,' she said.

'What about Cassie?'

'I know about her,' Molly said. 'I know she's not your child.'

'It's no secret,' Marie said harshly. 'I never pretended she was mine. We adopted her when she was a baby.'

'No,' Molly said gently. 'You didn't adopt her. I'm not sure why. Perhaps because you weren't sure you would get approval for the adoption. That's all much more formal, isn't it, than the way it worked out? More likely you ended up with this arrangement because the Grenvilles wanted to keep some control over her future.

They couldn't love Cassie but they still wanted some power to determine what would happen to her.'

There was a silence.

'I am right?' Molly said. 'Cassie is Joanna's daughter?'

Molly half expected vehement denials but Marie seemed too exhausted to make the effort.

'Joanna wouldn't give the baby for adoption in the ordinary way,' she said slowly. 'She couldn't bear the idea of strangers looking after her. This was the only way the Grenvilles could persuade her to give Cassie up at all.'

'Who was the father?' Molly asked.

'Not Simon,' Marie said. 'He never knew. Joanna insisted that he shouldn't. It was one of her lecturers at college. He was married and when he found out she was pregnant he dumped her.'

'Why don't you tell me exactly what happened?' Molly said.

Marie sat beside her, quite close, with her elbows on the table. She did not look at Molly.

'Joanna was an unhappy girl,' she said. 'Anyone with eyes and a brain could tell that. She was always nervy. She needed careful handling but no one seemed to see it. Except Ursula. If she'd been allowed to see more of Ursula that might have helped. When she went off to the art school I thought she might have the chance to sort herself out but she couldn't cope with the freedom. She'd had nothing but criticism from Olivia Grenville and that's no way to start off in adult life. She had no confidence, you know, no belief in herself.'

She paused again and Molly prompted her.

'She got into drugs,' Molly said. 'Is that it?'

'You know about that?' Marie looked directly at her for the first time and Molly felt she had never known such kindness. Even now, after all these years, the keeper's wife was moved by Joanna's loneliness. . .

'She came home one weekend and I hardly recognised her. You expect art students to be scruffy, don't you? I never had the chance to go to college but that doesn't mean I can't understand. But she was thin and miserable. She came to see me and she hardly seemed to hear what I was saying to her. She told me she had the flu . . . If I hadn't been so sheltered perhaps I would have seen what was happening to her but it never crossed my mind.'

She lapsed into silence. In the oven the stew gurgled and spat and the sweet smell of rabbit made Molly feel sick.

'She stole money from me that day,' Marie said at last, reluctantly. 'I've never told anyone else about that. I went to answer the phone and when I came back twenty pounds was missing from my purse. She needed it, of course, to buy drugs.'

'Did she tell her parents she was pregnant that weekend?' Molly asked.

'No,' Marie said. 'If she'd told them then she'd have been whipped away to an abortion clinic. She didn't tell them until it was too late.'

'What happened?'

'They took her out of college and sent her to a private nursing home for the rest of the pregnancy. She was in no state then to argue. They told us that she was ill – glandular fever, I think they said – and when no one believed that they said it was stress, a breakdown. There were rumours of course that she was coming off heroin but even that was better than people knowing there would be a bastard on the Cadver Estate.'

'When did the Grenvilles approach you to care for the child?'

'Not until after Cassie was born. They didn't have much contact with Joanna while she was in the nursing home. Mr Grenville was always busy and Mrs Grenville preferred to pretend that none of it was happening. The medical staff might have had some idea that Cassie would be handicapped but they never told Joanna. Perhaps they thought she was in no state to cope. The Grenvilles thought that as soon as the baby was born it would be taken for adoption and no one would be any the wiser.'

'But it didn't work out like that?'

'No,' Marie said. 'It didn't work out like that and I can't pretend I'm not glad. We love Cassie and she's the only chance I'd ever had to have a baby.'

'What happened?'

'It was clear to everyone, even to Joanna, that Cassie wasn't normal. She was an ugly-looking mite with a great, misshapen head. Joanna hadn't taken much interest in the child when she was pregnant. She had her own problems and was prepared to let everyone else take the decisions. But when she realised the baby was a misfit too things were different. She began to make a fuss. She said she would keep the baby after all. She would give up art school and bring the baby back to the Cadver. She blamed herself, of course, and thought if she hadn't been taking heroin the baby would be perfect. You can imagine what the Grenvilles thought about that. It was bad enough having an illegitimate grandchild. But a baby as ugly and deformed as Cassie in the Cadver was more than they could bear.'

'So they came to see you?'

Marie nodded. 'They knew that we couldn't have a family. You can't keep a thing like that secret in a place like this. They told us that Joanna had refused to give the baby up for adoption. She hated the thought of it being cared for by strangers and, besides, it was so handicapped she thought no one would *want* to adopt it. She couldn't stand the idea that it would spend its life in a hospital.'

She paused and for the first time she smiled. 'Mr Grenville took us to the nursing home to see Cassie and meet the doctors,' she said. 'It was like something in a spy film. He was so worried about keeping it secret that he picked us up after dark. Mrs Grenville wouldn't come at all. So far as I know she's never seen Cassie. Except perhaps at a distance through the ambulance window.'

'And you agreed to go along with it?' Molly asked.

'I wanted a baby,' Marie said simply. 'I suppose we could have adopted in the ordinary way, but I'd heard all those stories of couples waiting until they were too old to be considered. And there was no guarantee that we would be approved. And when I saw Cassie I fell in love with her. I'd have brought her home then if they'd let me.'

'What about Vic?' Molly asked. 'What did he think of it?'

She shrugged. 'He wasn't sure. He went along with it for my sake, but he wasn't really happy.'

'I thought there'd be trouble,' Vic Liddle said. 'And I was bloody right.'

He was standing in the doorway from the hall. They had been expecting him to come in through the kitchen and throughout the conversation Marie had turned towards the window looking out for him. They had not heard the front door open or his stockinged feet in the hall.

His wife looked at him helplessly. 'Vic . . . .' she said. 'I'm sorry . . .'

'No,' he said. 'I'm sorry. I should have known better than to trust that lot.' He stood behind her and clumsily took her hand. 'I know they want to send Cassie away,' he said. 'Mr Grenville told me today. He seemed to think we'd have heard from the school.'

'There was a letter on Friday,' she said. 'I meant to tell you. But I was so upset. I tried to pretend it wasn't happening. I should have told you.'

Her eyes filled with tears. She stood up and tore a square of kitchen paper from a roll on the wall and blew her nose.

'I'm sorry,' Molly said. 'I don't understand what's going on.'

'There was never any legal basis for us caring for Cassie,' Marie said. 'We *told* everyone that we were adopting a baby through social services because that's what the Grenvilles wanted. But although she's never taken any interest, Joanna has always been her legal guardian. We have no rights. The social workers were prepared to approve the informal fostering arrangement because of the special circumstances. But in law I'm no more than a bloody nanny.' The anger and bitterness which had been growing since she had received the letter from school on Friday gave force to the words.

'Yes,' Molly said quietly. 'I see that. But what happened on Friday to bring matters to a head?'

'Cassie came home for the weekend,' Marie said. 'She comes home every weekend. This time she brought a letter from the school.

It said that following instructions from Cassie's mother they had made the appropriate arrangements to transfer her to a private residential school in Dorset. All her records had been sent on. They said they would miss Cassie and asked if I would like to go in to say goodbye to the staff before the end of term. There were no details in the letter. They assumed of course that I knew all about it.'

'But you didn't?'

'No. It was a terrible surprise.'

'What did you do?' Molly asked.

'I tried to talk to Joanna,' Marie said. 'I hoped she might change her mind if she saw how happy Cassie was with us. I wanted her to come to the cottage to see.'

'That must have been at the library,' Molly said. 'And she wouldn't listen to you?'

'No,' Marie said. 'She wouldn't listen.'

'Did you tell Ursula?' Molly asked suddenly. 'She was here on Friday night after she'd been to the Cadver. Did you tell her then?'

Marie nodded. 'I was upset,' she said. 'She could see that, even though she was so angry. But I wouldn't have told her about Cassie being Joanna's daughter. I wouldn't have broken the confidence after all this time.'

'But she knew already,' Molly said. 'Didn't she? Not that the Grenvilles were planning to send Cassie to school in Dorset, but that Joanna was her mother.'

Marie nodded. 'That made it all right, somehow,' she said. 'I showed her the letter, told her everything.'

'What did she say?' Molly asked.

'That I wasn't to worry. She would talk to Olivia Grenville and make her see how cruel it would be to move Cassie when she was so settled in Appleworth. She seemed to think that it was all Olivia's idea.'

'Did she give you the impression that she intended to see Olivia immediately, that night?'

'I don't know,' Marie said. 'She was angry and we'd both had a lot to drink. I don't know what she intended to do.'

'Did you see where she went when she left here?'

'No. I presumed she'd gone back to Back Rigg.'

She turned to her husband. 'I couldn't tell you,' she said. 'I didn't know how you'd take it . . .' Then she stopped because how could she explain to him her fear that he had never cared for Cassie, that he had tolerated the girl for all these years for Marie's sake and that now he would be glad of the excuse to be rid of her?

Vic sat down beside her, awkward and purposeful. 'I've been thinking,' he said, 'that we could fight. You read about cases in the papers. Care orders, wards of court. I've been thinking we could find a solicitor and fight.'

'But you'd hate all that!' she said. 'The fuss. . .'

'All the same,' he said stubbornly. 'I don't think it's right for the child to be sent away.'

They looked towards Molly for advice and support. She stood up. 'Wait,' she said. 'Give me a day. It might not come to that.'

And they seemed reassured by that. Almost happy. So when she left them to eat their meal she felt a terrible burden of responsibility.

Chapter Sixteen

George bought a first-class ticket for his return journey to Appleworth. It was six o'clock, the train was busy and he needed to think. He sat in the almost empty first-class compartment, his head back, his eyes shut so that his fellow travellers probably thought he was asleep. But he was considering the events of the day, quite certain that he knew now who had killed Ursula Ottway.

He had arrived at King's Cross at mid-morning and phoned Lomax at his office in Westminster. It was a relief to find him there. It would be a long, wasted journey.

'I'd like to talk to you,' George said. 'Perhaps you could spare me half an hour. It's important. I've come to London specially.'

'Not here, George,' the MP said. 'I don't want you coming here. What would people say? You were always the one sent to sift out the bad boys, weren't you? You were the one they sent to plug the leaks and find out who hadn't declared *all* his interests. If you come here there'd soon be rumours that I'd been fiddling the petty cash.'

He laughed but was quite firm.

'What's it about then, George?' he said. 'Fed up with retirement? Want me to pull a few strings and get you back into the old service?'

'No,' George said. 'I'd like to ask about Kate Craven.'

There was a pause but no surprise.

'We'll make it a *private* meeting, shall we, George?' he said. 'I don't think it's something we should discuss over the phone. I've got to be home this afternoon anyway. Jane's at some charity do and the nanny's got the flu. Come at about two, then we can have a couple of hours of civilised conversation before the little buggers come back from school.'

So George had three hours to kill before he needed to set off to see Lomax. He was tempted to look up other colleagues to see if any rumours about Grenville's improprieties surfaced, but Lomax had sounded worried and he thought it was safer to be discreet. So he sat in the Shaw Library in the Euston Road, reading Dickens, only breaking off once for coffee and a Danish pastry in the basement café. At twelve-thirty he felt stale and stiff so he set off to walk to Lomax's home, with an A-Z in his pocket for reassurance, but not needing to look at it because he felt he was on old familiar territory.

The house was large and untidy with a view of Hampstead Heath. George had been to social functions there several times before. Lomax and his wife always had a big party on bonfire night and as he walked through the front gate George could remember, quite clearly, the smell of wood smoke and explosive. He had never seen the place in daylight and it was impressively shabby, the garden overgrown, the paint peeling. Lomax was the youngest son of an old and penurious aristocrat and would have considered concern about such matters frightfully bad form, but George wondered what Lomax's suburban constituents would make of the decay.

The door was opened by the MP himself. He was older, fatter, more careful than George remembered. He had always had the look of a boisterous school boy. George wondered if someone had warned him off.

'Come in!' he said cheerfully, and George stepped into a wide hall which contained three bicycles and a piano.

'Your children must be growing up now,' George said. He remembered them as violent and exhibitionist toddlers at the firework parties, bruising guests' shins with pedal cars and peeing on the lawn.

'Thank God! The youngest is eight. The oldest two are at the comprehensive round the corner. It's a bloody good school and it's great propaganda of course to send them there – it shows what faith we Tories have in the State system. And of course it saves us a bloody fortune in school fees.'

He was wandering on through the house, opening doors and expecting George to follow him. They ended up in a kitchen which was full of laundry. There was washing on a rack suspended from the ceiling, and underwear draped over a radiator under the window had caused the glass to steam up. In one corner a washing machine churned relentlessly. Absentmindedly Lomax took two cans of beer from the fridge and moved a pile of ironed sheets so George could sit down.

'What *is* all this about, George?' he said, peering cautiously over the rim of the can.

'You had a secretary,' George said. 'Kate Craven. She killed herself. I want to know all about her.'

'In what context, George?' He shuffled uneasily on the kitchen chair. He had definitely, George thought, been warned off.

'In the context of Marcus Grenville,' George said, deliberately.

'Ah!' He drank more beer and looked uncomfortable. 'I see.'

'I'm working for Marcus Grenville,' George said. 'He's hired me.'

'Oh, I see!' Lomax cheered up considerably. 'So old Marcus knows you're here.'

'I didn't say that,' George said. 'But I've got his interests in mind. There's every danger, you know, of his being arrested for murder. I don't think he's killed anyone and I want to prove it. Did he recommend Kate Craven to you as a secretary?'

'No,' Lomax said. 'Not exactly. But she gave his name as a referee. She'd been brought up on his estate in Westmorland. So I had a chat to him about her.'

'Had he seen her since she'd left home?'

'No,' Lomax said uncertainly. 'At least I don't think so. He just sketched in her background.'

'But he did get to know her later? When she started working for you?'

Lomas was an honest man despite his profession. He disliked lying. 'Look, George, this is off the record, isn't it? Marcus isn't a great chum but I don't want to land him in the shit. Besides, he's got a lot of important friends. . .'

George was tired and running out of patience.

'You should know by now that I'm hardly likely to go talking to the press.'

'Yes.' Lomax shrugged apologetically. 'Of course.'

George tried a different tack.

'Was Miss Craven a good worker?' he said. 'Did you get on with her?'

'She was one of the best!' Lomax was glad of a question he could answer unambiguously. 'Efficient, of course, but there are lots of efficient secretaries about. She was different because she was so *pleasant*. She made you feel good about going into the office in the morning. Pretty, too. I could understand. . .'

His voice trailed off.

'. . . why Marcus Grenville fell for her?' George completed the sentence. Lomax nodded unhappily.

'How did the affair begin?'

'Look here, George,' Lomax blustered. 'I never said anything about an affair.'

'I *know* they were having an affair,' Palmer-Jones said impatiently. 'And if you don't tell me about it I'll talk to someone less scrupulous.'

Lomax got up and wandered vaguely to the fridge to fetch another can of beer.

'I don't know how it all started,' he said. 'Marcus used to come into the office – we were on the same select committee – and he always had a fatherly word for her. I didn't think anything of it. Why should I? The man had been there at her christening. The age difference between them was immense. And her father had been one of his employees.'

'When did you suspect that he was taking more than a fatherly interest in Miss Craven?'

'I saw them together by chance,' Lomas said. 'I went to her flat quite late one night to pick up some papers. She wasn't there. I went to the car to wait for her and I saw them walking up the street together. He had his arm around her. It was raining but neither of them seemed to notice. He went into the flat with her and although I waited he didn't come out. I think by the end he was practically living there.'

'Was the affair common knowledge?'

'No,' Lomax said. 'I don't think so. They were very discreet. I think eventually some of his clever colleagues found out. You know what the place is like. It's impossible to keep anything secret. But I never heard it discussed.'

'Did you talk to Kate about Grenville after you'd seen them together?'

'No. I didn't think it was any of my business.' Lomax drank slowly from the beer can. The washing machine spun to a standstill with an unhealthy crash. Lomax got up automatically and pushed a button. 'Grenville talked to me about it, though,' he said.

'What happened?'

'He asked me out for a drink,' Lomax said, 'and that was unusual in itself. He never usually bothered much with me. I wasn't any use to him, you see. He knew I'd gone as far in the party as I'd ever get. My face didn't really fit. Marcus might look like a genial country squire but he's an ambitious man.'

'What did he want?' George asked.

'I don't know. Reassurance, acceptance. To explain. We got rather pissed, actually. I found the whole thing rather embarrassing to tell you the truth and it was the only way I could handle it.'

'What did he tell you?'

'That he loved her. That was it. I suspect that was the reason for the meeting. He wanted to put it on record and there was no one else to tell. Not even Kate.'

'Why couldn't he tell her?'

'Because he didn't want to lead her on. Although he loved her he knew there was no future to the relationship. I've told you he was an ambitious man. He wasn't going to risk scandal and losing the prospect of high office by leaving his wife.'

'Not even when he found out that Kate was pregnant?'

'You know about that?' Lomax looked at George cautiously, with respect. 'No. Especially not when she was pregnant. The press would have had a field day. He's very conscious of his image is our Marcus and he would have come across not only as a lecherous old bastard, but also as bloody careless.'

'Did Miss Craven expect him to marry her?'

Lomax shrugged. 'I don't know what she expected. She didn't discuss it with me.'

'But you knew she was expecting a baby?'

'Look, George! I've had six kids. I've got an instinct for these things.'

'You might have suspected,' George said. 'But did you *know*?'

There was a pause.

'Yes,' Lomax said in the end. 'I knew. I caught her sobbing her heart out at her desk early one morning. She told me then.'

'What did you do?'

'Nothing. What could I do? She knew Grenville would never leave his wife and make an honest woman of her. I expected her to go somewhere discreetly to get rid of it.' He paused again. 'I offered her money,' he said. 'She turned it down. I told her to think about it and come back to me if she needed help. She never mentioned it again so I presumed old Marcus had coughed up.'

Lomax would be a sympathetic employer, George thought. He imagined the MP trying to comfort the girl, desperate not to sound judgemental, distressed by her tears.

'You had no suspicion that she was considering suicide?' he asked.

'No.' Lomax paused. 'These days you expect girls to take something like that in their stride. They seem so sophisticated, so . . .' he groped for the word, '. . . unsentimental.'

But Kate Craven had not been sophisticated, George thought. She was a country girl. She wouldn't have the confidence of a Sarah Keays to come into the open and face the press. And her desperation was caused not only by the baby – as Lomax said, these days you could take steps to deal with an unwanted pregnancy. It had been Grenville. He had betrayed her and let her down when she needed him.

'I found her body, you know,' Lomas said suddenly. 'I was going to a conference in Brighton and I wanted her with me to take notes. I'd arranged to pick her up from her flat. She must have timed the thing so I'd find her. She'd known I'd be discreet...'

'Was there never any gossip surrounding her death?' George asked. 'Rumours linking her with Marcus Grenville?'

'There might have been some talk in the bars,' Lomax said. 'But it was the time of the by-election and no one wanted any fuss. No one cared about her, you see. She was a pretty secretary. Dispensable. I even heard one friend of Grenville's say that he thought she'd taken the honourable way out.'

He drained the can of beer. 'Enough to turn you into a raving feminist, isn't it? I don't know what Jane would have said.'

'The police must have investigated the death?'

'I presume so. But she'd got rid of everything in the flat belonging to Grenville and she didn't leave a note of explanation. It was soon forgotten. There are always new scandals.'

No, George thought. It wasn't forgotten. Not by Daniel Craven. Of course Kate had confided in him. She always had. Craven would know about his sister and Marcus Grenville. He had an excellent motive for revenge. His anger had built up in the two years since her death and he had come to the Cadver with the intention of paying Grenville back. Why had Marcus taken him on? George wondered. Surely not through guilt. Perhaps he thought it would be safer to have Craven on the estate where he could keep an eye on him. Perhaps he had hoped it would all blow over.

'What's the word in the bars on Marcus Grenville?' George asked. 'What do people say about him?'

Lomax answered readily. It was the sort of gossip he was accustomed to and enjoyed.

'They think he'll definitely make the Cabinet next time round,' he said. 'Unless he does anything stupid. Of course his wife's a liability, but that doesn't matter so much these days.'

'Why is Olivia considered a liability?' George asked.

'Well, you know, she's practically an agoraphobic recluse. A Tory MP's wife is expected to get out into the constituency, open jumble sales, hold garden parties. You know the sort of thing, George.'

'Yes,' George said. 'I know the sort of thing.'

He was interested in the marriage Marcus and Olivia had devised together and for the first time felt some sympathy and admiration for Grenville's wife. Why should she be her husband's social secretary? It must have taken a certain courage to stand up against the party machine. He would have liked to follow up the line of questioning. But there was no opportunity. The front door was pushed open with tremendous force and two solid young boys in designer trainers and brightly coloured jogging suits burst in on them demanding food.

'Why don't you stay, George?' Lomas said hopefully. 'Meet the other four.'

But George said that he had a train to catch and took the tube to King's Cross.

As the train sped through the darkening countryside he considered the events of the day. He stretched his legs and opened his eyes and thought he would treat himself to a Scotch. He was quite certain that Daniel Craven had murdered Ursula Ottway, and that by the end of the next day it would all be over.

He was the only person to get out at Appleworth station and after a moment of shouts and banging doors the train moved away and he was left alone. After the city the place seemed very quiet and clean. A tawny owl flew out of the trees on the other side of the track. He felt quite awake and wanted the investigation to be finished. From a call box he telephoned the police station, thinking there was a chance that Benwell might be working late. If he was still on duty they could get a warrant and go to Craven that night. They could have the thing over by morning. But no one from CID was on duty and he had to drive on to Back Rigg, keyed up and impatient, unable to relax.

'But I don't understand,' Molly said, 'why Craven killed Ursula.' They were sitting in the dim light of the kitchen. She had been waiting for him on his return, wrapped up in the faded candlewick dressing gown she must have had for thirty years. She made milky drinks and listened to his story patiently. He was excited and full of all that had happened. Then she could keep quiet no longer. 'I can see why he put the poisoned bait on the hill to coincide with the Conservation Conference. That was to embarrass Grenville in front of the delegates. It was obviously Craven who phoned the police about the buzzard and Craven who leaked the story to the press. If he believed Grenville was responsible for Kate's death it would be quite a satisfactory means of revenge. But where does Ursula come into it?'

There was a silence. George had to admit the force of her argument but he was committed to the idea that Craven was a murderer. He searched desperately for an explanation.

'I'm not sure,' he said at last. 'Perhaps she found out that he'd been putting down the poison.'

'So what?' Molly demanded. 'Why should Craven care if he was discovered? He need only say that he was acting under Marcus Grenville's instructions and he could cause even more embarrassment. It might have meant him losing his job but he doesn't seem to have bothered much about his own position.'

'I don't know,' George said unhappily, too proud to dismiss his theory without a fight. 'There must be an explanation. Perhaps he'll tell us when we talk to him in the morning.'

'Listen,' she said and she told him the story of Cassie and Joanna. 'Doesn't that seem a more potent motive for murder?'

'What are you saying? That Joanna killed Ursula because Ursula found out that Cassie was her illegitimate child? I thought you said they were fond of each other?' He made his voice as cruel and mocking as he could manage. This time it was Molly's turn to sound uncertain.

'I don't know,' she said. 'Perhaps you're right. Perhaps that's ridiculous after all.'

They went to bed very late in tense ill-temper, hardly talking to each other.

Chapter Seventeen

Benwell arrived at Back Rigg early the next day in response to the message George had left at the police station. They heard his car driving up the track and he was unusually excitable, quite convinced of Craven's guilt. He accepted George's offer of breakfast and the men sat together at the table, being loud and male, making jokes, excluding Molly from the conversation. She was not too offended. She put the rudeness down to nerves and exhilaration. But she was worried for them. She was quite sure that they had the whole thing wrong. It was at the same time more complicated and more simple than they seemed to think. She regarded them as school children who have to learn by their own mistakes, and watched them go off with a sigh.

George felt overcome by a sort of temporary madness. It had something to do with his admiration for Benwell. They got on so well together and there was the pleasure of working again as part of a male team. The madness was of the kind that provokes respectable men to shout and scream at rugby matches. He felt that the case would soon be over and then they could celebrate with pints of beer and reminiscence.

When they approached the Lodge the mood left him quite suddenly and he became serious. He thought they were not adequately prepared and Molly's question 'Why would Craven want to kill Ursula?' took on a greater significance. He was glad that he had no real responsibility and that Benwell was in charge of the investigation. Benwell seemed typically unworried. He knocked loudly on the door and waited patiently for a reply. No one came. He looked at his watch. It was eight o'clock.

'Perhaps he's already at work,' George said. He was quite relieved. He wanted to pull back and take the time for further thought.

Benwell knocked again and put his ear to the door to listen for movement. There was none. He turned the handle slowly and pushed open the door. The room was empty and when they opened the doors into the kitchen and the bathroom it was clear that Craven had already left. The main room was untidy and there was the stale, sour smell of unwashed sheets. Little attempt had been made to provide comfort – there was a chair, a rented television on legs, a settee. It was as if Craven had been camping out there.

'Do you think he always leaves it in a mess like this?' Benwell said. 'Or was he especially in a hurry this morning?'

'He's depressed,' George said. 'I don't suppose he makes much of an effort.'

Benwell began searching in a methodical way and George, embarrassed by the official intrusion into Craven's privacy, wandered through to the kitchen. The draining board was piled precariously with clean crockery and pans, a whole week's washing up. There was one dirty plate and mug on the table, so presumably the cycle was about to start again.

'There's a letter here from his sister,' Benwell called. He walked through to the kitchen with a sheet of blue paper covered in fine writing.

'What does it say?' George said. He preferred not to read it.

'See for yourself.'

It was written when Kate Craven was at her happiest. She did not know how the affair had started, she wrote. Marcus had been such a figure of fun when they were young and now that she adored him it was as if he was quite a different person. She had no unrealistic expectations. She did not expect him to leave Olivia. But he spent most of his time in London anyway and she had no reason not to think that they could not be happy together for ever.

'Are there any other letters?' George asked.

'No,' Benwell said.

'He must have kept this specially to fuel his anger.'

'It's proof anyway that Craven knew about the affair,' Benwell said. 'If he wanted to get his own back I wonder why he didn't go straight to the press with the story.'

'Because he cared too much for Kate's reputation,' George said, 'even though she was dead.' He felt an obligation to defend the man and realised that he was being persuaded by Molly's arguments. 'Why should he have wanted to kill Ursula?' he said, almost to himself. 'He had no quarrel with her.'

Benwell had begun to search through almost empty kitchen cupboards and did not answer directly. He knelt on the grimy floor and began to pull open dresser drawers.

'What do you think of this, then?' he said, standing up triumphantly, dusting down his trousers. George's question was forgotten.

Underneath a roughly folded linen tablecloth was hidden an empty cardboard egg box and a hypodermic syringe.

'That's the evidence we need,' he said. 'We've got him!'

'You'll probably find traces of phosdrin in the syringe,' George said slowly. 'I'm sure that's what Craven used to inject the eggs he used as bait on the hill. But there's still no proof that he poisoned Ursula.'

Why had he kept the needle? George wondered uneasily. If he'd poisoned Ursula why hadn't he thrown the thing away? Especially when he'd taken the trouble to return the empty jar of phosdrin to Vic Liddle's shed.

'It'll do to be going on with,' Benwell said. 'It gives us enough to get him to the police station for questioning. Do you want to come?'

'No,' George said. 'That's a police matter, isn't it?' He wanted to talk to Molly, felt even that an apology was in order. But when he got back to the farm the house was empty and there was a note on the table telling him that she was at the Cadver.

At nine o'clock Molly left the house and walked briskly down the track. The day was heavy, still, unnaturally mild for the end of March. As she approached the road, Vic Liddle passed her in the estate Land Rover and she remembered that he had said something about burning a strip of heather on the hill. She stepped off the track to allow him to pass, and waved, but he did not stop.

At the Old School House she looked to see if Simon Barton's car was parked in the yard. She had no wish to see him. At this point, she felt, he would only get in the way. The yard was empty so she opened the gate that had stopped generations of Crowford children from running out into the road at the end of class and went to the front door of the house. She rang the bell. There was no reply. She looked in through the downstairs windows but saw nothing unusual. The bedroom curtains were still drawn but perhaps that only meant that the Bartons had left in a hurry. She left the house and crossed the yard to the pottery. The door was locked and she could see nothing through the small dusty windows. Joanna was not at work.

Molly knew that there were any number of possible reasons for Joanna's absence – she had gone shopping, to see friends, to visit one of the galleries that sold her work – but the locked and empty pottery made her uneasy and troubled her for the rest of the morning. She took a scrap of paper from her pocket and wrote:

Joanna. Come to tea. I'll be in all afternoon.

Then she was unsure where she should leave the note. Was Joanna more likely to go to the house or the pottery when she came home? Finally she folded it and pushed it through the letterbox of the house.

When Molly arrived at the Cadver she refused to be intimidated by its magnificence. She overcame any lack of confidence by manufacturing a sense of moral outrage. What had Olivia ever *done* with her life? she thought. Nothing, except for tending the house and brooding on the changes that had taken place in the valley. It was common knowledge that she seldom crossed the boundary of the estate into the real world. So, fortified by indignation, Molly climbed the stone steps and rang the bell.

The door was opened by the housekeeper, a small, anxious woman.

'Mrs Grenville?' she said in response to Molly's inquiry. 'I'm not sure if she's free. If you'd just wait here. . .'

She hurried away in mid-sentence and disappeared into the room where they had sat for coffee on the evening of the dinner party. Molly prepared for a fight. She was just in the mood. She would demand to see Olivia if some excuse were made. Of course the woman was free. What else was there for her to do? But no battle was necessary and when the housekeeper returned Molly was led immediately into Olivia's presence.

Olivia was sitting on a window seat, looking out on to the garden. She sat quite still, with her hands in her lap, until Molly came right into the room. Then she stood up to greet her.

'Thank you for seeing me, Olivia,' Molly said. 'I hope I'm not interrupting anything important.' The sarcasm was spoken almost before she had realised it but Olivia seemed not to notice.

'No,' she said. 'Nothing important.' She paused then added unenthusiastically. 'Perhaps you'd like some coffee?'

Why not? Molly thought. Why don't we go into the kitchen and make it for ourselves with granules from a jar and boiling water. Like ordinary people. But it would not do to antagonise the woman yet. 'Thank you,' she said. 'That would be very pleasant.'

Olivia nodded to the housekeeper who scuttled away, Molly supposed, to do the business with the grinder and the percolator.

Olivia walked away from the window and they sat in armchairs on either side of the fireplace. The grate had been cleaned and a bowl of dried flowers stood in front of the hearth. Olivia said distantly that the weather was very warm for so early in the spring. Molly agreed and resisted the temptation to observe that she supposed Olivia would prefer a downpour to discourage the reporters still camped out at the end of the drive. The housekeeper came into the room, pushing the door open with her back. She was carrying a tray with pots and cups and biscuits. It looked very impressive but when Molly tasted the coffee she decided it was instant after all and she smiled.

'How can I help you?' Olivia asked. The encounter with Molly was difficult for her. She did not know quite what line to take with the woman. Her parents had been friends of the family and Marcus seemed to think that Palmer-Jones could be useful to them, but she sensed that Molly was dangerous. She was like Ursula in many ways and Olivia did not trust her.

'I was wondering if you'd had a phone call from Ursula on the evening of her death,' Molly said.

The question shocked Olivia. 'No!' she said. 'Of course not. I've already told the police everything about Friday night.'

'If she *did* phone here after she left the Cadver that night,' Molly went on, 'really it would be best to say so now. The police can check with the telephone company, you know, and find out.' Could they? she wondered. Probably not for local calls. But it hardly mattered. Olivia had been taken in by the confident statement. She became stem, autocratic. And defensive.

If Mrs Ottway *did* make a call, she said, it was about a personal matter and had nothing to do with the police. She hoped that Molly would respect her wish for privacy.

'Of course,' Molly said easily. 'Because it's not only your privacy that we have to worry about, is it? Vic and Marie have rights too.'

Olivia Grenville stood up sharply. Her cup rattled on its saucer. To give herself time to respond she walked to the table and set it on the tray.

'I don't understand,' she said evenly, 'what you mean.'

'I know about Cassie Liddle,' Molly said. 'I know that her name is Cassandra Grenville. I know that she is your grand-daughter.'

In the silence that followed, Molly wondered if she had been too theatrical in her accusation. After all, she hoped for Olivia's cooperation. She wanted Cassie to be allowed to remain with the Liddles. She added more gently:

'Ursula did talk to you about Cassie, didn't she, on the night of her death?'

Olivia remained silent. Her unlined, beautifully cared-for face was quite still. At last she turned towards Molly. 'I suppose you intend to make mischief with this information,' she said bitterly. 'Don't you think the family has suffered enough unpleasantness?'

'Which family are we talking about here?' Molly asked. 'Are we talking about the Bartons? Or the Liddles? Or are we talking about you and Marcus?'

'We did what we thought was best,' Olivia said. 'We knew that Joanna could never care adequately for a child.'

How could she? Molly thought. She'd not had much practice at being a member of a family.

'You couldn't have made a better decision,' she said. She leaned earnestly towards Olivia. 'Marie has been a wonderful foster mother. I don't understand what prompted you to change the arrangement after all these years. And to do it in such a heartless way, without any consultation. Marie only heard about it from the school.'

'The Liddles wouldn't have lost out financially,' Olivia said. 'We would have continued to pay the allowance for caring for the child.'

'Money?' Molly demanded. 'Do you think that's what this is all about? Vic and Marie haven't thought about money. They love the child. They want to keep her.'

It had never occurred to her that Olivia could be quite so stupid.

'Tell me,' she said, trying to keep her anger under control, 'exactly why you decided to move Cassie from the school in Appleworth. Were you dissatisfied with the care she was receiving?'

Olivia regarded Molly with a cold and disapproving stare.

'The education at Appleworth was perfectly adequate,' she said, 'but it's unsettling for Joanna to see the girl in the valley. She feels guilty. It's a terrible strain. While she's still Cassandra's legal guardian there's always the possibility that she will do something stupid, decide even to try to care for the girl herself. That would be disastrous for everyone. Her marriage would never stand the stress. So we persuaded Joanna that it might be better for Cassandra to be at a school with excellent resources in Dorset. It would be less distressing for everyone that way.'

'But why now?' Molly persisted. 'I can see that the situation isn't ideal, but it's worked well enough for all these years. It would work better, of course, if the thing were out in the open. Then Joanna could visit her daughter, get to know her. The Liddles wouldn't mind that. But at least the present arrangement gives Cassie a degree of stability. Why change things so radically now?'

Olivia hesitated and Molly thought she would refuse to answer, but she spoke not looking at Molly, in a very flat and formal voice.

'Our decision was prompted by my son's relationship with one of the teachers at the school. The head teacher there is very discreet but there are records to which Miss Theobald would have access. We were frightened that if she acquired an intimate knowledge of the family she would reach certain conclusions about Cassandra. We knew that she disapproved of my husband's hunting and shooting. We were not sure that we could trust her discretion. She would have a vested interest in causing the family embarrassment.'

'And because of that risk you decided to move Cassie?' Molly was astounded by the paranoia. Olivia seemed to have the thing quite out of proportion. She had lost her grasp on reality.

'It was Joanna's decision,' Olivia said flatly. 'Her father and I advised her. That was all.'

'You should know,' Molly said, 'that the Liddles intend to fight the decision. They will go to a solicitor tomorrow and ask for wardship proceedings to begin. If Cassie becomes a ward of court you'll lose all influence over her. Any judge coming to a decision about her future will take into account the fact that the Liddles have had everyday care and control since she was a few weeks old.'

Olivia seemed frozen in her chair.

'I knew,' she said bitterly, 'that you were here to make mischief.'

'I had nothing to do with the decision to take legal action,' Molly said. 'It was Vic's idea. Of course if you decide to reconsider your position he won't need to go to court.'

'It has nothing to do with me!' Olivia said sharply. 'You should talk to Joanna.'

'Yes,' Molly said. 'Perhaps I should.'

She stood up and Olivia, relieved that the discussion was almost over, rose too.

'Who else knew about Cassie?' Molly asked.

'There was a friend of Joanna's, Kathleen Prime's niece, Alexandra. She used to visit Joanna in the nursing home when she was pregnant. But Joanna seemed convinced that she would keep the confidence. There was no one else. Jeremy was away at school. He never knew.'

'And Ursula?' Molly asked. 'She did phone on Friday night to persuade you to change your mind about Cassie?'

Olivia nodded. 'And I told her exactly what I've told you. That she should talk to Joanna.'

'Did she agree to talk to Joanna?'

'I never found out. Our conversation was interrupted. She told me that there was someone at the door and she would have to go.'

'Who could be visiting her so late at night?'

'I don't know,' Olivia said. 'I thought the call was an impertinence. I was glad of the excuse to ring off.'

She saw Molly to the front door herself. She seemed unrepentant, still certain that her judgement had been sound. Perhaps it was to shake the woman's confidence that Molly spoke, just as Olivia was about to close the door.

'Does the name Kathryn Craven mean anything to you?'

Olivia opened the door and said, readily enough: 'Wasn't she the girl from the estate who committed suicide?'

'She was Daniel Craven's sister,' Molly said.

'So she was! They both left the valley as soon as they left school.'

Olivia shut the door and Molly was left on the step, uncertain whether the woman knew of Marcus Grenville's affair or not.

Eve Theobald had slept fitfully and woke early with the decision still not made. It was impossible at a time like this to know who to trust. The Animal Rights Group had talked about secrecy and loyalty at all costs and Jeremy with his anachronistic notions of duty had seemed equally certain. She was not sure. She was aware that she was trying to cover her back to save herself at the expense of others and the indecision came because she did not want to think of herself as a coward.

She would have liked to trust George Palmer-Jones but he had seemed so much a part of the male, middleclass establishment that she could not see how he would understand. Then she had been tempted to confide in his wife, the woman in the scruffy anorak with the little Billy Bunter specs who had been waiting for her outside school. She had the air of someone who would not by shocked by anything. But in the end Eve had said nothing and that silence seemed a crime on its own.

At seven o'clock she got out of bed and showered. The gas boiler had only just switched on and the water was hardly tepid. She dressed carefully. At eight o'clock she phoned the Cadver and asked to speak to Jeremy Grenville. A woman, presumably the housekeeper, said flatly that he was not available.

'Could you tell him that I'd like to see him,' Eve said and left her name.

'Of course,' the woman said. But Eve had left similar messages the day before and she had heard nothing from Jeremy.

Immediately afterwards Eve phoned the house number of the special school's head teacher.

'I'm terribly sorry,' she said. 'I've got a lousy stomach bug. I've been up all night. I think I'll have to stay at home today until it clears up.'

The head teacher was sympathetic. Eve hadn't been looking well for a few days, she said. She should take as long as she needed to get better.

Eve replaced the receiver and left her flat. There were few people in the town. It was before the start of the season and many of the tourist shops stayed closed until after Easter. The Deux Chevaux was off the road again. She walked out of Appleworth on the Crowford Road. When she reached open countryside she walked more quickly, sticking out her thumb to hitch a lift whenever she heard a car approaching.

Jeremy Grenville immersed himself in work and tried not to think of Eve Theobald. He had had years of practice at distancing himself from unpleasantness. Before breakfast he went on to the hill to look at the strip of heather Vic Liddle was proposing to burn. It was not that he questioned Vic's judgement. Vic knew more about keeping and the countryside than he ever would. He wanted to prepare himself for the day's work. He had watched Vic burning on the hill when he was a child but had never before taken part. He was worried about appearing ignorant.

When he returned to the Cadver his mother was already eating breakfast in the dining room. There was no sign of his father and when he asked where Marcus was his mother seemed not to know.

'Miss Theobald was on the telephone for you,' Olivia said. 'Again.'

Jeremy said nothing.

'She really is a persistent and ill-mannered girl,' Olivia said. 'You should be pleased to have discovered in time how unsuitable she is.'

Jeremy ate bacon and sausage and concentrated on the plans for the day's work on the fell. He thought Vic would burn against what wind there was. The fire would move more slowly that way. Vic prided himself that a Cadver fire had never got away from him.

'Jeremy!' Olivia said. 'I'm talking to you!'

He cleared his plate, stood up abruptly and left the room.

Simon Barton had not come home all night. He had phoned Joanna at eleven to say that a meeting in Carlisle had taken longer than he had expected and he would stay on at the hotel where it had been held. Joanna accepted his explanation without question and asked no awkward questions about the meeting.

'I'll see you tomorrow night,' Simon said cheerfully. 'At about eight.'

In the morning Joanna woke unusually early and decided she would go to see Alex at Monk's Wood. Alex wouldn't mind, she thought, despite the previous day's phone call. They were supposed to be friends, weren't they? And if she was still in bed when Joanna arrived it would serve her right for being so bloody unfriendly the day before. She deserved to be woken up. Joanna needed to talk to her about Cassie. She needed reassurance that her bloody parents were right and the private school in Dorset was the best place for the girl.

All the same, when she got to Monk's Wood it was still very early so she decided to park by the pub and walk down the lane to the house. It would give Alex an extra quarter of an hour in bed. The day was still and cloudy, very mild. There were already midges under the trees so she could imagine that it was summer, like the time she had first walked with Simon on the hills.

She saw his car parked outside the house. Before she had time to consider the implication of it, the front door opened and he came out, dressed in a suit all ready for work, his hair still wet from the shower. He carried a briefcase. Alex was behind him. Joanna saw that she was taller than him. She wore a silk dressing gown with an extravagant oriental design embroidered on the back. Her hair was loose, longer than Joanna could ever remember having seen it. Simon put down the briefcase and kissed her. He pushed his hands underneath the dressing gown so it swung open and Joanna could see the long freckled legs and the greying pubic hair. They turned and she saw his hands moving beneath the silk so the pattern seemed to come to life. They broke apart. Alex was laughing. Simon picked up his briefcase and drove away, without seeing Joanna watching him from the trees.

Alex stood by the door to wave him off. As she turned to go back into the house she thought she glimpsed something moving across the grass between the trees, but when she looked again she decided she had imagined it. Upstairs the baby began to cry.

Chapter Eighteen

When Molly returned to Back Rigg the house was empty. George was on the hill watching the heather being burned. As she walked round the house to the kitchen door she could see his silhouette moving across the fell to join the Land Rover and the small group of men already there. She supposed he was afraid of missing out on some excitement but thought he was wasting time that could be better spent.

It annoyed her that although she knew all the facts surrounding Ursula's death, all the secrets in the valley, she did not know who had killed her aunt. She could guess, of course, but there was no certainty. George, with his logical mind, might be able to make something of it.

When the knock came on the front door she supposed it would be Joanna, who had read her note and was too impatient to wait until teatime. But when she opened the door it was Eve Theobald, flushed and dusty in jeans and a sleeveless T-shirt with a sweater tied round her waist.

'I'm looking for Jeremy,' she said. 'I didn't like to go to the Cadver. They don't approve of me. Do you know where he is?'

'He's on the hill watching the heather burning,' Molly said. Then, sensing the girl's anxiety, 'He's quite safe. My husband's with him too.'

'I ought to talk to him,' Eve said. 'There's something he should know.' She bent double so her hands were on her shins and breathed deeply. 'I'm terribly unfit,' she said. 'I hoped to get a lift but in the end I had to walk most of the way.'

'Why don't you come in and have some tea?' Molly said. She

opened the door wide so Eve could see the dark hall. 'Perhaps I can help.'

Eve hesitated. 'I don't know,' she said. She thought that she would end up telling everything once she was in the kitchen drinking tea with the kind old lady. She remembered what her friends in the Animal Rights Group thought of traitors. 'I don't know,' she said again.

Molly said nothing. She left the door open and walked through the house to the kitchen. Eve heard the splash of water into a kettle, a clatter of spoons. It would not hurt, she thought, to rest for a few minutes and have some tea. Then she could go on to the hill and find Jeremy.

But as soon as she came into the kitchen she began to talk.

'I'm sorry,' she said in the end, when she had told it all. 'I'm no good at secrets. This really screwed me up. I expect you think I'm really silly.'

'No,' Molly said. 'Not silly at all.'

'What will you do now?'

'I have to go out. I want you to wait here for me. Will you do that?'

Eve nodded.

At the door Molly stopped and turned back to the room. 'If Joanna Barton comes, will you ask her to wait for me? I want to talk to her. She might seem a little overwrought but she's just unhappy. She's not dangerous.'

As she left Back Rigg and began to walk down the lane she saw the smoke rise above the hill. It hung in the still air, like a grey curtain, blotting out all that was going on beyond it.

When Vic Liddle began to burn the heather Danny Craven was still there to help him. Benwell had decided against an immediate arrest after all. He said he would go back to Appleworth and try to get an analysis done on the syringe he had found at the Lodge. He seemed to have been affected by George's doubt.

'You'll be here, George, won't you?' he had said when they sat in the car outside Back Rigg after searching Craven's house. 'You can see them working from here. If Craven makes a move you can give me a ring.'

George, who had always taken responsibility seriously, said he would go on to the hill and watch what was happening, but he thought if Craven had intended to run he would have gone by now.

When he arrived at the strip of long heather Vic Liddle was preparing to start burning. He had unloaded his equipment from the Land Rover. Danny Craven and Jeremy Grenville stood, listening to his instructions, obviously impatient to start.

'I've never had a fire get away from me yet,' Vic said. 'And I don't intend to start now. We're in no rush.'

He gave them long-handled, wide-bladed beaters that he had made years before from flattened oil drums.

'Don't go waving them about,' he said. 'You'll just fan the flames. Shuffle them along the ground like this to keep out the air.'

Craven swore under his breath.

'Have you got a problem, lad?' Vic demanded.

Craven shrugged. 'I know what I'm doing,' he said. 'That's all. I don't need to take orders from you.'

'You can do as I say,' Vic said. 'Or you can get out.' He turned to Jeremy. 'That's right, isn't it? He does what he's told or we manage without him.'

But Jeremy was staring down the valley at the lane and seemed hardly to notice what Vic Liddle was saying.

They started the fire with a flame thrower. The heather caught easily and soon there was the crackle of flame and charred vegetation and the smell of charcoal. They walked on each side of the strip to be burned, flattening the flames with beaters, preventing the fire spreading to the new growth. It seemed a terribly risky business to George to set the hill alight. As the fire spread birds flew out of the heather with raucous alarm calls. Behind them the black stalks and bare earth smouldered.

'It's a bit of a mess now,' Vic shouted, 'but it's got to be done. Overgrown heather's good for nothing. Not even for wildlife. If you don't manage the moor it dies.'

Danny Craven allowed the fire to spread deliberately. They realised that afterwards. George thought he should have guessed that the temptation to cause more embarrassment to Marcus Grenville was too much for him to resist. A big hill fire would scar the moor for years. The first George realised that something was wrong was when Vic Liddle shouted and they saw Craven, through the smoke, standing with the beater above his head, the flames seeming to lick around his feet.

'For God's sake, man, what are you playing at?' Liddle shouted. 'You'll have the whole hill alight.'

'I'm doing my best,' Craven shouted back. But he swung the spade-shaped beater over his head with full force and the flames leapt as if blown by a bellows and spread into the green shoots of the new heather.

Later Vic was to say that if it hadn't been a cold damp spring they might have lost the whole hill. As it was, the damage was contained. He gave George a beater and they ran behind Craven, stamping on the flames with their boots, stifling them with the spades. Craven stood apart, watching them, and George could not tell if he was disappointed or relieved when they had the fire under control. It was only when the crisis was over and they stood, choking and reeking of smoke, that George realised that Jeremy Grenville had gone.

Olivia Grenville let Molly into the Cadver. She said nothing but stood aside to let her in. Upstairs, far away, there was the whine of a vacuum cleaner and as Olivia led her down the corridor to the drawing room Molly heard Marcus behind a closed door saying heartily into the telephone that it was a storm in a teacup and would all blow over. But the house was so big that when they sat together in the drawing room they felt quite alone.

'Well,' Olivia said unpleasantly. 'You're becoming quite a regular visitor.'

'I know what happened on Friday night,' Molly said.

'You might think you know,' Olivia said calmly. 'But you can have no proof.'

'There was a witness.'

'I'm sorry,' Olivia said, as she might have done to a tradesman who had sold poor quality goods. 'But I don't believe you.'

'Tell me,' said Molly quietly. 'How did you manage it?'

'Look,' Olivia said. 'If you know as much as you do you must realise that I can have had nothing to do with it. I never leave the house.'

'You were responsible.'

'No,' Olivia said sharply. 'Ursula was responsible. What right did she have coming here, disturbing our evening, making threats?'

'So you arranged to have her removed. It would solve all sorts of problems, wouldn't it? Back Rigg would be available for Marcus's shooting parties. You never could stomach the idea, could you, of the Cadver as a glorified guest house with loud Italian businessmen playing snooker in the library? The threat to go public about the poisoned buzzard was just the final straw. You decided to get rid of her.'

'No, no,' Olivia said. 'You don't understand. I never meant to have her killed. That was a typical example of incompetence. I wanted her off the estate. I made it clear that was what I expected.'

'But you do know who killed her?' Milly said. 'You're a clever woman. You do know that. And you must have known there was a danger.'

Olivia smiled. 'Of course I know who killed her,' she said. 'But there's no proof. And I'd admit it to no one else.'

They sat, looking at each other. Molly thought she heard a car engine but the room was at the back of the house and she could not be sure.

'Well,' Olivia. 'And what do you intend to do now?'

'I'll go to the police,' Molly said.

'Do you really think they'll believe you? With the influence we have in the country?'

'You're out of touch,' Molly said sadly. 'This isn't the 1930s. Things have changed.'

'Not here,' Olivia said. 'Things haven't changed here. Not at the Cadver.'

'Tell me,' Molly said. 'Did Ursula tell you who was at the door when you were speaking to her on the telephone on Friday night?'

'Of course,' Olivia said. 'I asked her. I wanted to find out if . . .' She paused.

'. . . your instructions were being followed,' Molly said.

Olivia shrugged.

'You've outstayed your welcome,' she said. 'I think you should leave.'

She stood up and walked towards the door. As she opened it there was the sound of footsteps running and a door slamming. Immediately afterwards there was an explosion. Molly, who knew very little about these things, thought at first that it was a bomb. The Animal Rights Group had got Marcus after all. Then, more rationally, she realised that it was a gun fired in an enclosed space and she ran from the room towards the noise. Upstairs the vacuum cleaner still whined and a woman screamed.

Eve Theobald sat in the kitchen at Back Rigg and waited for Mrs Palmer-Jones to return. She had given up the idea of going to look for Jeremy on the hill. The walk from Appleworth had left her quite washed out. Besides, she trusted the old lady to sort it out for her. She sat in the comfortable chair by the range. The room was very hot and she must have fallen asleep.

She was awoken by the sound of the kitchen door being opened and because there had been no knock she assumed it would be Molly or George. She tried to compose herself and turned to greet them. Jeremy Grenville stood just inside the door. His face was streaked with black and he smelled of smoke.

'I saw you from the hill,' he said. 'Walking up the track. What are you doing here?'

'I wanted to talk to you,' she said. 'You wouldn't answer any of my calls. I was worried.'

'Worried? What could you have to be worried by?'

She noticed then that there was no stammer. He spoke so fluently, with such confidence and determination that he seemed like a different man.

She did not answer.

'Go on!' he said. 'What's bothering you? Why don't you tell me? Don't you trust me?'

'I don't know,' she said carefully. 'I'm not sure any longer.'

'Look,' he said. 'Tell me if something's wrong. Perhaps I can clear it up.'

He walked further into the room and stood beside her.

'I saw you,' she said. 'On Friday night.'

'I don't understand what you mean.'

'After I'd let you out of the car at the dam I felt lonely. I thought we'd had so little time alone together that evening. I wanted to walk with you. It seemed a romantic thing to do, walking together by the lake in the dark. I parked the car and followed you. But before I could catch you up I saw you go up the track to Back Rigg.'

'What did you do then?'

'Nothing,' she said. 'I didn't want to be involved in any argument over estate business. I was on Mrs Ottway's side. I felt awkward. I went back to the car and drove home.'

He moved closer to her and crouched on the floor beside her chair.

'Have you told anyone about this?' he asked. He began to caress the hair on the back of her head.

'No,' she lied. 'Of course not. I never betray my friends. You know that.'

'Do you want to know what happened at Back Rigg that night?' he asked.

'I'm not sure,' she said. She was frightened, and wanted to give an answer that would please him. 'Only if you want to tell me.'

'My mother sent me there,' he said.

'Of course,' she murmured under her breath. 'She would.'

'Mother talked to me while you were getting ready to leave,' he said. 'She explained what an embarrassment it would cause to the family if Ursula's allegations were made public. She said I was the only one to stop her.'

'Of course,' Eve said again, bitterly. 'It was your duty.'

'Yes!' he said, apparently surprised by her perception. 'That's right. So you understand.'

'Did your mother tell you to kill Ursula Ottway?' Eve asked. If I keep him talking, she thought, Mrs Palmer-Jones will return. Someone will come.

He considered the question seriously. 'I'm not sure,' he said in the end. 'Probably not in so many words.'

'What happened, then?' she said. 'Tell me about it. I want to know.'

'Do you?' he said. 'But perhaps I shouldn't tell.'

'All right, then,' she said hurriedly. 'It doesn't matter. Whatever you think.'

'No,' he said, stroking her hair again. 'I think I'll tell you. You need to understand. . .'

He sat like a boy, clasping his knees to his chin. 'Where shall I start?'

'At the beginning,' she said. 'You went to Back Rigg to stop Ursula making a fuss about the buzzard. What did she say?'

'Too much,' he said crossly. 'She was drunk, you know, and she said too much. When I arrived she was on the phone and I waited for her in the kitchen. But as soon as she came in she started.'

'What did she say?'

'That my mother was a wicked woman. It was something about the Liddles. I didn't understand.'

'But your mother is a wicked woman,' Eve said, forgetting for a moment to be careful.

'No!' he said angrily. 'No, she isn't. She just does what she thinks is best.'

'I'm sorry,' Eve said. 'Of course. Go on.'

'Ursula had been to Keeper's Cottage,' Jeremy said. She'd found a jar of poison in Vic's outhouse. She waved it under my nose. Forensic science was so sophisticated these days, she said, that they'd be able to compare the chemical in the buzzard with the actual solution in the jar. There'd be no doubt then that the poison had been put down by someone on the estate. She said she would go to the police and the press.'

'Would that have been so terrible?' Eve cried. 'Was that a reason to kill her?'

'Of course,' he said seriously. 'It would have been a disaster.'

'For the family,' she said.

'Yes. For the family.'

'What happened next?' she asked.

'She started to lecture me,' he said. 'She told me that I should leave the estate and get a job somewhere else. If I stayed in the valley I might end up like my sister. Then she fell asleep. Almost in the middle of a sentence. I told you she was drunk.' He spoke in an irritated way as if Eve had not been paying proper attention.

'Yes,' Eve said. 'You told me she was drunk. What did you do then?'

'I poured some phosdrin into her glass of whisky. That gave her a chance, you see, of survival. It meant that I wasn't wholly responsible. If she carried on sleeping without drinking more whisky she wouldn't die. I left it to fate.' He stared blankly ahead of him. 'She shouldn't have been so greedy,' he said. 'If she hadn't wanted more to drink she'd still be alive now. When you think about it, it was all her fault.'

'What did you do then?' Eve asked. 'Did you go straight home?' Why doesn't somebody come? she thought. Where is everyone?

'No,' he said. 'Of course not. Do you think I'm a fool?'

'No,' she said carefully. 'I know you're not a fool.'

'I was wearing gloves,' he said, 'so there would be no fingerprints. I put the poison in a plastic bag in my pocket. Then I knew I'd have to find the buzzard and the cats.'

He paused and looked at her, expecting her to take an interest, wanting her to ask a question.

'Did you find the buzzard?' she asked.

'Yeah!' he said. 'No problem. It was in the freezer. I knew it would be there.'

'And the cats?' she asked. 'Did you find them?'

'No,' he said. It was an admission of failure and he did not like it. 'They weren't anywhere in the house so I reckoned Ursula must have buried them. I couldn't risk anyone seeing me in the garden so I left it. I thought if she'd buried them no one else would find them either.'

'No,' she said. 'Of course.'

'Then,' he said, 'I had to keep my nerve. It wasn't much fun walking back to Keeper's Cottage with a half-frozen buzzard corpse under my jacket.'

She thought he might be attempting a joke and looked at him carefully to see what response was expected but his face was still serious.

'Why Keeper's Cottage?' she said. 'Why did you go there?'

'Because I didn't know what else to do with it,' he said. 'I wanted to replace the poison bottle and it seemed a good place to hide the bird. I knew if Vic Liddle found it, it would be in his interest to keep it secret. But his shed's such a tip I didn't think it would come to light for years. I wasn't to know that my father would ask Palmer-Jones to start snooping around.'

'No,' she said. 'Of course not.'

'Now,' he said. 'I've only got one problem left.'

'What's that?' She turned to face him.

'You,' he said. 'I've got to decide what to do with you. It'll have to be an accident, of course. A car accident might be best. We'll say you were driving my car and you weren't used to it. Instead of braking at the corner you hit the accelerator and shot straight into the lake. And I know you can't swim.'

'You can't do that,' she said. 'I won't let you.'

'I'm sorry,' he said. 'You won't have any choice. You'll be dead, you see, before you get into the car.'

He continued to stroke her hair with the palm of his hand. He slid his hand down to the back of her neck and with the other grasped her throat. She tried to scream but there was no sound.

By the time they arrived she was almost unconscious. Secretly George blamed Benwell for that. If he had not been so eager to hear all the details they might have interrupted the conversation earlier. As it was they arrived in time. But the girl had been given a terrible shock and he wasn't convinced it was justified. Then he blamed Molly. Where the bloody hell was she? he thought. What was she thinking of leaving the girl on her own?

Molly was still at the Cadver. She stood in the small white bedroom where Joanna had slept as a child and watched Marcus Grenville kneel on the floor and cry over the body of his daughter. Shock and a terrible guilt paralysed her.

'It's my gun,' Marcus said. 'Why did she have to take my gun? For God's sake, I taught her to shoot with it.' Then he looked at Molly. 'You don't think it could have been some sort of accident?'

Molly shook her head. There was a patchwork quilt on the bed and blood on the carpet. Why didn't I see, she thought, how desperate she was, how ill? I knew she was unhappy but I've had experience enough to recognise the danger of suicide. I was too wrapped up in the ridiculous competition with George. I should have made more effort to help.

'Why did she do it?' Marcus cried. 'I thought she was settled. My little girl . . . I didn't realise . . . Why didn't she come to me?'

Because you'd caused damage enough, Molly thought, but she said nothing. There was little point now in going over all the details.

By the door Olivia stood, dry eyed, and watched them.

Ursula's funeral was held two days later. It was a quiet affair. Sally arrived just in time for the service and disappeared immediately afterwards to Manchester Airport to catch a flight to Frankfurt.

'It would serve her right,' George said, 'if Ursula had left all her money to a cats' home.'

But he was glad to see the back of her.

The Liddles were there and came back to the farm afterwards to drink whisky and talk. Marie stood uncomfortably in a black dress that was too tight for her and tried to express her grief about Joanna's death.

'The poor girl,' said. 'I suppose it all got too much for her. After all those years.'

No one ever discovered what had triggered Joanna's sudden breakdown. The police had made half-hearted inquiries to discover where she had been on the morning of her death but Alex had not come forward. She managed to persuade herself that she had not seen Joanna in the garden at Monk's Wood. She went to Ursula's funeral but stood apart at the graveside and declined Molly's invitation to go to Back Rigg with the other mourners.

'We've decided to go for wardship proceedings after all,' Marie said. 'Not out of spite. But to give Cassie a bit of security. I shouldn't think the Grenvilles will oppose it. Not after all they've been through.' She paused. 'They say that Marcus wants to sell up but Mrs Grenville won't hear of it.'

George had been worried that Ursula's funeral would be disturbed by the press. With Jeremy's arrest and Joanna's suicide the newspapermen camped out by the Lodge had been ecstatic. The story had almost everything – passion, class, drama. There had been headlines of: DOUBLE TRAGEDY FOR MP'S FAMILY. Only sex was missing. Because they never found out about Kate Craven or Alexandra Prime it was impossible to inject a satisfactory element of sex. That meant that the story was quickly forgotten and the friends of Ursula Ottway, who gathered at the funeral to say goodbye to her, were left in peace.

Lightning Source UK Ltd.
Milton Keynes UK
UKHW010725310122
397961UK00001B/11

9 781447 289005